VENGEFUL VOWS

ELLIE HALLARON

Cover design by Ellie Hallaron

ISBN: 979-8-9990397-3-6

First edition, 2025

Vengeful Vows

Book Three of the Syndicate Series

For rights, permissions, or inquiries, contact:

EllieHallaron.Author@gmail.com

To all the ones who stay quiet when they really want to scream and fight. May you find your inner strength to become who you want to be. Even if that person is a little crazy and sometimes stabs her husband.

Content Warning

This is a dark romance intended for mature audiences. It contains themes some readers may find triggering, including abuse from a parent, a mother's suicide (in the past and off page but briefly discussed), patricide, forced marriage, and violence. The heroine's story begins in a bad place for her, but she quickly becomes a strong and fierce woman. The hero begins the story disgusted with the idea of marriage, specifically towards the heroine, but quickly has a change of heart. They never planned on marriage, they never wanted it, but it's what they never knew they needed.

This is not a sane romance, but it is a satisfying one.

If you crave reluctant vows made under duress, the push and pull of enemies joined through matrimony, and a wife putting her husband in his place...

Let me introduce you to Mr. and Mrs. Dominic Montclair.

Prologue
Dominic

The hardened faces of the other bosses of Boston's crime families scowl at me around the table.

We're holding a meeting to discuss the impending war that my brother foolishly started. Of course, the one family that needs to be here isn't.

I stare at the empty chair that Viktor Sokolov, Pakhan of the Boston Bratva, should be seated in. For fuck's sake, he and I are the only ones who are needed for this meeting. The war is between us. But he isn't here.

I don't think he's even interested in peace, even though he's already gotten his revenge.

Roman, my younger brother, wrongfully attacked the Bratva. They retaliated, but it isn't enough. We unintentionally declared war. If I can't find a way to end it, then the destruction and death on both sides will be devastating.

Lorenzo Del Vecchio, the Capo of the Boston Mafia, clears his throat. Typically, it's me who starts the meetings. Even though I'm one of the youngest in the room at thirty-seven, I tend to be the mediator. But, since it was The Syndicate that fucked up, I keep quiet.

"We all know why we are gathered today. The Syndicate wrongly attacked the Bratva, and the Bratva retaliated. We need to discuss this war and what it'll mean for our families," Lorenzo starts.

"We have nothing to do with this war. And we intend to keep it that way," Cillian O'Connell, head of one of the numerous Irish Mobs, states.

I look at his fellow brethren to see how they respond. As expected, they all nod in agreement.

Sean Callahan leans back in his chair as if he doesn't have a care in the world. "We're not looking for a fight. Especially not with the upcoming wedding." He shoots a hard gaze at Kieran Donovan.

Ah, I guess there'll be another Irish wedding coming up. I'll have to see if I can send a gift and avoid the event altogether. They have far too many weddings. The Irish Mobs are constantly shifting. Marriage alliances combine families, then fallouts between brothers break them apart. It feels as though each time the leaders meet, there are different Irishmen at the table.

Except for the one that's always here.

Malachy Finnegan.

The old bastard's been around since before my dad started the Syndicate. He looks as weathered as his age. But he's still stern as ever.

"This is not the Irish's fight. None of us will step in. We will never align with the Bratva, on principle alone, but we also can't back the Syndicate since your family carries all the blame," Malachy Finnegan speaks on behalf of his kin.

The Irish have tiffs amongst themselves, but at the end of the day, they're family. They share Irish blood, and all respect the elder, Malachy.

I swing my gaze to the Cartels at the table. Their allies are seated next to each other across from their sworn enemies. The Capos of the Cartels of each country have strong allies and even stronger enemies. Unlike the Irish, they're much less likely to form alliances. They're dangerous, and I tend to avoid working with them.

Esteban Herrera, don of the Mexican Diablos Llorando Cartel, sitting between Alejandro Ramírez, don of the Peruvian Fuego del Sol Cartel, and Luis García, don of the Guatemalan Víboras Venenosas Cartel, whispers to them. Those three tend to stick together. They don't compete in imports and seem to respect each other.

Ángel Santos, don of the Venezuelan Ángeles del Infierno Cartel, ironically named Angel despite his gruesome nature, and Emiliano Torres, don of the Colombian Portadores del Dolor Cartel, oppose them. They're an alliance that I don't involve myself with. Honestly, I try to stay away from the cartels altogether, only interfering if they break our stringent rules.

Even if they offer help, I don't want it. I don't trust them, and they play by a different set of rules.

"We will back the Syndicate in this war against the Russians," Esteban offers with a sly grin.

I know the Russians compete with some of the drugs those three deal. It's not an offer on my behalf at all, and I know they'll stab me in the back the moment I turn around.

"Then we will have no choice," threatens Ángel.

I knew this was coming. They'll forever oppose each other.

"You scum of the earth Venezuelans," spits Alejandro. "No tienen ni columna ni lealtad. Manga de cagones."

"Amarre esa lengua, Peruano, o amanece sin ella." Emiliano reaches into his waistband as he spits out Spanish threats.

I don't need to speak the language to know the situation is escalating.

The Peruvian stands to his feet so quickly, his chair topples.

Lorenzo tilts his head at me in a silent warning. I know what he's saying. If the cartels get involved, it'll be a bloodbath for the entire city, not just the underground families.

"I thank you for your offer, gentlemen, but I don't think it'll get that far. I intend to make peace with the Bratva. I want no more situations like my brother's wedding attack. I refuse to lose any of my men over this misunderstanding," I state calmly. I can't let anyone see the anxiety swirling in me. I've spent years masking my emotions to the point where even my family doesn't think I have any.

"What will you do?" Lorenzo demands.

"I'll figure something out," I say carefully, not wanting to let on my lack of a plan. If Viktor didn't even show up to this mediated peace discussion, a part of me worries that he has no interest in peace.

I look around the room, and my eyes settle on two of the Irishmen discussing an upcoming marriage alliance.

The thought curls my stomach. I've never understood marriage. While my brothers seem happy with their wives, the thought churns my stomach. Having someone invade my personal space, someone constantly around, sounds like hell.

But it seems to work for the Irish, so maybe there's some substance to it.

"Stop this war by any means necessary. Violence is not the answer this time," Lorenzo stresses. He's almost as old as Malachy, so I know this comes from experience.

As the meeting goes on, Lorenzo's words echo in my mind.

'Stop this war by any means necessary.'
How far am I willing to go for peace? To protect my people?
There isn't a line I won't cross. No matter the sacrifice.

Chapter 1

Katerina

I watch Vova play with his catnip fish and can't help but be envious of my grey tabby.

He's so free, even though he's confined to this room with me. He couldn't care less that this luxurious room is merely a gilded cage, trapping us in this lavish nightmare.

I'd give anything to be free.

From the outside, Katerina Sokolov lives a privileged life. Taught by the best private tutors, clothed in designer, fed by accomplished chefs, wealth beyond measure...

But it's all just a farce. This life is built from dirty money accrued from horrific deeds. I know who my father is, I know what he does.

I know what he's done.

I hate the man. Loathe him.

And one day, I will watch Viktor Sokolov die at my own hands.

Not because of the nefarious things he does outside the walls of this haunted mansion, but for the things he's done inside of them.

I'm just relieved he got rid of Мама before she could see how much worse he's gotten.

He wasn't bad when Pyotr, Petya to me, was around. My father respected my brother too much to show his darker side around him. But everything worsened when he moved out. With him being twelve years older than me, he was gone by the time I was six.

That's when things shifted.

He started getting angry. At first it was a tight grip on my arm or seething words. But soon the threats stopped being empty.

Мама was on the receiving end. She endured the worst for as long as she could. Until one day when I was ten, she couldn't take it anymore.

I don't blame her. I became his target when she was gone. I didn't realize how much she was taking. How much she was shielding me from.

It's just been him and me in this haunted mansion ever since. The ghost of her still roams these halls in the touches of her left behind, the silver and crystals, the portraits on the walls, the décor that she picked out. But now, it's accompanied by the gaudy and tacky things he added later on.

This ugly house was once refined and classy. But he took down much that she put up to wipe her memory. I don't know why he kept the few things he did, but I'm grateful for the reminders of her.

The sound of the food dispenser, and Vova's greedy response mark my cue to leave. I set his dinner timer at our dinner time.

I glance in my mirror on the way out of my room to ensure my makeup is pristine and my dress spotless. Viktor has strict rules on my appearance. Pastels and perfection.

The Bratva Princess must always look the part. She must be sweet and kind. She must hold her tongue. She is to be seen and not heard. She must always be presentable. She will wear light pink makeup and pastel dresses. She must never be seen as negative. She must be weak. And meek. And pathetic.

She must be a lie.

I hate her.

I hate the Bratva Princess, and all that she stands for.

I hate being the Bratva Princess.

But he's beaten her into me. All that I am is the Bratva Princess.

Katerina Sokolov doesn't exist anymore, if she ever even did. All I know is the girl Viktor made me to be. And I want her dead almost as much as I want him dead.

I enter the dining room and sit to his left. The seat to his right always remains empty in honor of Мама. It infuriates me. How dare he honor the woman he led to deaths door! The woman he broke. The one he killed.

I wonder if he'd honor me if I left just as she did.

It doesn't matter. I'll never let him win. I will defeat him one day.

I look at Viktor as I sit and shoot him a saccharine smile. The fake love and sweetness from his perfect daughter enrage me, but I know the consequences of dropping the mask.

Yelena comes in with plates of zharkoye iz dichi for dinner. Even after years of eating the roast game, it still unsettles me. It's too ostentatious of a dinner, too pretentious. He feasts like a god when he's really a demon. It disgusts me.

We eat in silence, as we do most nights. The sounds of forks scraping the plate are music to my ears as opposed to the alternative of speaking to the demon king. But good things can only last so long.

"Katyusha, what have you done today?" Viktor muses.

I go rigid. Fuck him for calling me that. My mother called me Katyusha, and that's the only reason he does. He only started calling me it once she passed, and only when he's trying to start a fight.

But I won't show a reaction. The last set of bruises only just healed, and I won't give him a reason to give me more.

The question itself is also set to piss me off. There's nothing for me to do in this godforsaken prison. He keeps me locked up, and recently, he's banned me from leaving. I used to be able to get fresh air, but that's no longer an option.

I know something's going on with his Bratva. He's been even angrier recently. More stressed, on edge. And he takes it out on me.

"I've been working on a paper for class," I say as briefly as possible. When his eyes narrow, I relax my posture and soften my tone. "Thank you, Отец, for letting me get my masters. I appreciate it."

The words taste like ash in my mouth, but they appease him. After a few more minutes, he continues.

"Sergey will be joining us for dinner tomorrow. Be presentable." His demand comes with an evil grin.

I feel nauseous at the mention of Sergey.

Viktor has been hinting at a marriage between Sergey and me for a while now. I was given until I finished college to marry. I had hoped getting my master's degree would prolong my time. At twenty-three, the idea of marriage disgusts me. But the idea of marrying Sergey is even worse. It's inconceivable.

Sergey is in his forties, and he's already had two wives. Both have *disappeared*. But he's close to Viktor and currently single, so I don't think Viktor cares. All Viktor cares about is keeping his men happy. Not about the wellbeing and safety of his only daughter.

But why would he? He doesn't care about my wellbeing or safety. For fuck's sake, he beats me weekly.

"Thank you for informing me, Отец. I will be well-dressed." I hesitate a moment, gaging his response. When he continues eating, I push my meal away and ask, "May I be excused, Отец?"

I know better than to just leave. A good daughter always asks for permission.

He just waves his hand dismissively.

I jump up and make my way to his side. I give him a light kiss on the cheek, choking on the smell of cigarettes, and scurry out of the room.

Only once I'm back in my bedroom with Vova can I breathe again.

Sergey's coming tomorrow.

I need to mentally prepare.

Chapter 2

Dominic

Stefan steps into my office with a loose grin.

"Hey, Dom, what's up?" my second in command asks.

"Shut the door, Stefan." I can't have anyone overhearing this conversation.

His smile drops as he turns to close the door.

"So, this isn't a good meeting. What's wrong?" His easy grin drops as he takes a seat across from me.

"I have a solution to the Bratva war," I say grimly.

"Then why do you look so stressed?" Stefan's usual jovial nature dissolves into worry. It's an unsettling thing to see. Even in battle and on missions, even when being fired at, Stefan still cracks jokes.

My lips are barely tilted at the sides, the only indication that something is amiss, yet Stefan catches it. He's my oldest friend, my second in command, the only one I trust fully. He can read me better than anyone, and I'm still able to hide much from him. But not this. I'm too distraught to care.

"Because I don't like the solution." I sigh and rub a hand over my face. I take a deep breath and spit it out. "I'm going to suggest a marriage alliance between the Bratva and the Syndicate."

Stefan's eyes widen as he absorbs the information. He's so shocked, he's speechless at the news.

"And who's going to get married?" he demands. "Dom, I love the Syndicate, but I'm not wedding some Russian scum just to end this war. I'd rather just slay them all and be done with it." He looks truly ill at the prospect.

His green pallor reflects what I'm feeling inside.

"I am," I say firmly. I won't have one of my men suffer when it's something I can do. When it's a sacrifice I can make for my family.

"Dom... I know how important ending this war is, but this is not the way to do it." His grip tightens on his chair.

"I will not have any of my men die over my brother's mistake. This is not up for debate." My voice steels. I won't have anyone questioning me.

Instead of shrinking back and heeding my words, Stefan looks me in the eyes.

"No. You've sworn off marriage. Fuck, you've sworn off women. Do you even remember the last time you spoke to a woman you're not related to? A woman you were interested in?" He says it as though the thought of me with a woman is ludicrous.

I don't blame him. I haven't involved myself with any woman since my twenties. Once I took over the Syndicate and realized all the lives that are in my hands, my priorities rearranged, and woman didn't make the cut. I don't have time for the frivolity of that kind of company. And I can't risk being betrayed by one.

"This is simply business. The woman can do whatever she wants. I'll stay out of her way, and she'll stay out of mine. I have no interest in romance and intimacy. I don't have that luxury. This is what must be done." My stomach clenches at the idea of a woman in my space. I'll put her on the other end of my house and leave her alone. We'll live separate lives and not interact. I think that's the best way to go about it.

"What makes you think this can work? What woman would want that life?" Straightening in his chair, he questions me further.

"It works for the Irish!" I argue. "They have marriage alliances constantly. They have no issue with it." I take a breath. "What woman wouldn't want a life of wealth, with the only stipulation being my wife? I know... I know I'm not made to be a husband, but I wouldn't stop her from being with other men. All I'd need is for her to remain by my side in the public eye to uphold this alliance."

I've mulled over this for days and come to the conclusion that giving her complete freedom in the confines of the Syndicate is the only fair thing to do.

"Yeah, but they have real marriages from them. They don't just avoid their wives." Stefan throws his hands in the air. "Who are you even going to marry?"

I sigh and lean back in my chair. My gaze steadies in the corner of my office in resignation.

"It doesn't matter. Whoever Viktor chooses. Maybe he has a niece or one of his higher ups has a daughter." All I need is a woman from the Russians to agree to this.

Even if I knew the women of the Bratva, I wouldn't have a preference. Women all the same. What difference does it make who it is?

"Viktor has a daughter. What if that's who he chooses?" he asks curiously. "You couldn't trust her. There's no way his daughter would just abandon him and become loyal to the Syndicate."

"His daughter is young. There's no way he'd have her marry me." At thirty-seven, I don't feel old. But for a girl in her twenties, that's a ridiculous age gap. "But you do make a good point. There's no way to prove the allegiance of a Bratva daughter. I'd have to keep her at arm's distance. I'd never trust her."

He relaxes in his chair, sagging unprofessionally in relief. If he were any other of my men, I'd scold him for such lack of composure in my presence. We have a standard and reputation to uphold as Syndicate members. And I will not have my men looking lazy.

But it's Stefan, so I don't give him shit about it.

"So that's that? You're really getting married?" He runs his hand through his hair and sighs. I just nod. "Fuck, man. I never thought I'd see the day."

My gaze remains locked on the corner of my office. I spiral into thoughts about what this means. Into the horror of what I'm about to do.

Because, Stefan, neither did I. I never thought I'd be here.

I'm not meant for marriage.

But I'm willing to do anything to save my family, my Syndicate.

So really, how big of difference can one woman make on my life?

Chapter 3

Katerina

I'm researching business hierarchies for my end-of-term paper, but I can't stay focused. All I can think of is Sergey's creepy remarks and wandering eyes.

He knows I'm his. Not yet, but I will be.

I don't know how much longer I can live like this. Belonging to men. Whether it be Viktor or Sergey, it doesn't matter. I'll always only be property in their eyes. A pretty smile and punching bag.

I want to run away. I want to sneak out and leave this all behind. I need to.

But I can't.

I know Viktor would find me. He'd prowl through all corners of the earth to get me back, if only so he could enact his revenge. His fury over embarrassing him by leaving would be unmatched.

But that's not the real reason I stay. I'd gladly risk his wrath if only for a moment of freedom. A taste of life outside this cage.

But I won't leave. I can't leave. Not until I get my own revenge. Until Viktor is dead. Until I kill him.

It's not even about freedom. I know the minute I kill him, I'll have signed my life over. The minute he's dead, his precious Bratva will end me. But I also know in those last minutes, the sweet taste of vengeance will satiate me. I'll finally avenge my mother. I'll be deserving to sit at her side in the afterlife. I can tell her it's over, that he got what he deserved.

Vova runs to the door and crouches in a fighting pose, ready to attack. Knowing what this means, I quickly grab him and throw him in the closet before Viktor is on the receiving end of his wrath.

My door flies open so quickly it slams against the wall. And there he stands, in all his sinister glory.

"Katerina, I have an important man coming over for a meeting. You are to look presentable if you leave this room. If I see a single hair out of place, you'll feel it for a week. Do you understand?" he demands.

I mull over what he's saying. He seems almost... uneasy. His hands tremble, and there's a sheen of sweat on his forehead. His face is an even lighter shade than his regular pallor. I momentarily wonder who could be coming over that causes him this much distress, then brush it away with my indifference.

I must be quiet for too long because before I know it, Viktor has me by the throat. His tight grip is sure to leave a mark. There's no warning. He's restricting my airflow. I resist the urge to struggle, knowing it'll only worsen his wrath.

"Katerina, do you understand? I will lock you in this room for a week without meals if you embarrass me! This is no trifling matter." He's so pissed that his spit hits my face as he speaks.

I try to squeak out a response but can't get the sounds out with his grip on my neck.

He loosens his grip just enough for me to let out a meek, "Yes, sir."

He throws me to the floor and slams my door on his way out.

I gasp for air on the floor and think over what he said.

Part of me wants to put on something obnoxious and risqué to parade around the house just to piss him off. But the rational side of me shoots down the idea. The consequences wouldn't be worth it. And it's not like I even own anything near that. I don't even own pants or shorts. Viktor doesn't think a lady should wear those.

Fuck Viktor! I'm so fucking done with him.

I'd do anything to get away from him and this hell he has me suffering in.

Chapter 4

Dominic

The gaudy office overflows with extravagant items that clash hideously. Viktor Sokolov has no taste. It looks as though he bought every expensive thing he could find and threw them in here with no care of cohesion.

There's a metal desk sitting on an ornate rug that insult each other. The rest of the room is just as unmatching.

The whole house looks this way. I recognize some of it from our rescue mission for my sister-in-law a few years back, but at the time, I wasn't focused on the décor.

Viktor stands when I enter, welcoming me into the room.

"Viktor, thank you for having me. I'm here to offer an alliance," I shake his hand, then sit. I don't waste time on mindless conversation. Neither of us are men that enjoy pleasantries in subtlety and introductions.

"We had an alliance. Your brother destroyed it, desecrated my men, and reveled in it." He sneers and rubs his beard in aggravation.

"Again, I apologize for his actions. They were made out of desperation. His woman was gone." I don't understand it. I can't comprehend how one woman can bring a man to such insanity. How he can lose all sense when she's gone.

"From what I understand, she left of her own volition." He snorts at the irony of the situation.

"It was a miscommunication." My voice remains even as his obstinance drives me to anger.

"One that my family paid for," he shoots at me.

I rub a hand down my face. We aren't making any progress. I need him to hear me out, but I'm starting to think he has no intentions of doing so.

"Again, I have come to apologize and offer a truce in the form of an alliance," I say in a patient voice, despite the urge to strangle him. Roman's the hothead of the family or at least was before his wife calmed him down and made him start meditating. It's a bullshit thing to see. I'm the calm, cool, collected one. I don't show any emotions, but Viktor is testing my patience at the moment.

"What makes you think we are interested in a truce after what you've done?" His eyes are sharp as he throws it at me.

As much as I want to, I don't mention what his men did to my family. How they destroyed my brother's wedding and almost killed another one of my brothers.

"I come with a new offer." I keep it vague to gage his interest. When he leans forward slightly, I internally grin. I've got him.

"And what would that be?" He tries to appear uninterested in his stoic facial expression, but I can feel his excitement.

"I'm proposing..." I hesitate, knowing the minute I say it, it's solidified. Knowing there's no going back after this. "A marriage alliance."

It's a gamble. The Irishmen do it often, but no other families have done it as far as I'm aware of. He could take offense to it.

"Explain." The glint in his eyes tells me he's interested.

"Someone from the Bratva will marry someone from the Syndicate. It'll be a peaceful union in front of both families. Our men will see that we seek an alliance built on the most important thing to us: family."

"Hmm..." he mulls over the idea. "Who are you offering up in this marriage?"

This is it. There's no going back.

"Me. As the head of the syndicate, I will" *bear this burden* "get the privilege to join the families."

"Interesting." I can tell he's already decided. "And who do you wish to marry?"

I can sense the trap. If I were to select a Bratva woman, he'd take offense on behalf of all the others. And, technically, I shouldn't know any Bratva woman. But I do. I wouldn't be a good leader if I didn't know my enemy. And my youngest brother, Sebastian, has computer skills that come in handy in obtaining knowledge we shouldn't have.

"I have no preference. I trust whoever you select will make a fine wife." I doubt it. They'll be Bratva. And God forbid they're related to him.

The room descends in silence as he thinks. I can practically see his wheels turning. Only when his expression morphs into a sinister grin does my heart accelerate.

"You'll marry my daughter," he says gleefully. "She is the perfect candidate. Young, beautiful, pure. There's no finer Russian girl. She's been raised to be the perfect Bratva Princess. She will do you well."

My stomach drops. So, I'll be marrying Katerina Sokolov, the girl in her twenties. Viktor's young daughter.

"Thank you for this honor," I say calmly and call up a grateful smile. "I will treat her well."

"Yes, I'm sure you will," he says flippantly. "My Katerina will be a good, subservient wife. She listens well and will be at your command. She's untouched by any man, an unadulterated virgin. She won't give you any trouble."

A subservient wife? Listens well? At my command? I've never thought much of what I'd want in a wife, but it would've probably been something along those lines. A woman who respects me and obeys me seems ideal.

But for some reason, the thought of it disgusts me. I don't know what I want, but a wife who's basically my servant is not it.

And a virgin? That sounds like a nightmare. I don't want some young, inexperienced girl. I don't need someone who still has to grow up.

The way he speaks of her makes me sick. What kind of man can so easily get rid of his daughter? Sell her without a second thought. Without even discussing it with her.

"Thank you." I nod in acceptance. "Let me know when she has decided." I give him the chance to prove he's not a total piece of shit father.

"I have decided. She'll be your wife," he assures me. He doesn't even hesitate or take her feelings into consideration.

Despite not knowing or caring about the girl, I'm furious on her behalf. For fuck's sake, this is the twenty-first century. Women get a say in who they marry. And a daughter should be protected by her father, not sold like cattle.

"Let's talk logistics." I switch the topic because any more talk of his slave daughter, and I won't be able to stop myself from throwing a punch. "What do you want on your end?"

"Ever the businessman." He laughs. "I want a ceasefire. Not one more of my men should have a finger laid on them. None of your men are to interact with my own. I need you to stop monitoring my activity. When we agree to peace, the threat will be gone, so no more observation is required... And your brother must pay for what he's done."

I nod along until the last one.

"I agree to all the terms except the last one. Roman has done his penance in the form of being shot, twice, by your men. No more will be asked of him." My tone leaves no room for argument. My family is off limits. It's my job to protect them.

"Fair enough," he concedes.

"Do you have any more demands?" I need it all on the table now.

"Port control. I want your ports near mine to be handed over. I have more... *product* being delivered, and with a higher supply, I need more docks." His stern eyes show this isn't negotiable.

"Deal. I want the same terms as the previous treaty. Total ceasefire. No men of mine are to be harmed. Any of your men found in our territory are at risk of being interrogated. If you start any wars, then the treaty is over. Also, you are required to attend every meeting of the families." I add the latter as a precaution if things go south.

"My men can be interrogated but not killed." When I nod, he proceeds. "I agree to these terms."

I stand and shake his hand.

"My lawyer will draw up a contract and send it to you," I say. I don't trust him to make the contract.

"It's been a pleasure doing business with you." His grin makes me anxious. This was almost too easy. "Should we celebrate over a glass of vodka?"

He's already making his way across the room towards his cabinet. I'm not a vodka man, but I know better than to turn him down. I can't risk offending him.

"Thank you,'" I say tightly.

He grabs the hammer and brush that match the bottle and proceeds to open it in a way I've never seen before. He pours the clear liquid in two tumblers and hands me one.

"To the upcoming nuptials," he says.

"Cheers," I say tightly as I lift my glass to his.

"Za zdoróvye!" he says in return as he clinks his glass to mine.

I wait until he's taken a sip before I bring mine to my lips. In my line of work, you never drink something offered to you until you're sure it's clean.

I take a sip and am surprised by its smoothness. There are hints of honey, oats, and vanilla. It's certainly not the cheap stuff we drank as teenagers.

"This is from the motherland. Beluga Gold Line. Drunk by the elites and oligarchs. One of the finest vodkas in the world." His proud, celebratory tone has me feeling victorious.

"Thank you for sharing it with me."

"This is means of celebration. After all, by next month, you'll be family." He slaps me on the back jovially, and I almost choke on the vodka.

"Next month?" I knew the treaty needs to happen soon, but I didn't consider the wedding would be in the next month.

"Of course. We don't want to waste any time." His eyes shine with victory, and it lessens the feeling of mine.

"Yes. Next month, I'll marry your daughter." Through the smile, I take a long sip of the vodka and note how my life is about to change forever.

Chapter 5

Katerina

I'm too hungry to stay hidden in my room simply because Viktor is having a guest over. He didn't say I have to stay hidden, just that if I leave, I need to look appropriate. Or, well, his level of appropriate.

I put on my soft makeup and a light pink dress that ends below my knees. I fix my white-blonde hair into loose curls that fall down my back to my hips.

Looking in the mirror, I sneer at my reflection. I look like a doll. A doll that Viktor controls. This pink-clad sweet girl isn't me. I turn away from the mirror before I break it and abandon my room.

On my way to the kitchen, I hear voices from Viktor's office. Despite knowing better, I linger, trying to listen, to see if I recognize the other man. I know some of the men that work with him. None of them are men I'd choose to be around. But if it's my brother or his men, then I'll gladly say hi.

My brother runs other parts of the operation. I know he's taking over when Viktor steps down. The men he surrounds himself with are much kinder and more approachable. They don't make me feel uncomfortable like Viktor's men do.

I'm so caught up in trying to hear who it is, that I miss their footsteps towards the door. I barely turn down the hallway when the door opens.

And out walks the sexiest man I've ever seen. He's tall, at least six foot five. That leaves him six whole inches taller than me. Not many men are tall enough that I could wear heels and they'd still tower over me. He has dark hair and scruff. It's sexy on him. His eyes are so dark they're almost completely black. His olive tone leans towards European or Mediterranean decent. This man is certainly not Bratva. That only makes me like him more.

"Katerina!" Viktor hisses at me. I quickly avert my gaze.

"Sorry, Отец," I mumble and bow my head reverently.

"This is the girl of the hour. Dominic Montclair, meet my daughter, Katerina." Victor's voice is so cheerful, I stumble.

What in the hell has him so happy?

I glance at the man, Dominic, and he's eyeing me disapprovingly. He's studying me like it's a test, and I've already failed. His nostril rises in so much disgust, I have to look down and make sure I still look decent.

What the fuck is his problem?

This asshole can just fuck on right out of my house. How dare he come in here and look at me like this! *This* is the asshole that had Viktor nervous but now has him grinning?

"Katerina," Dominic says coldly as he offers me his hand.

I grab it lightly and shake it weakly when what I really want to do is crush his hand in mine and jerk his arm off his shoulder. I give him the sweetest, most demure smile I can muster, when what I really want is to growl and glare at him. I know what

Viktor expects of his Bratva Princess though, so I'm an angel on the outside.

Dominic, the asshole, just continues to look at me disapprovingly. Fuck him. I can't even shake his hand correctly! Asshole.

He pulls his hand from mine, *wipes it on his pant leg*, and turns from me dismissively towards Viktor, ignoring me. Just as my father does. "It was a pleasure meeting with you. I look forward to our alliance." He starts to stride out of the room, stops, turns to me, looks me up and down one more time, sneers, shakes his head, turns, and leaves.

Viktor follows behind the asshole and walks him out of the house. I run to the kitchen in an attempt to avoid Viktor. Even though he's in a good mood, I can smell the vodka on him, and I don't want to be anywhere near him when he drinks.

Unfortunately, Yelena finds me a few minutes later and tells me Viktor is waiting for me in the dining room. I guess we're having dinner together. *Fuck.*

...

After ten minutes of silence, Viktor speaks.

"You're getting married next month," Viktor says casually.

I choke on my stroganoff, hoping I didn't hear him correctly.

"What?" I whisper.

"You're getting married next month," he repeats just as calmly.

I swing my gaze to him as tears gather in my eyes. They evaporate the moment I see the glint in his. He wants a reaction from me. He knows what this is doing to me. I won't give him one.

"To Sergey?" I ask casually, looking at my plate. I take another bite, pretending the taste isn't ash in my mouth.

"Not this time." He chuckles.

What the fuck does that mean?

"This time?" I keep my tone disinterested.

"You're marrying Dominic Montclair."

My stomach drops. I'm marrying the asshole from earlier? There's no way. There's just no way Dominic wants to marry me. He was so disgusted and disapproving of me. He looked like he couldn't stand to be in my presence.

"The man from the hallway?" Confusion laces my words. I just can't make sense of it.

"Yes. He's an important man, and your marriage will be the perfect opportunity." His voice is dripping with glee.

"Who is he? What opportunity?" I beg for clarity.

"He's the enemy. The head of the Syndicate. And you're going to be his demise." Delight devours his demeanor, and I can tell he's already plotting his betrayal.

I've heard of the Syndicate. They're horrible people. Barbaric. Just earlier this year, they brutally killed many of our men. And he's going to marry me off to the monster that leads them?

My stomach twists at the thought. If Viktor, a rather reasonable man, can beat his daughter senseless daily, I can't imagine what that barbaric man would do to his wife. I wonder if I'll even survive a year of marriage before he kills me.

"I don't want to marry him," I whisper, more to myself than anything.

I don't even see it coming. The sting from the slap across my face takes over. He hits me so hard my face hits the table and sloshes into my meal.

"You don't have a choice, you ungrateful bitch!" he seethes.

I straighten my spine and muster up all my courage.

"I won't marry him!" I swear on everything that I have that I won't do it.

Viktor stands so fiercely that his chair swings back onto the floor. He's on me in an instant. He pulls me up by a tight grip on my hair. The burn of my scalp brings more tears to my eyes. He raises me until we're at eye level, and he's so furious, his face is red.

"You will marry him, or you'll join your mother. Those are your two options. Take your pick."

He throws me to the floor and stands over me. The hate in his eyes burns into me. He stopped being my father a long time ago, but I can't quite put a finger on when dislike turned to loathing.

"Fuck you!" I yell and spit on his shoes.

He lifts his leg and kicks me so hard in the stomach, that I have to curl into a ball to catch my breath. The pain is unbearable, but it's also familiar. And that makes me hate him even more.

"You will marry him. You will earn his trust. You will reveal to me everything about his shitty operation. And with that information, I will take out the Syndicate." The glint in his eyes as he tells me his grand plan makes me uneasy.

"Then what?" I spit out.

"Then I kill Dominic Montclair and his filthy family." Viktor cackles at that.

But for me, I feel hope. If I can stay alive in my marriage to that asshole, then maybe, once Viktor kills him, I'll be free.

"Then I'm free?" Hope against all odds fuels me.

Viktor throws his head back and laughs again. Then he crouches down until he's at my eye level.

"Then you marry Sergey." His grin, the glint in his eyes, his rosy cheeks... this bastard is ecstatic. And I couldn't hate him more than in this moment.

"Fuck you!" I say one more time. This time it's weaker. But I won't stop fighting. Because my bad situation just got so much worse.

Viktor does what I knew he'd do. He starts kicking me again. Cursing me out. Calling me a spoiled brat. He hits me. Spits on me. And at some point, I pass out from the pain.

But it's better than the alternative.

It's better than complying. Even if fighting back only gets me pain and leads me to the same place, at least I fought.

Because if I don't fight this, I'll have betrayed myself.

Chapter 6

Dominic

I don't want to do this.

I don't want to marry that porcelain doll.

So fragile, so inadequate.

She was sickly sweet, wearing that ugly pink dress, with her big, blue eyes gazing at me so innocently.

At first, I could've sworn she was looking at me with interest, but it was quickly overtaken by an angelic look.

This life has no place for angels.

She seems like she has no idea what her father does. What I do.

How am I supposed to explain to a wife like her what my life is like? How can she possibly understand the horrors that lie beyond the walls of her hideous mansion?

The fragile doll isn't built for this. She won't survive my life. She won't survive me.

She'll break under the slightest pressure. And I don't have time to coddle her.

I have to be the leader. The Syndicate is my only priority. I don't have it in me to be sweet and patient with the breakable doll. And that seems to be what she needs.

I think I did a good job masking my disgust at the sight of her. It'd be inconvenient for my wife to think I dislike her, but her feelings aren't high on my list of things to care about.

This is simply business, a treaty. If she agrees to this marriage, then she has to know it's nothing more than an alliance.

She can do whatever she wants. Whoever she wants. I won't stop her, nor will I intervene. I won't rob her of her life as long as she stays out of mine. I'll place her in the wing on the other side of the house, far from me. I want nothing to do with her. This marriage is in name only.

I feel more at ease with that decision. To not involve myself with her. I'll fund her life and put her on my card, but besides that, we'll have no interactions.

Despite this, I still can't alleviate the pit in my stomach.

I don't want to do this.

I don't want to share my space and live with her. I don't want to be tied to her. I don't want to be around her.

It's not often I get to do what I want. But it's even rarer I have to do something I don't want to do.

Being the boss, duty tends to take over my life. I don't have time for galas and festivities like Matthias, my younger brother, who runs Syndicate Enterprise, our legal front. Nor do I have time to start a family like my other brother, Roman. Despite being the enforcer for the Syndicate, he still found the time to marry his woman and impregnate her. Our youngest brother, Sebastian, works on both sides of the law, but he still manages to do... *I'm actually not sure what he does. I barely see him outside of work and family dinners.*

Matthias and Roman are both married. And they seem happy in their marriages. But that's not in the cards for me. I've never seen myself as a married man. A wife seems like more of an inconvenience than anything else. Especially that young, tiny, timid woman.

It's not that she isn't beautiful, she is. With hair so blonde it's almost white, eyes an icy blue, and fair skin, she's breathtaking. But all that pink shit on her ruins it. And she's tall. I've always preferred women who can look me in the eye without craning their necks. She must be almost six feet tall. She'd be perfect if she weren't so skinny. Not that being thin is an ugly thing, but her lack of muscle shows how weak she is. I'd break her if I ever took her to my bed.

I shudder at the thought. There's nothing I'm less interested in than sex with Katerina Sokolov. Her father's boasting of her being 'pure' and 'untouched by any man' had the opposite reaction on me than intended. I don't want some young, inexperienced woman in my bed. It'd be a chore to teach her everything.

But that won't be an issue. I truly don't remember the last time I was with a woman. They're distractions, and I don't trust any of them.

Which is another issue with my marriage alliance plan.

Trust.

I don't trust her. I can't trust the spawn of Viktor, even if she seems clueless to the Bratva. This porcelain doll will surely be loyal to her father and would betray me for him.

I'm going to have the enemy living under my roof, taking my name, and I have no clue how to address it.

Ignoring her is a given. If I pretend she doesn't exist, then maybe she'll be less concerned with me.

I'll have to be careful as to which meetings I take outside my office. My home office is soundproof, but the rest of the house isn't. I also need to install biometric locks on all the weaponry around the complex.

I live on a huge complex that houses the Syndicate. The gated community is guarded and patrolled at all times. There's the main house where I live, then a few barracks around the acres of land for guards. Stefan has his own house on the grounds as well. There's also a gym, gun range, and running trail open at all hours. We have an indoor pool and many armories on the grounds. My fortress is perfect for running the Syndicate. However, the only private office I have is in my house. I figured there was nowhere more secure than my home which is heavily guarded. I never foresaw the enemy moving in.

This is a fucking nightmare. And it's one I designed.

But I've handled worse. I've been shot, tortured, and stabbed.

If I can handle those, then surely, I can handle a sweet, kind woman.

Chapter 7

Katerina

"Nik, I can't do this!" I cry out as I throw a shoe across my bedroom.

"Calm down, babe," Nikolai, my best friend, chides me. His words only piss me off.

I change my aim and throw the other shoe at him instead.

The bastard, of course, catches it.

"How am I supposed to calm down when I'm being married to an asshole that runs a crime family?" I cry out.

I continue digging through my closet, looking for my favorite sweatshirt. Viktor is away for the weekend, which means I get to dress like a normal girl for once. But that also means finding my contraband clothes.

"At least he's a sexy asshole who happens to run a crime family." Nik winks at me. I point another shoe at him threateningly. "Hey now, you're the one who said he's hot!" He raises his hands defensively.

"I said he wasn't bad looking, and you're the one who pulled it from me!" I huff, pissed that it's true. Pissed that he's hot.

"At least he's better than Sergey," Nik offers. He picks up my lilac kitten heel and curls his lip at it.

"We don't know that," I counter, mostly to be obstinate. I know I'm picking a fight with him, but it's because he's the only one that'll let me.

Vova rubs against me, comforting me.

"Yes, we do. Sergey's an old creep that kills his wives. Dominic Montclair is a sexy crime boss."

I snort, and Nik throws the heel back at me. I duck in time to miss it but still glare at him.

"Ugh! I'm just so pissed!" I hop on my bed and scream into a pillow. Better that than Yelena thinking Nik's killing me in here. "I can't believe this is happening. I can't believe when I'm finally free of this hellhole, I'm moving in with another controlling, abusive bastard. Out of the frying pan and into the fire."

Nik grunts at the mention of abuse. He hasn't mentioned the bruise on my cheek, nor the way I flinch and groan when I move. I know he notices them, but with Viktor as his boss, there's not much he can do. But I know he hates it.

"I wish I could be there for you. Then, at least, I could protect you from the abuse if he tries anything. I can't stand by while another man hurts you. I don't give a damn if it's your husband causing the pain." He sighs, and I know he means it.

It gives me an idea.

"Wait, Nik, what if you do come? Viktor wants me to spy on Dominic and the Syndicate. I bet I could convince him to bring one of his men with me to help on the mission. He'd probably even like the idea of having control over me even when I'm married. I could ask him if it can be you!"

I jump up and start pacing, letting a plan take form. I'll have to ask carefully, so as to not give away how much I want this.

Nik's my personal Bratva guard. He has Viktor's trust but is loyal to me.

"You might be onto something. There's nothing Viktor gets off more on than control. And having eyes on his Bratva Princess would make him ecstatic. I bet he'd even want me to spy on you, which of course, I'll only tell him what you want me to." Nik jumps up and wraps his arm around me. "This is great! We just have to hope Viktor can convince Montclair."

I'm soaring at the possibility of having my best friend, my comfort, with me when I go. I give him a kiss on the cheek, and he ruffles my hair.

"This could work. I might survive if I have you by my side." I give him a tight hug, and sigh in relief. This could be it.

"You're strong, Katya. You can survive anything. Fuck, you've put up with Viktor for this long. You're a fighter," he tells me as he squeezes me.

"Thanks." I blush at the compliment, not used to them. "Maybe there are some hot Syndicate men to ogle while we're there" I tease him, changing the subject.

He throws a hand over his heart dramatically.

"A man can only dream," he says wistfully. "Is it bad that I'm hoping the Syndicate men are hotter than the Russians? My own people just aren't doing it for me."

"They aren't doing it for me either. Imagine having to fuck Sergey!" I blanche at my future.

"I can't believe he's making you marry Sergey after Montclair. It's ridiculous. You really can't catch a break."

"Ooh idea! What if you get me pregnant right now, then I have to marry you instead of the others! Then we have a happy lavender marriage raising our kid!" I sigh longingly at the absurd, unrealistic vision.

"Nope!" Nik says as he drops me to the floor. "Neither of us wants a kid, and I actually would like to live to see my twenty-sixth birthday. Viktor would kill me for adulterating his 'perfect, virgin daughter.'"

Nik pretends to vomit at my preposterous idea, and I just laugh.

"Let a girl dream. There's nothing I'd want more than to marry my best friend, even if the sex would be awkward." I tease him.

"The sex would be nonexistent. You're not my type," he looks me over with a similar disgust as Dominic Montclair did.

"You're not mine either. Remember, Russian doesn't do it for us?" I scold him.

"I take that back. Pyotr does it for me. Oh, he really does it for me!" He wiggles his eyebrows at me then laughs at my revulsion.

"Hey now, that's my brother!" I throw another pillow at him, but he just swats it away.

We spend the rest of the day hanging out, and I pray that Viktor lets him go with me so we can have more days like this.

Chapter 8

Dominic

I take a deep breath then walk into my parents' sitting room.

It's our weekly Sunday dinner, and despite holding it in, I know it's time to share my upcoming nuptials.

I look around the room at their cheery faces. Even Roman is happy. He used to be the other grump, but now I'm alone in my misery.

Matthias and his wife, Margot, sit on a couch with Sebastian next to them. Roman and Cecilia, his wife, sit on a loveseat that's too small for both his muscular frame and her petite one, so she's almost on his lap. Mom and Dad are in armchairs looking lovingly at their family. There's one seat open, but I stay standing.

Everyone's attention lands on me when I clear my throat.

"I have an announcement." I keep my voice neutral.

They look at me expectantly, but I'm frozen. I don't know how to tell my family. I hate their disapproval, and I know that's the reaction I'll receive.

"Go on, honey," Mom tells me kindly as she reaches up and squeezes my hand.

"I'm getting married next month." I spit it out in one rushed breath.

The room freezes. No one moves a muscle. It's as if everyone's too scared to breathe.

"What do you mean?" Mom asks, this time more hesitant.

"I'm marrying Katerina Sokolov next month," I explain. I run my fingers through my hair and yank at it, needing the prick to set me straight.

"NO! This can't be happening! Dom, no!" Roman jumps up so quickly, Cecilia tumbles to the floor. He rushes to pick her up and place her back on the seat, then marches up to me.

"There has to be another way." He's pleading with me. His eyes hold so much desperation, but I know it'll fade.

"There's no other way. It's the only thing Viktor would agree to," I explain.

"No! I forbid it!" He exclaims, then shakes me. "Wake up, Dom. This is the last thing you want. You can't do this to yourself."

I know this is his guilt talking. He can't bear knowing that because of his fuckup, I'm now having to enter my worst nightmare. I have to sacrifice everything to fix his mistake.

"Oh fuck," Bash whispers as realization dawns on him. "Do you really have to?"

"Yeah. It's all that's left to do. The war has to end."

Matthias whispers to his wife, and I see the moment Margot finally understands.

"How could you marry *his* daughter? After all he's done! How could you do this to us? How could you welcome her into our family?" The look of betrayal on Margot's face is a punch in the gut. I never considered what this would mean to her. Her trauma with Viktor Sokolov runs deep, and here I am, cutting open her barely healed wounds.

A single tear slides down her cheek then she looks at me with such a broken expression that I realize I'd rather be shot than hurt my family.

"I'm sorry. I can't do this," she whispers then runs from the room.

Matthias instantly stands and looks at me. "I'll explain it to her."

Then he's gone too. The front door opens, and I realize for the first Sunday in years, the whole family won't be together. And it's my fault.

"Honey, it's going to be okay. What's she like? Why don't we have her over for family dinner next week?" Mom offers after Dad explains the situation to her.

"No, that's not necessary. I've barely even met her. She's just some stranger I'm marrying. It's just business." I reach down and pat Mom's hand comfortingly, but she pulls back and slaps my hand.

What the fuck?

"Absolutely not! You will know your fiancée. Marriage is not business. It may not start out as love, but you never know where it may lead to. Unless you ignore her, then it'll go nowhere. I'm disappointed in you, Dominic." She shoots out of her chair mid-scolding and glares at me.

I haven't been reprimanded by my mother in a decade and a half. What the fuck is happening?

"You don't understand. This is literally business. It's for the Syndicate. I–" Before I can finish the sentence, she's in my face.

"No! YOU don't understand! This woman is going to be your wife. And you'll treat her as such. I will not stand for a son of mine to treat a woman poorly, especially not one he's marrying." Her eyes narrow as her nostrils flair.

"But–" I start.

"Dominic Daniel Montclair, you listen to me! You may think you're some big hotshot running the Syndicate, but I'm still your mother. I don't care how old you are, you were raised better than this. I taught you to respect women, and your father and I showed you what a healthy marriage looks like. I expect you to at least try!" Mom leaves the room, and Dad looks at me sternly before following her.

I stare at the floor in astonishment. I didn't expect it to go well, but I definitely didn't foresee it crushing Margot and upsetting Mom too.

I hear someone approach me, then a large hand grabs my arm.

"I'm so fucking sorry, Dom. I don't even know what to say. Fuck," I look up and see Roman run his hand over his buzzcut, "I know I messed up. I thought Matthias's wedding would be the worst of it, but–"

"I don't want to hear it. What's done is done." I cut him off. I don't care to hear his guilt, let Cecilia deal with that.

The two of them exit the room, leaving me alone with Bash.

He just stares at me for a few minutes then sighs.

"Need a drink? I can make you one," he offers plainly, and I smile at my sweet younger brother.

While I'm cold and stoic, Matthias is cocky and arrogant, and Roman is hotheaded and wrathful, Bash is unlike us. He's laid back and calm. Happy. If not a little nerdy.

"I'm good. Let's get through this dinner sober," I sigh knowing alcohol won't help my feelings.

He stands and slaps me on the back.

"If you ever need to run from her, you're welcome at my house," he tells me with a grin.

I snort at the idea of running from the porcelain doll. "She's not that kind of woman. There isn't anything intimidating about her. Plus, I don't want to visit your suburban house. Don't you miss the penthouse?"

Bash unexpectedly moved from his penthouse in the city to some middle-class suburb. None of us know the reason. It's weird as fuck and such a downgrade, but he seems happy.

"Nope. This house has everything I could ever want." He has a faraway look in his eyes when he says it and the creepiest grin on his face. He leaves the room looking excited... *at the idea of his house?* I don't even have it in me to figure out what the fuck is wrong with him.

...

We're eating dinner, ignoring the two empty seats that should be occupied by Margot and Matthias. Mom keeps shooting glares at me, and Dad keeps mediating. Bash has been a godsend. He redirects the conversation every time it starts to come back to my marriage.

And Roman and Cecilia seem to be in their own world as usual.

Looking at them laughing together, the way he looks at her... Could Mom be right? Could this marriage amount to something like that?

I've never been envious of my brothers and their wives. I've never so much as been tempted by it. I see the way Bash looks at them longingly, and I know he wants what they have, but I never have. Maybe there's something wrong with me, but I just don't have it in me to care for a woman. There's too much risk and not enough reward.

But maybe something good could come from this marriage.

What the fuck am I saying?

No, I'm not like them. I don't get to marry some woman off the streets. This is Katerina Sokolov. I'm marrying Viktor Sokolov's daughter. The enemy. There can be no trust there. And there certainly can't be any love.

On top of it all, I could never feel anything for that fragile, perfect porcelain doll. Just the image of her has me indignant.

Marriage to her is my burden to bear as the leader of the Syndicate, and that's all there is to it.

I just pray she doesn't drive me crazy with her saccharinity.

Chapter 9

Katerina

Boxes litter my bedroom floor. They're full of my possessions. Which are mostly just clothes and cat toys. I don't have many other things.

I can't believe I'm moving in with that man in just a couple weeks. I keep praying that I'll wake from this nightmare, but I know it's not the case. I've succumbed to my new reality.

I've been trying to tell myself that this is better than the alternative. But how can I be sure? Sergey is the monster I know. This man is a stranger and the head of a barbaric organization. He's the enemy. What if he hates me simply because of my relation to Viktor?

I pull another hideous dress off its hanger and fold it. Vova starts scratching a box, so I abandon the dress and pick him up. He hisses at my hold, and I *tut* at him.

"Hey, buddy. We're moving to a new house soon. You may even be allowed to roam the whole place instead of just a bedroom. We'll have to see. But at least we'll be away from Viktor," I tell him soothingly.

I'm distracted playing with him, so I don't hear him approaching until it's too late.

My bedroom door swings open, and Vova hisses. His hair raise, and he jumps out of my arms. He's on Viktor in seconds, scratching his legs and biting his pants.

Viktor curls his nose in disgust and kicks my cat away. Vova whines but recovers quickly and is back attacking him.

"Control your pest, or I'll get rid of him," he hisses.

"Yes, Отец." I rush to Vova and pick him up. He's hissing but stops struggling when I pick him up. He'd never risk hurting me.

I stare at Viktor, waiting for him to tell me why he's here. I haven't seen him in a couple days. It's been peaceful.

"I don't want any communication between you and Dominic before the wedding." He glares at me skeptically when he says it.

I just raise a brow. Why on earth would I want to talk to that asshole? How would I even talk to him? It's not like I have his number.

"Okay," I say slowly.

"You haven't spoken to him, have you?" he interrogates me. His distrust is nothing new, but this subject is.

"Of course not. I've only ever seen him once, and that was in the hallway with you." It's obvious. I don't know what has him paranoid.

Viktor sighs, and his shoulders drop.

"Yes, I believe you haven't. You're many things, but stupid isn't one of them. He invited you to his family dinner." He pauses to gage my reaction. When there isn't one, he continues. "I declined, telling him until there's a treaty signed, you aren't leaving the premise. I won't risk my only bargaining chip."

Bargaining chip.

He doesn't care about his daughter's safety, only his leverage.

"If he wants to get to know you once you're married, that's fine. Let him think he has your trust. But at the end of the day, remember where your loyalties lie. This man will not be your savior; he will not be your salvation. You are a Sokolov, and he will burn you the first chance he gets. You are Bratva, and you will return home when we win this war. You will help us win it. Do you understand?"

The threat is as evident in his voice as is his distrust for me. And I realize this is the perfect segue.

"If you're so concerned about my behavior over there, why don't you send my guard with me. Then you'll have an additional set of Bratva eyes and ears over there. I don't know what you want me to look for. I don't even know why this marriage is happening at all." My voice comes out sarcastic, as though this stems from distrust in the spur of the moment.

The pensive look that comes over his face feels like a victory in itself. He doesn't realize this was my plan.

I hold my breath for what seems like eternity as he mulls it over.

"See, I knew I raised you to be smart. That's the way the Bratva Princess should think. Nikolai will be sent with you. I'll negotiate with Dominic, tell him that it's the only way I can ensure my daughter's safety." Viktor's glee is palpable.

I bow my head in response, because I know if I open my mouth, my excitement will be obvious.

Viktor glances around the half-packed room and nods.

"Finish up packing. You only have two weeks before you move." He turns on his heels, but before opening the door, he abruptly halts.

He fishes into his jacket pocket and pulls out an envelope.

"Dominic sent you a letter when I declined the invitation. I took the liberty of reading it. Nothing unexpected is here, but it looks as though he wants nothing to do with you. It makes sense, but you can't let it happen. Figure out a way to make him trust you."

Viktor tosses the envelope at me, and I leap forward to catch it. Vova is dropped from my arms, but before he can attack Viktor again, he's out of the room and shutting the door behind him.

I look down at my name and address written in neat cursive across the front.

I don't remember the last time I received a handwritten letter. I flip it over, and note that as Viktor said, it's already been open. I'm a little pissed that he read what was meant for me, but I wouldn't expect anything less from him.

I take a deep breath and open the letter.

For some reason, this feels like a big moment. Whatever is in here, Viktor didn't like. Which makes me hopeful. Maybe it's good news for me.

Dear Katerina,

I am writing to you since your father has made it clear I won't be seeing you before the wedding. There are some things that need to be said, clarity that needs to be shed, before we wed. I was hoping to discuss this at family dinner, but here it is.

What I'd like to address are the expectations for our marriage. First and foremost, I'd like to thank you for agreeing to this treaty. I understand the sacrifice. Not many would be willing to forfeit their future for their family.

Secondly, our marriage is simply a business transaction. We will only be husband and wife in name. I know what this is, and I want to ensure you're on the same page as me.

You must move into my house on my estate, but you will be staying in your own suite on the other side. You will have your own area, and there are no expectations of you. You are free to do as you please. To go where you'd like, see whatever and whomever you please, and live freely. I will not stop you, nor do I have any demands of you. You will be added to my card, so there are no limitations to your spending.

Be aware, I am not a man of feelings. I have no intention of changing that. The Syndicate is my priority. Nothing and no one has ever nor will ever come before it.

In giving you your freedom, I expect the same in return. You will not question me on my whereabouts or doings. We owe each other nothing.

I hope this pleases you. Seeing as you are marrying a stranger, I see no reason for you to want to know me, and I certainly have no interest in knowing you.

Thank you for doing business with me,
Dominic Montclair

I take a deep breath and reread the letter.

My heart is racing. My hands are sweating. My head is swirling.

This... this is too good to be true.

Is there truly a possibility that this man will give me freedom, just like that? That I won't be his wife or whore? That he'll let me be?

It's too much to wish for. I never even considered the possibility that once he gets his alliance, he'll have no more use for me. I would've thought he'd at least force me into his bed. But to just leave me alone, it's all I could ever want.

Viktor's words echo in my head. He wants me to go against this. He wants me to worm my way into Dominic Montclair's heart. To help bring him down.

But what if I don't? What if I just live my happy life and abandon the Bratva?

What if Dominic Montclair is my key to freedom?

Chapter 10

Dominic

Gathered around the conference room are the higher ups of the Syndicate. Some men from my father's reign still are active members. A few, I think, will die before they retire. A good portion of the men present are people I've selected throughout my time as the leader of the Syndicate. They're the ones loyal to me. The ones that trust me. They won't be as hard to convince.

"I brought us together today to discuss an upcoming change." The room silences as I begin speaking. "I've brokered a peace treaty with Viktor. In ten days, we will no longer be at war with the Bratva."

There are murmurs throughout the room. Most of my men seem relieved, but a few seem agitated. Their faces are pinched as they talk rapidly among themselves. It concerns me. A few of my men have been too eager during this war. Almost as though it excites them.

"What are the terms?" Mark asks. He's a younger guy but is eager to learn. He's going to make a great member of the Syndicate one day.

I glance at Stefan just for him to shoot me a knowing look. We both know how this is going to go.

"The alliance depends on an arranged marriage between the Syndicate and the Bratva," I tell them honestly. They're going to find out anyway.

The room breaks out in chaos. Some men are demanding answers. Others talk among themselves. But overall, the consensus seems to be anger.

"QUIET!" I yell, effectively silencing the room.

"Dom, who do you propose enters this marriage? Surely you cannot ask this of one of your men," Daniel inquires. He's older, having been around since my father's rule. But he's a strong ally. He's someone whose suggestions I tend to consider.

"You're right. I would never ask that of one of you. I will be marrying Katerina Sokolov." As expected, the room erupts into chaos once more.

"Your father would never do this!"

"This is preposterous!"

"She'll betray you. It'll be the end of the Syndicate!"

Men shout their opinions over one another. I'm not sure who's saying what. Most of the criticism I expect. But that last one, yelled by young Alex, the threat of her betraying me, stabs through me like a knife.

Not because I didn't consider it, but because it's the only thing I've thought of since agreeing to this.

She is the biggest threat to this plan.

And the only defense I have is distance from her.

"ENOUGH!" I shout over them, but they keep going.

I pound loudly on the table. The loud *bang* grabs their attention.

"It has already been decided. Papers have been signed by both Viktor and me. This is not up for debate. You will not change my mind. And you will not question my decision. If you have legitimate concerns," I glance at Stefan questioningly, and he nods. "If you have any legitimate concerns, go to Stefan. He'll investigate and report to me any that have merit."

I look around the room, meeting my men's gazes. My cold tone leaves no room for questions, and most seem to understand that. A few men brood, furious about our alliance with the Bratva.

When my gaze lands on Olly, an older member from my father's time, he braves up.

"You don't know what you're doing, boy. You'll ruin us," he threatens.

My hand tightens into a fist, tempted to use it on him. But I take a deep breath and refrain.

"It's 'boss' to you," I hiss, not standing for the disrespect. "I know exactly what I'm doing. I'm going to every length to ensure no more of my men lose their lives to these bastards."

It's a lie. But it's one that quiets him.

I have no idea what I'm doing. I know in my gut that this is a terrible idea. But it's the only one I've got.

Chapter 11

Katerina

I slip on the same ugly dress I wore two days ago. Because all my clothes are packed in boxes. It's been cleaned, but it's still an annoyance.

I can't believe this weekend I'll be married.

But I also can't believe this weekend I'll be free from Viktor.

Granted, it'll only be so another man can control me. But better the beast I don't know, right?

I pick up Dominic's letter again and just hold it. I've read it so many times that I have every word memorized by now.

I've done my best to not let myself believe it's true, but I can't squash all my hope.

Because what if it is? What if this is really my key to freedom?

If this man is bearable, if what he says is true, then I'll abandon Viktor and live a happy life.

Granted, I'm not sure I'll be reporting anything back to him. He doesn't deserve it.

But what if he retaliates? What if he comes after me?

I need to make Dominic like me enough, or at least be protective enough of his wife, that he won't let Viktor hurt me.

A man like him has to care enough about his wife, right? Even if it's just the image of her.

Vova jumps into my lap, and I pet him. He knows something's changing. I haven't packed his things yet, but he knows.

I don't think he wants to move. But he doesn't realize anywhere is better than this tacky prison.

He's already torn into multiple cardboard boxes. So many that we had to start packing in plastic ones.

He meows as I scratch him behind the ear.

"It's going to be okay. We're going to be okay." I'm trying to convince myself just as much as him.

A knock at the door interrupts us, but Vova doesn't fly out of my arms, so I know it's not Viktor.

Yelena walks in before I can answer.

"Get up, girl. You have your final fitting!" She rushes around me, trying to get me up off the floor.

Right, the fitting. For the world's ugliest wedding dress.

I didn't get to pick it.

I didn't get to pick anything.

Hell, I don't know a single detail about the wedding.

But knowing Viktor, it'll be tacky, gaudy, and miserable. Just like my life with him.

The seamstress enters with a bundle of white tulle in her arms. I start undressing, knowing the assignment.

Once the monstrosity is on, I look in the mirror and have to stifle a gag. Out of all the hideous dresses Viktor has picked out for me, this is by far the worst.

If I got to pick a wedding dress, it'd be sleek. Form fitting. Classic white, no lace. It may have a modest neckline but a low back.

It certainly wouldn't be a ballgown with three bows. Three! It wouldn't be covered in the ugliest lace pattern. Nor would it look like it's fit for the eighteenth century.

If I didn't know Viktor's ego and his obsession with his Bratva Princess's image, I'd think he did it on purpose. That he chose this eyesore as some sort of humiliation ritual for me.

No one except Viktor could find this dress attractive. In fact, even the seamstress curls her nose as she works on it.

Actually, maybe it's a good thing. There's no way Dominic could look at me lustfully in this. Maybe he won't be tempted to touch me.

My one goal is to avoid being his concubine. I won't whore myself out to him, even if I am his wife. I don't care how many beatings I take, I won't give myself away like that.

"Straighten your back! Shoulders straight and powerful! Look straight ahead!" Yelena snaps at me.

I do as she says, and she analyzes me for more errors.

"No man wants a troll stomping down the aisle to him. Have a little decorum," she huffs at me.

I roll my eyes.

I damn well might just stomp down the aisle. Show them all what I think of this.

But then Dominic might not want me. He could back out. And I wouldn't get my freedom.

But will this freedom come with strings?

I just don't know.

There's so much uncertainty on this path. I have no idea what to expect. It worries me so much.

I look down at Vova and pray our new home won't be the same hell as this one.

I don't know how long I can last as sweet, quiet, pathetic Katya, the Bratva Princess.

Chapter 12

Dominic

Black minivan entering Gate 1

The message appears on my smart watch just like every security alert does.

Who the fuck is entering my fortress in a minivan?

And how the fuck did they get through the front gate?

I retrieve my gun from my waistband and hold it at eye level as I creep towards the front door. With the tablet installed on the wall next to it, I pull up the surveillance cameras of the driveway. And sure enough, there's a black minivan with tinted windows pulling up to my house.

But what startles me the most is when it parks, my brother emerges from the driver's seat.

Why the fuck is Roman driving a *minivan*? Nothing could make me degrade myself in such a way.

Matthias steps out of the passenger seat and Bash from the back.

The three swagger up to my door, but instead of knocking, they let themselves in.

"Hey, James Bond, you can put the gun away," Roman smirks at me.

I put it away, but not because he told me to.

"Why do you have a gun trained on us?" Matthias raises a brow in question.

I glare at them. First, they show up uninvited at my house, and now, they're questioning me.

"Because an unknown vehicle entered my gate without my approval," I snarl at them. Then, I take a deep breath and control my emotions. "Roman, where's the Suburban? Why are you driving a minivan?"

It's mostly curiosity that has me asking. What reason does my bloodthirsty brother have to drive such a humiliating vehicle?

"Dom, my wife is pregnant. *With triplets.* Three girls." He sighs and runs his hand over his face. The worry of his situation is taking its toll on him. "We need a car that can hold all of us. I had it custom made, fully bullet-proof. Nothing's ever touching them."

It still throws me off hearing him say 'wife.' We've known Cecilia for a while, but with their *unconventional* eloping, I forget they're married. And now that she's pregnant... I don't know how he's going to do it. It'd be my personal hell.

"Hmm... Why are you guys here?" I want to settle whatever needs to be done, then kick them out.

I planned on drinking and despairing tonight. The wedding is tomorrow. Doomsday is here. I'll have a wife, someone invading my space. That porcelain doll.

Sneering at the reality of my situation, I turn around and make my way back to my den, needing another sip of whiskey.

"Bachelor party!" Bash says excitedly lifting a poker set.

Mattias holds up a bottle of liquor, and Roman grips a piece of paper. They're all wearing matching grins.

I can't stop the curse that escapes my lips.

"Look, I appreciate the sentiment, but no. I'm not in the mood to celebrate." My even voice conceals my annoyance. There's nothing I want to do less than have a party. This is commiseration, not commemoration.

"Don't care. We're here anyway," Matthias says as he follows me into the den.

"We knew you'd say no, that's why we didn't ask." Roman looks around then frowns in disappointment. "Do you have any snacks?"

"Oh yeah. I could do a pizza!" Matthias suggests.

"I'm down for that. Want me to place an order?" Bash adds, his phone already in his hand.

"STOP! No pizza! No poker! It's time for you to go! All of you!" I raise my voice, desperate for some alone time. I need to fully process tomorrow. Make sure I've planned for everything that could occur, not just tomorrow, but also in this marriage.

But instead of listening, all three of my godforsaken brothers make themselves at home in my den. In my house. Where they've shown up, uninvited.

"I've got four large pizzas coming. They'll be here in thirty," Bash says with a grin.

"Perfect! Let's grab the table," Roman fetches my poker table.

Matthias gathers four tumblers for the whiskey and starts pouring drinks.

"None for me. I'm not drinking during the pregnancy." Roman stops Matthias before he pours the fourth drink.

I stare at him incredulously. Is he fucking serious? He doesn't even have the baby in him. I'm astounded, but Matthias just nods understandingly.

"What the fuck?" I blurt out, unable to hold back.

"I want to support Cecilia. Also, triplets make the pregnancy high risk. I need to always be coherent in case she needs me." He smiles softly at the mention of his wife.

With three of the four chairs filled and whiskey poured, I succumb to my fate. I guess I won't be spending the evening alone.

After an hour of losing my money to my brothers, I sigh and lay my cards down. It's not that Bash is beating us, he always does, it's tomorrow's events that have me upset.

"What am I going to do with a wife? How can I have the enemy in my own home?" I sneer and take another sip. The burn doesn't calm me in the slightest, and I know I need to slow down; I refuse to be hungover in the morning.

"Here's some advice from a married man: happy wife, happy life." Matthias grins proudly, as if he came up with the ridiculous motto.

I just snort in derision. There's no fucking chance my happiness is dependent on the doll's.

"No, no. He's right," Roman cuts in. He pulls out the piece of paper he was holding earlier and waves it in my face. "I made a list of suggestions for a good marriage. Or really any relationship since you've never had one."

At the mentions of a relationship, Bash perks up.

"I don't need your fucking advice. If I remember correctly, your wife didn't even choose to marry you." Throwing their elopement in his face is a low blow, but he doesn't fall for the trap.

Cecilia has calmed and mellowed his formerly wrathful demeanor. Normally it's a good thing, but right now, when I'm itching for a fight, it's pissing me off.

"First, spoil her. Treat her like a princess. Women are gifts, and we don't deserve them." Roman begins.

"Work hard to earn her!" Matthias cuts in.

"I don't want your advice either. You fucking kidnapped Margot!" I seethe.

They just ignore me.

"Learn to do things she likes to do." Roman continues. "Oh, and don't expect her to do things for you. She's your wife, not your maid."

I gesture around my mansion, conveying that obviously I have a team that cleans, cooks, and upkeeps the house.

"Make sure she's always protected. Don't ever let her out of your sight without protection." Matthias's voice gets serious.

He's referring to what happened to his wife. It's been almost two years since that situation, but he's still scarred.

"That won't be a problem. Her personal guard is coming with her. It's not ideal to have a full-fledged Bratva member in the house, but I thought she'd feel better if she had some semblance of normalcy." I was against the idea when Viktor first suggested it, but then I realized it was the only thing Katerina has asked for, so I gave in.

"Don't lie to her. Don't hide anything," Roman says.

I roll my eyes. There's no way I'm telling her anything. She's the enemy. She doesn't get to know any Syndicate information.

Now, I understand why Roman hid so much from his wife. It all makes sense. In fact, what seemed ridiculous now seems reasonable.

"If she tries to fight you or run away, she will forgive you for cuffing her to the headboard, just until you know she's sensible again." Roman chuckles as if it's a fond memory for him, and to my upmost surprise, Bash nods along as if it has merit.

"That's a good one. I just slept on top of her. She can't stab me in my sleep if she can't get out from under me." Matthias grins.

They're all fucking psychotic. Even Bash, who would typically be scolding them for such behavior.

I just consider my hand. Instead of placing a bet, I fold.

I look at Bash expectantly, but he's on his phone again.

"Bash! It's your turn!" I huff, annoyed at him. This is the third time he's gotten distracted by his phone.

"Got it," he says with a grin as he puts it away.

"What are you doing on there? You've been glued to it all night. Is it something for the Syndicate?" I'm hoping it is, begging for the distraction.

He shakes his head, only to be interrupted by Matthias's curiosity.

"Is it something for Syndicate Enterprise?" He sounds disappointed by the thought. I guess work's not as exciting when you have a wife at home.

It's not something I'll experience. There's no way Katerina will ever come between me and the Syndicate.

"No, it's not any of that. It's... personal." Bash's vague answer piques my curiosity, but when he refills my tumbler and hands it to me, I drink away my interest.

I drink away all my emotions until I'm just as frigid and detached on the outside as I am on the inside.

Chapter 13

Katerina

The morning passed in a blur. My anxiety has passed and now I'm just numb.

I stare at my reflection in the full-length mirror in the church's dressing room. The Orthodox church the wedding is held in is the one used by all the Russian weddings I've attended. I'm sure it has Bratva connections.

The door slams open and in marches the devil himself.

"Katerina, you're not going to fuck this up, understood? I expect only the best from you. This is the start of the Syndicate's downfall." Viktor looks me up and down, then grins. "The dress looks good. I chose well."

I knew he picked this monstrosity out, because no one else could have this horrible taste in fashion.

I just stare past him. I can't form a sentence right now. I can't do anything. I've turned off all emotions. All feelings. I'm empty.

Viktor scowls and stomps across the tiny room. He grips my arms tightly and shakes me.

"Do. You. Understand? You will do this for me. For my Bratva. You useless girl." Spit sprays my face as he speaks, but I can't move to wipe it away.

"Yes, Отец," I whisper.

He shakes me one last time, then squeezes me hard enough to make my fingers numb.

"I will make your life hell if you mess this up. Your only worth is what you can do for me." He snorts then drops me.

His hatred awakens my own.

"Fuck you. You're lucky you have me as a bargaining chip!" I spit back at him.

"Why you little–" He raises his hand, ready to slap me, but my words stop him.

"Uh uh! You don't want to damage the product before you sell it. Dominic Montclair might not like that." My grin takes over.

Is this my new protection? Could Dominic care enough about the state of his wife that he wouldn't allow Viktor to harm me anymore? Even if he doesn't care, Viktor doesn't need to know that. This could change everything.

"There's more I can do to you than just physical violence. I don't care whose last name you have or whose wife you are, you will always belong to me. Just as your worthless mother did."

With those words, words that make my blood boil, he storms out of the room.

The mention of Мама crushes me. I wish she were here. Even though I didn't get a choice in any of this, not even in my groom, I still wish she were here for my wedding.

I wipe the spit from my face and pull myself together.

Yelena is the next one to enter the room. She holds up a vodka shooter and hands it to me.

"Za nóvoye nachálo i udáchu na putí," she cheers, then clinks hers to mine.

I nod at the salutation of new beginnings and luck on the road ahead, and then I throw back the shot. She does the same.

Yelena steps back and looks me over. She straightens my sleeves and pats my cheek.

"You can handle this man. He is nothing compared to what you've already conquered." Yelena meets my eyes once more, then leaves me alone.

It's the first time Yelena's ever spoken ill of Viktor to me. I've never suspected she harbored any negative feelings toward him. I guess her stoic front hides opinions that align closely with mine.

After twenty minutes of doing nothing, there's a knock at the door.

I look up in confusion.

I truly have no idea who it could be. No one respects me enough to knock and wait for my permission to come in.

The cute, patterned knock happens again, and I speak up.

"Come in," I say hesitantly.

A short, curvy woman with dark curly hair comes in first. She's almost as pale as me, with extremely rosy cheeks.

A tan woman with long dark hair comes in. The first thing I notice about her is the baby bump. She has a hand placed over it, but it's still noticeable.

These two look around my age. The third woman that comes in is old enough to be my mother, but there's no mistaking who she is.

The tall brunette has the same hard cheekbones and stature as Dominic Monclair. This is clearly his mother. But on her, their shared features look kind.

But I know better than anyone how deceiving looks can be.

"Hi..." I pause, not sure where to go with this. "Can I help you?"

"I'm Margot! I'm Matthias's wife," the short one says as she bounces on her feet. She seems so hyper, I'm not sure if this woman is capable of standing still. When it's clear I don't know who Matthias is, she continues. "I'm Dom's sister-in-law."

"I'm the other sister-in-law, Cecilia," the pregnant one says softly.

"And I'm Evelyn, Dom's mother."

Oh, I get it. They're here to threaten me. They don't want me in this family any more than I want to be in it. This day just keeps getting worse.

"Katerina, we're here to welcome you into the family. We were sad you weren't able to make a family dinner before today, but we understand the circumstance," Evelyn tells me. Her voice is sweet but stern. I can tell she's a force to be reckoned with.

"Thank you. It's an honor to be a Montclair." It most certainly is not, but it can't be worse than being a Sokolov, right?

"I'm so glad Dominic has someone now. He's never been close to a woman before. It soothes my heart that he'll have you. He needs a woman. And aren't you just beautiful." Evelyn looks me over with a soft smile. "Some motherly advice, he may seem callous on the outside, but that's just because he's good at hiding his emotions. If you dig a little, you'll find a man capable of love."

I glance at the other two women, but they don't seem as confident as Evelyn.

"Dom's not a bad guy, per se. He's a little... icy on the outside, but maybe there's more underneath," Margot chips in.

"Oh yes, Dom has a steady head on his shoulders. He's a great leader. I'm sure he won't be a bad husband," Cecilia adds.

Neither of them seems too sure of their compliments of Dominic.

Perfect, not even his family thinks he's a good guy to marry.

I'm about to marry a man who's been described as 'emotionless' and 'icy' by his family. This is going to be a shit show.

Chapter 14

Dominic

I straighten my bowtie on my tux as my brothers lounge around the room carelessly. Only Roman seems solemn about my current situation.

He's barely looked at me today. I know he's ridden with guilt. He knows this is his doing, and I'm having to make this sacrifice to fix his mistake.

But I don't have the energy to deal with him.

Dad walks in and looks at us.

"My sons. You boys looks so handsome," he says, and I swear I see his eyes glisten.

This man used to lead the Syndicate, and now he's teary-eyed over his sons in tuxes. It's ridiculous what love does to someone. I just don't understand it.

"Dom, I'd like to have a word with you," he tells me.

Dad leads me outside to the garden behind this church. I've never been to an Eastern Orthodox church, but it's where Katerina wanted the wedding. It's a mix of American and

Russian architecture and has a lot of Russian writing throughout it.

"What is it?" I ask him.

I'm prepared for his lecture on the importance of keeping the Syndicate away from Katerina. On how I cannot trust her and must separate the two. She's the daughter of the enemy and must never get close.

"You need to give this girl a chance," he says with a sigh.

I whip my head back.

"What?" I demand, caught off guard.

"This girl didn't have a choice in this either, I'm sure." I try to deny it, not letting the possibility that she was forced become a reality, but he talks over me. "Hush, son. I dealt with Viktor long enough to know he forced his daughter into this. As I was saying, this girl didn't have a choice either. In fact, you orchestrated this, and she's merely a pawn. Be soft with her. Show her tenderness and affection. Don't give her the cold shoulder. Don't lock her on the other side of the house and sentence her to a life of solitude. And as much as those actions are for her, I think they're also what you need. Let her be that lightness for you. Look at how happy Roman is with Cecilia. Maybe Katerina could be that for you."

I stay silent because he's so wrong.

There's no way the porcelain doll could be anything but an inconvenience for me. And I certainly don't need her.

"Thank you for the advice," I say curtly. "I need to get to the church."

I see the disappointment in his eyes and try not to let it affect me.

I can't be that man. I have to put the Syndicate first.

...

The massive church mocks me from my spot on the altar.

Unlike at my brother's weddings, I stand alone. It's symbolic of how I feel. How alone in this I am. How alone I always am.

I may be close to my brothers, but they don't understand the levity and toll the Syndicate has on me. To rule it alone is a feat they can't comprehend.

Stefan is the closest thing I have to a friend, but even our relationship is more business-based.

Music starts to play, and my heart stops as I'm filled with dread.

This is it.

The doors open, and there she is.

Katerina Sokolov stands at the end as a beautiful bride.

Well... she's beautiful. Her dress, though, is hideous.

Her face is stoic, and although her gaze is in my direction, it seems to shoot straight through me.

She glides down the aisle seamlessly. Every part of her, every one of her movements, are immaculate.

I should feel excited. Hopeful. Loving.

But instead, all I feel is... nothing.

As I look at the porcelain doll, I feel empty inside.

There's no disdain for her despite my hatred for her family.

There's no affection for my future wife.

I'm just empty.

Closing my eyes, I take a calming breath, basking in this last moment of freedom.

Chapter 15

Katerina

Every step fills me with a heavy dread. My stomach is cement, holding me down.

I finally focus my gaze on Dominic, trying to meet his eyes, only to see them squeezed shut. His face is pinched and his lips pursed.

When he opens those dark eyes, he looks at me with boredom and disapproval.

To anyone else, he probably appears stoic, serious. But I can tell. I see the way his nose is slightly upturned, the way his eyes seem empty. He has no desire to be here.

I end the march to my demise next to Dominic.

Only days ago, I had been filled with hope. The visit from the women in his family ignited it. But looking at him now, all of it is gone. His blank stare, the way he mindlessly stands here, it's as though he's in a trance.

He wants a wife as much as I want a husband. This is simply a means to an end. I can handle that.

But I don't know if I can handle the disapproving and dismissive way he stares at me. It's not just a wife he doesn't want; it's me he doesn't want. I don't know what his problem is, but he's pissing me off.

The priest greets us and hands us blessed candles. I hold mine in my clammy hands. I have to squeeze it tightly, so it doesn't slip.

He starts praying over us in Russian, and it brings a smile to my face that Dominic won't understand his wedding.

I glance at him victoriously, but he doesn't seem to care. Fuck him.

The priest holds the rings and begins blessing them. As he goes through the rounds of blessings, I try to decipher if he knows this is a sham. That all of this is fake.

I decide he either doesn't know or is too afraid of my father to let on that he does.

Our rings are exchanged. The priest places Dominic's gold ring on my finger and my silver ring on Dominic's finger three times.

Finally, we switch the rings, placing the correct ring on the other's finger. Dominic places mine on my left hand, the American tradition, but I stare at him cooly as I move it to my right hand.

I look down at the silver band, and for the first time, I realize I don't have an engagement ring.

It makes sense. Why would he have bothered buying one?

The priest begins the Crowning Ceremony. He leads us to the center of the church while chanting psalms.

When the priest looks at me, I know it's my time to vow my life away.

"Have you good, free, and unconstrained will, and have you promised yourself to no other?" the priest asks me.

I pause. This is the moment. The one that changes my life.

"Yes, with God's help," I repeat the traditional Russian response.

It's a lie. All of it. I'm not here of my good, free, or unconstrained will. I'm not able to promise myself to no other. I briefly glance at Sergey and refrain from shivering.

The priest guides us to hold each other's hands, and as my warm one connects with Dominic's, goose bumps spread across my body. I expected his hands to be as cold as the rest of him, but to my surprise, they're warm. And large. They're also full of callouses. And for some reason, that coarse skin comforts me.

The crowns are then placed on our heads three times. They symbolize martyrdom and eternal unity.

It's bitterly ironic how true that first part is. I truly am a martyr in this marriage. All alone with no options. Forced by my father to make this sacrifice for his precious Bratva.

I feel the weight of the ridiculous crown. It's a fucking mockery of me. Of the Bratva Princess.

I zone out as the priest reads scriptures and prays. I'm a monotonous robot as I drink from the common cup. I don't register my movements as I do the ceremonial walk around the lectern.

But I do feel the weight lifted as the priest removes the crowns. I feel slightly lighter, as though I can breathe.

That is, until he instructs us to kiss.

My entire body goes rigid. Dominic's does too. I glance around the room and meet Viktor's gaze. He's glaring at me, urging me to proceed.

Dominic leans in, grabbing my attention.

My eyes widen.

The air is lost in my throat.

I barely get an exhale out before his lips touch mine.

They stay there, unmoving, for three seconds. Three long seconds.

Then he pulls back.

His eyes are dark and annoyed.

He rakes his eyes over me one last time and curls his nose.

Then he drags me down the aisle by my hand, out the door. All of it in silence.

It's worse than I anticipated. I don't know what I expected, but a wedding kiss from a man who's disgusted by me isn't it.

By the time we get into the limousine, my hands are shaking in rage.

How dare he humiliate me in such a manner? In front of my father, my people? How dare he treat me like this?

After a long stretch of silence in the limo, I finally crack.

"What? You can't even look at me?" I demand, furious that his apathy is getting to me.

He slowly rakes his eyes towards me, but unlike other times, there's interest in them.

"I didn't know the doll could speak with such fire," he muses. He arches a brow in intrigue.

"Don't fucking call me a doll!" I seethe. How dare he! It's fucking worse than 'princess.' At least with 'princess," I can pretend to be royalty. He's referring to me as an inanimate object. It's demeaning.

"I'll call you whatever I want. Don't forget who you're marrying." His smirk is victorious, and my palm itches to slap him. I barely refrain, and only because I don't want to show up to my reception with a black eye.

"I know what I married. A man who can only get a wife by buying her!" I throw back at him.

I realize my mistake the moment his grin drops, and his impossibly black orbs darken.

But I stand my ground. I don't shrink back or flinch, even though I'm expecting a punch.

I'll take it like a woman. A badass woman. I'm not starting this marriage as the weak woman who takes beatings.

But instead of hitting me, he leans forward, so close that I can feel his breath on my lips.

"Let's make one thing clear, doll. I didn't buy you. In fact, I have no interest in you. You were merely a means to an end. A way to obtain peace. After tonight, I have no more use for you. You can go live your spoiled little life funded by my hard work on your end of my house, and I'll lead my men on my side." He chuckles darkly, then pushes a strand of my hair behind my ear. "I mean, look at you. Why would I ever buy a porcelain doll?"

I raise my hand and swing. But the fucking bastard catches my wrist before I can make contact.

"Aghh!" I scream in frustration.

"Nice try, doll. But you'll have to be faster than that to get me." He drops my hand and moves back to his seat as if nothing happened.

"You fucking mudak," I seethe.

I should be excited about what he said, that I'll get to live my life away from him. It's the dream. But I can't look past the insults. The mockery of me.

I'm fucking sick of men underestimating me.

He chuckles again, just as darkly. Then waves his hand dismissively at me. He pulls out his phone and starts typing.

I'm speechless. I honestly don't know what to say. I'm used to being dismissed by powerful men, but for some reason, I can't handle it from him. My blood boils.

I finally get my bearings, having come up with a killer comeback, when the car jolts to a stop.

"Not now," he says then closes my mouth. "It's time to smile for the party, doll."

I grind my teeth and hold back the urge to bite him. I know the urge stems from hatred, but I can't ignore the way his cologne affects me. Biting him would be purely out of anger, not because I need to get closer to that smell.

"Listen–" I start again, only for the door to open and him to pull me out of the limo. I lose my balance and tumble into him. He grips my arms, hauling me into his chest. Once I steady, I pull back and push him.

"Get your hands off me, mudak! You don't get to touch me. Ever!" I warn him under my breath.

I swear on my life this infuriating man will never get the privilege of my body. No man deserves it. I doubt any will ever earn me.

"We'll see about that," he whispers it in my ear, and I can't help but notice he's tall enough that he needs to lean down to reach my five-foot eleven frame. "I'm Dominic Montclair. I get whatever I want. And if that's your body, then I'll have you begging for me."

"You vile man! I will never beg for you. You're not even worth my time." The blush on my cheeks isn't from his sexy grin, but from the gall of this man. The anger he elicits from me.

But instead of fighting back, he throws his head back and chuckles. He leads me to the entrance of the building, and I pause at the door. He rolls his eyes but opens it for me. *Rightfully so. A man will always treat me with respect and chivalry.*

I take a deep breath before we enter the reception, needing to center myself before facing Viktor. Needing to get the rebellious fighter under wraps before Viktor beats her out of me.

It was beyond exhilarating to talk back. To be sassy. To be my real self. And to not face consequences because of it.

In fact, Dominic seemed humored by it. Even thrilled.

Maybe this is my chance at freedom.

But I can't let Viktor in on it.

Chapter 16

Dominic

I sit at the head table next to my intriguing wife.

Katerina isn't just a pretty face, a porcelain doll, after all. She has fire in her.

Granted, the little fierce dragon doesn't spit enough to burn me, but it's entertaining.

Her little episode in the limo changes everything. She's sparked my interest. I want to see her spit fire at me again. I want to piss her off just to see the way those blue eyes fill with heat.

Good God, when she tried to hit me, it was the most excited I've been in as long as I can remember. Not because of the risk of pain, but because she tried to come after me. Because I was able to get under her skin enough to crack that boring exterior.

Some parts of me may have gotten a little too excited from it. I had to get some space from her before she saw it. Or before I did something I'd regret.

I don't understand how kissing this woman did nothing for me, but her fire, her violence, fuels me in a way I haven't felt before. Maybe there is something wrong with me.

I've been trying to rile her up all evening, but I've been unsuccessful. There've been a few times I've seen her lips purse or her fist tighten under the table, but she always remains composed.

It's infuriating. I hate the porcelain doll she becomes. She doesn't speak unless spoken to. She's timid and quiet and pretty. I don't want that. I want sassy and bold and rebellious. I want fierce and sexy.

Someone approaches our table, and Katerina stiffens. She straightens in her seat, pulling her shoulders back in perfect posture.

Interested in seeing who elicits such a response, I look up and see none other than her father.

"I wanted to give my congratulations to the newlyweds," Viktor says with a smirk.

He holds his hand out to me, and I shake it. He tightens his, but it's not enough to concern me. I refuse to flinch at the bite. His little game of dominance won't work on me.

He speaks to me for a few minutes but never addresses his daughter. It's starting to piss me off. How can a father talk business at his daughter's wedding? How can he just ignore her on such a special day?

I finally snap.

"Are you going to miss having Katerina around the house? I'm sure it's a hard day for a father." My voice bites. I don't know why I care, but I can't ignore it.

But Viktor just waves his hand dismissively at his daughter.

"I'm sure she'll be of better use to you," he says with a wink. Katerina scoffs in disgust, catching her father's attention.

"Slushay syuda, ty, malenkaya suka. Ty budesh' yego ideal'noy zhenoy, ili za eto zaplatish'. Sleduy planu, inache Sergey budet naimenshey iz tvoikh problem." His endearing tone doesn't fool me. The way he says it through clenched teeth, and Katerina's reaction are a dead giveaway.

She blanches, then nods jerkily. Only when Viktor sees her cower and comply, does he turn from her. But I see the way her fists clench. I hear the way she mutters curses under her breath.

"I'll let you two settle in. Have a wonderful night." Viktor sly smile brings to mind the distasteful way he spoke of his daughter.

He's disgusting, and it pisses me off.

As soon as he's out of hearing distance, I turn to her.

"What did he say?" I demand.

"Nothing important," she says quickly, but she won't meet my gaze.

"Tell me." I leave no room for argument.

"No. It's none of your business," she spits out, and it comforts me to hear her back to her bitter self.

I reach out and grip her chin. I turn her towards me more aggressively than I intended. I lean forward until our noses are almost touching, ready to demand answers. With my other hand, I twirl a lock of her long, white-blonde hair around my fingers.

"Actually, my wife is my business. So, tell–" I whisper lowly, but am cut off.

"Look at them! How adorable!" a female voice says, then a flash of light blinds me.

I pull back, one hand reaches for my gun, and my other arm goes across Katerina in protection.

I scan our surroundings for the threat, only to find Margot and Matthias standing at our table. Margot has her phone out, and I realize that the light was her taking a picture.

Katerina grips my arm that's trapping her against her chair and digs her nails into it. Even through my suit, I can feel the pricks of pain. They shoot a jolt of excitement through me. Then she violently pushed my arm off her.

"Kat! You looked beautiful up there! And this reception, it's just amazing!" Margot continues to talk, never one to be quiet. It appears she may also be fueled by alcohol. "I'm so glad we got to talk earlier. I'm so excited to have you in the family! Welcome to the Montclairs!"

As she rambles, my brother looks at me helplessly. He pulls her into his arms, as though he can't go minutes without touching his irritating wife.

I look at my wife, and note she's looking at the couple with the same confusion as I am. I guess my wife doesn't understand happily-ever-after either.

Margot mostly speaks to Katerina, and to my surprise, my wife actually entertains the conversation.

Soon, Roman, Cecilia, and Bash find their way to us.

The women keep talking, and it seems they've pulled Bash into the conversation as well. He's just as animated as they talk about... *are they talking about the time Roman, Matthias, and I conned our entire middle school class into a Ponzi Scheme? What the fuck?*

I open my mouth, ready to put an end to the conversation, when I witness something breathtaking.

Katerina throws her head back and lets out a stunning laugh. My heart stops. It literally skips a beat. I paw at my chest, sure something's wrong.

I find myself softening, seeing her so calm and happy. I've seen perfect, pretty, porcelain doll Katerina. I've seen fierce, sassy, sexy Katerina. But I realize I've never seen her happy.

I watch her converse for a few more seconds then realize what I'm doing. I scowl at my behavior and turn to my brothers.

They're both grinning at me.

"What?" I question them harshly.

"It's okay, big bro. It took us both by surprise," Roman says cockily. "I'm so glad this turned out well."

"What took you by surprise?" I grit out, pissed he's being vague.

"Being in love. Neither of us expected it, but it's the best thing that ever happened to us," Matthias cuts in, adding his opinion.

I scoff offendedly.

"I am not in love!" I seethe in a whisper, not wanting Katerina to hear. "This is just business." I start to add that I could never be attracted to that porcelain doll. It's what I've been telling myself for weeks. But I realize how untrue that statement is. I am attracted to her, and it's because she's not a porcelain doll.

"You'll see," Roman says ominously. I glare at him, but he just laughs.

"This is just the beginning. It's going to get so much better." Matthias laughs too, then turns to Roman. "I bet he's going to be the worst of us. I bet he's going to be the craziest one."

"I'm not like you!" I hiss out. I'm not like them! I'll never be as psychotic as they were about their wives.

My brothers open their mouths, but I'm done with this conversation.

I grab Katerina's hand and stand up. She must not be expecting it, because she doesn't pull away. She just looks at our joint hands questioningly, then raises those scrunched brows to me.

"It's time to go home." It actually isn't. The reception doesn't have an end time, one of the perks of owning this establishment. But I'm ready to bed my wife.

She follows me without protest. As she slowly stands, I realize how tired she must be. It's been a long day for her.

As we walk through the crowd towards the back doors, an older Bratva man grabs her wrist. I recognize him as Sergey Petrova. He's a higher up, close to Viktor.

What the fuck is he doing grabbing *my wife?*

"U tebia yest' odin god s nim, chtoby razrushit' Sindikat, potom ty budesh' moey. Esli net, ya ub'yu ego, a potom zaberu tebya," he spits out at my wife.

Katerina scoffs at him, then clenches her fist. I can see her warring with herself. Does she play sweet and innocent or does she fight back?

"Fuck off, Sergey!" My beautiful wife straightens her back as she bites into him. I couldn't be prouder of her.

Until this fucker raises his hand as if to hit her.

Without a second thought, I push in front of Katerina, pulling her behind me, effectively breaking his hold on her.

I grab his throat, tightening my grip until no air can get through. He claws at my wrist, but he's no match for my strength.

"If you ever raise your hand towards my wife again, I'll end you. There will be no other warning." It's not an empty threat. If he, or anyone, touches my wife, they won't live long enough to regret it.

I drop his worthless ass on the floor, grab my wife's wrist, and storm out of the fucking party with her dragging along behind me.

We get in the limo, and she tries to speak, but I put up a hand, silencing her.

"Give me a minute," I grunt out, needing to calm myself, so I don't project my anger onto her.

"Too bad. I'm not a dog, don't fucking order me with your hand," she says as she swats my hand out of the air. "I don't need you to pick fights on my behalf. I'm a big girl. I can handle it on my own."

My body tenses, my fury now justifiably aimed at this beautiful fool.

"Are you insane? He was going to hit you!" She doesn't get it.

"I know. And I can handle it!" She continues to push into me.

"FUCK THAT! YOU'RE MY WIFE! NO ONE HITS MY WIFE! I WILL ALWAYS DEAL WITH ANY MAN THAT TRIES!"

She scooches out of her seat and thrusts a finger in my face.

"In name only. I am your wife, in name only. I can fight my own battles, so stay in your lane." She then straightens the finger with the rest of her hand and lightly pats my cheek. It's the most condescending thing anyone has ever done to me.

It's unacceptable.

I crawl across the bench seat until she's pressed against the window, and I'm caging her in.

"Don't ever fucking slap me again. I will always protect my wife. Deal with it," I seethe in her face, speaking in a low, threatening tone. This tone has had grown men cower.

But she just laughs bitterly.

"Oh, big boy can't control his emotions." She makes a pouting face, then *flicks my forehead.*

How dare she?

I'm about to... I don't know what I'm about to do. But I'm cut off by the car stopping abruptly, then the door opening.

She almost falls out of the car since she was trapped against the door, but I grip her waist, holding her to me.

I won't let her fall.

No matter how infuriating this woman is, I'll never let her get hurt.

Chapter 17

Katerina

"Take your hands off of me," I demand as I roll my eyes.

I'd rather fall on my ass than have him catch me.

This man, my husband, is infuriating. He swore he'd let me live my life separately. I have the letter that proves it. And in the limo earlier he even repeated it.

But in the past few hours, all he's been is extremely annoying. It took everything I had to keep my composure at the reception, and it was only possible because Viktor was there. I won't risk his wrath just to bite back at my husband.

Dominic is not at all the man I thought he was. He's maddening. I don't know how long I can last before I do something I regret, well more than hitting him. Actually, I don't regret hitting him, even if he hits me back harder.

But he hasn't yet. I wonder if he's just waiting until we're in the privacy of his home before he punishes me. But I won't let him beat me into submission.

"I just stopped you from falling!" He scoffs as though he was doing me a favor by gripping my waist.

I roll my eyes because, technically, he might have been.

I push him off of me and step out of the car, taking in the castle he lives in.

I wasn't paying attention when we entered the gate, but now I am. It's breathtaking in a gothic sort of way. It feels just like Dominic, dark and brooding, but still expensive. I just stand there and stare.

"Welcome home, Katerina Montclair." I can feel his smugness in his voice.

I cringe at the name. I hated being a Sokolov simply because of Viktor, but I never expected to replace it with a name so far from my roots. And I certainly never expected to call home a place with no ties to Russia. It's an odd feeling.

As we walk up the steps, an older man opens the front door. He's tall and bald and so stoic. I can't get a reading on him.

"Welcome home, Mr. and Mrs. Montclair," he says sternly.

He holds the door open for us, and Dominic walks through first. I scoff at the lack of chivalry. Even if someone else is holding the door open for us, a man should always let his lady through first. Looks like someone wasn't taught basic manners.

"Thank you," I tell the man as I enter.

He nods slightly and closes the door behind me.

"Would you like me to show Mrs. Montclair to her chambers?" the butler asks.

"Yes, please do. And call me Katerina." I can't stand hearing any last name associated with my name. Maybe I'll become like Madonna and just not have a last name.

Instead of showing me to my chambers, the man stares at Dominic, waiting for his instructions.

Assholes. Of course he's not going to listen to me. How silly of me to forget only men are worthy of giving orders.

"No, Harold. She'll be staying with me," Dominic says after a moment of contemplation. His smile at his decision enrages me.

"Yes, sir," Harold says with a nod.

"No! You said I'd have my own side of the house! That I'd get my own privacy and my own life!" I don't care that I sound like a whiny, petulant child.

He's taking away the freedom he promised me. He gave me hope, only to squash it. It's not fair.

"I changed my mind," he says it as though his decision is concrete. That there's no changing it.

"No, no, no. That's not how this goes. You said I'd get-" I start, but I must piss him off.

"I don't care what I said. I'm now saying that I changed my mind." He runs his fingers through his hair, tugging at the ends. "So, follow me. It's late. Let's get to bed."

"I'm not following you anywhere. Harold will show me to my room. And I sure as fuck am not going to your bed!" I start to raise my voice, unable to contain my rage any longer.

"Harold, you're excused for the night." Dominic waves his hand, and my last shred of hope leaves with him. "You're coming with me to *our* bed. My wife will be by my side on our wedding night. Now you can either come on your own two feet, or I can take you. It's up to you."

I'm furious now. I see an ugly black and gold vase within arm's reach and pick it up.

"Fuck you, mudak!" I throw the vase at his head in rage.

His eyes flare as he watches it crash to the ground. It breaks into thousands of tiny pieces. He didn't even have to move because my aim was terrible.

"Bad girl," he muses.

Within a blink of an eye, he has me thrown over his shoulder and is marching down the hallway. I can't keep track of where we're going.

I punch his back and kick his stomach but eventually stop because his muscular body is so hard it's hurting my fists and toes.

He finally opens a door, and we enter a room with a giant bed. The room is dark and mysterious. The main color is black, with accents of gold throughout it. It's manly but not gaudy.

He throws me onto the bed, and I bounce. Then he prowls onto it until he's hovering over me, trapping me.

The fury in his eyes would make a lesser girl shrink back, but I've faced angrier monsters. I can handle Dominic Montclair.

"Is this how our marriage is going to go, *husband*?" I hiss out 'husband' in disdain. "Are you going to boss me around, and when I don't listen, you'll manhandle me and overpower me by brute force? Not very nice of you. Imagine what Evelyn would say."

I cackle afterwards. There's a catharsis in my mania. In being able to fight back. It's a high I've wanted to chase my whole life, and now that I finally have, no pain will take it from me.

"You're the most maddening woman ever. But I'll break you in, and I'm going to start with this tempting body. I'll tame the Bratva Princess." His grin is unmistakable, but I just scoff. If he thinks a beating is going to break me, he's delusional. And fuck him for using that name.

"Hit me all you want. I'll never back down." I cackle, but it fades at his furious expression. If I thought he was angry before...

"I'm never going to hit you. I'd never bring you any pain." His expression holds so much promise. I can feel the levity in it. He looks appalled by the suggestion.

But I roll my eyes. I know men. When they don't get their way, they force it with their fists.

He shakes me enough to grab my attention.

"I will never hurt you. But that doesn't mean I won't break your resolve with my cock." He lowers himself onto me, and I can feel his hardness press on my leg through our layers.

I gasp instinctively. He's fucking huge. That monster isn't going anywhere near me.

"You sick fucker, getting turned on by our fighting!" It comes out breathy, and that pisses me off.

"I see the flush on your cheeks. I see your eyes dilating, and your breath catching in your throat. You want me just as much as I want you," he demands.

And sure enough, he's right. I'm fucking turned on by our anger. I can't help it if my husband is hot when he's pissed.

"You're delusional! Why would I ever let you touch me?" I throw back at him.

My breath is coming in pants, and he presses more of his weight onto me. He's grinning, but I can see my effect on him. He's red, and his pupils are blown out too.

"It's our wedding night. We have to consummate our marriage," he says cockily. *What a dumbass.*

"This isn't the eighteen hundreds. I'm not 'consummating our marriage.'" I'm appalled he even suggested it. Mostly.

"It's our wedding night," he repeats dumbfoundedly.

I bring my wrist up and cup his cheek. He leans into it. The stupid mudak thinks I'm giving in.

"You don't have any right to my body," I say sweetly, then I pat his cheek condescendingly. Once, then twice.

"I'm your husband. I own your body," he says darkly. He pulls my hand from his face and traps it on the bed in his own.

"You don't own anything." I struggle against his hold as I refute his medieval claim. I'm so sick of men thinking I belong to them. It's ridiculous.

"I own this virgin cunt. And I'm going to take it." He pauses for a moment, then leans in. "No. You're going to give it to me. You're going to be begging for me to take you."

He grins, and I roll my eyes, knowing how much the disrespect pisses of the big bad Syndicate Boss.

"I'll never beg a man for anything." I swear, and it's the truth. I will never give a man that pleasure. "And I'm not a virgin." I lie with a big grin on my face. And it's so worth it.

He exhales sharply as his eyes darken. His grip on my wrist tightens.

"That's not what I heard," he muses.

"You think I'm telling daddy when I fuck someone." I'm riling him up on purpose. After hours of pissing me off, it's fun to dish it back to him. "A girl has to keep her escapades to herself, no matter how delicious the man is. And boy were they delectable. Sexy, hard, big men. All begging for me. Their dicks–"

"ENOUGH!" he roars. It's the first time he's raised his voice, but instead of scaring me, I'm thrilled. It means I'm winning. "I won't hear about any other man with you."

He's panting. His eyes are wild. They're so dark, I can't make out pupil from iris. He's furious. And it makes me giddy.

"Oh, right. That's our agreement. We keep our private lives separate, as long as we don't flaunt it in front of each other." I mock him with his rules. Even though I want my freedom, the private lives thing isn't important. There will never be a man I'd risk my freedom for. And now the appeal of him focusing on other women isn't as good anymore. In fact, the thought of him bringing other women to our home and having them in our bed pisses me off. I'm the one who brought it up to get to him, but now it's angering me. *Great, I'm pissing myself off.*

"Excuse me?" He doesn't look as though he wants to be excused.

"In the letter. You made it clear that we can live our separate lives in private," I remind him.

"What exactly are you saying?" His calm voice can't hide his body's reaction. He's tense, a spring wound up, ready to uncoil.

"We can fuck whoever we want." At this point, the idea is pissing me off as much as him. But I'm not letting that stop me from winning this argument. From letting it enrage him.

"Let me make one thing clear, doll. If another man so much as looks at you, I'll gift you his eyes. The same goes for every part of him that touches you." A soft smile grows on his face, but his wild, black eyes reveal his craze. He's insanity incarnate.

"Excuse me?" I repeat his words from earlier, disbelief clouding my understanding. There's no way this man in this tuxedo is capable of such a thing.

Then I remember how barbaric the Syndicate is, and realize, yes, he probably is.

"You are my wife. I will not have any other man near you." It's a promise and a threat wrapped in one.

"In name only. I'll do as I damn well please on my own time," I fight back. It's addictive. The fight, the adrenaline, the power. I can't get enough.

"Then their blood is on your hands. Every man you so much as look at will pay the price. In fact, I'll make you watch as I dismember them." He looks content with that and sits back.

I just stare at him, mouth agape. Because he's not threatening to hurt me. No, he's threatening to hurt men that want me. And I think it's because he wants me. I can feel the promise in his words. And for some reason, it thrills me.

I must take too long to respond because he winks at me and walks to what must be the adjoining bathroom.

"You're a sick fuck!" I throw at him, but he just chuckles.

"Doll, you haven't seen anything yet."

Chapter 18

Dominic

This fucking woman.

How is the porcelain doll I married this crazy? This infuriating? This alluring?

I scrub my teeth harder than necessary as I replay tonight's events.

It was fun. The fighting. It was fun until she started mentioning other men.

Her being a virgin didn't matter to me. In fact, it was an inconvenience. Why would I want a woman who I'd have to train? I don't want some inexperienced girl.

But as soon as she started mentioning all the other men she's been with... my vision started darkening around the edges. How dare any man touch my wife? How dare they try?

Even if it was before our arrangement, they shouldn't be near her. She's too perfect for any of them.

She's perfect for me.

And no other man gets that perfection. My fiery dragon is mine. And I won't share.

I don't give a damn what that fucking letter said. I wrote it before I knew her fire. Before I knew how irresistible she is.

No man is going near her. There will be no private lives.

She's my wife. She's going to start acting like it.

It's going to be hard, but I know I can tame the beast.

I just need her controlled enough to respect me in public. I won't even squash her fire. Her rebellion, her sass, has my blood boiling in the best way.

I'm addicted to the high of fighting with her. Her passion and fury fuel me.

I think I'm looking forward to my life with my wife.

Chapter 19

Katerina

I wake to an empty bed.

Last night, I quickly changed into one of Dominic's t-shirts and boxers when he was showering. I had to use a knife to cut myself out of that hideous dress. No way was I asking him for help undressing. When he left the bathroom, I showered and brushed my teeth.

The way he stared at me when he saw me in his clothes... he looked hungry. Starved. He didn't look at me that way in the wedding dress. Maybe Viktor was onto something only allowing me to wear dresses. Because the heat from his gaze at me in boxer-shorts and a t-shirt scalded me.

I climb out of bed and look around. The room is pitch black with the curtains closed. Opening them, I revel in the sunlight.

After brushing my teeth, I leave the bedroom to explore the house. Making my way down the hallway through rooms, taking random turns, I get lost. I have no idea where I am.

The few men I pass must be Syndicate. They either glare at me or avert their gaze. I guess I'm not going to be popular around here. Not that that's a surprise.

Dominic's unmistakable voice booms through a wall, so I go to the door. I listen for a minute but can't make out what's being said.

Fuck it.

Opening the door, I step inside.

My husband sits behind a dark desk, and there's a man across from him. They seem relaxed... until Dominic's head whips in my direction.

The other man turns to me but drops his gaze and turns back around as soon as he sees me.

"WHAT THE FUCK ARE YOU DOING?" Dominic yells at me.

He stands so abruptly, his chair wobbles backwards. He's around the desk in the blink of an eye and crowding me against the door.

"Excuse me?" It's sassy. A tone I know I shouldn't take with him in front of his men. But I don't care.

"You can't walk around in that!" He's already taken off his jacket and is now trying to put it on me.

I shrug it off and let it tumble to the floor. His scowl deepens.

"Well, what do you expect me to wear? My clothes are in my bedroom, and you refuse to show me where it is," I counter with a grin.

He knows he has no choice but to bring me there.

"You can't walk around like this. You're practically naked!" His hands run through his hair, and he pulls the ends.

"I'm not naked! And no one I've seen so far has had an issue with it." I bat my eyelashes innocently at him, but he isn't deterred.

"Who the fuck saw you?" Dominic's gritted teeth barely make the words comprehendible.

I ignore him. It's not like I know the names of any of the men. I squeeze out from between him and the door to walk towards the man still sitting in the chair. His back is to us, clearly giving us privacy. But I walk in front of him.

"Get back here!" Dominic demands. He's practically shaking in his fury.

I continue to ignore him as I face the man, noting he's quite handsome. I thrust my hand out, but he ignores me.

"I'm Katerina, the wife. But in name only." I wink at him as I say it suggestively, but he continues to ignore me. This one's not dumb.

"KATERINA! GET BACK HERE! NOW!" Dominic's almost to his tipping point. It's just going to take one more little push. "Stefan, don't fucking look at her!"

I sit myself on Stefan's lap and put my arms around his neck.

"So, it's Stefan. A strong name for a strong man." I shamelessly flirt with this stranger in front of my fuming husband. I squeeze his biceps as I say it. "Aren't you going to introduce yourself? I'd love to have a friend around here." I pout my lips and run my fingers through his dark hair.

Before either of us can react, I'm ripped from his arms. To give Stefan credit, he never looked in my direction. And he was seconds away from pushing me off.

Dominic has me cradled in his arms and turns his back on Stefan, making sure none of me is visible.

"GET OUT, STEFAN!" Dominic roars at the man, and he scurries from the chair.

"Good luck, Dom." Stefan sounds delighted at my husband's misfortune in a wife, and it almost makes me feel bad for using him.

"OUT! NOW!" Dominic growls at him, and I swear I hear Stefan's laughter behind the door.

Dominic dumps me in the chair next to the one Stefan was sitting in and crowds me.

"You've gone too far. You parade around this house in fucking boxers and no bra! Then you throw yourself at my second!" Dominic's wild eyes only spur me on.

"I have nothing else to wear. I don't know where my room is. Hell, I don't even know where any food is." I sigh dramatically, then make eye contact. "And my tits are so small I don't need a bra."

Dominic's gaze drops to my breasts at the last comment, and his nostrils flare.

"I can see your fucking nipples poking through my goddamn shirt. Fucking dress yourself!" His fists grip the leather of the armrests so hard they squeak.

"Then bring me to my room so I can change!" I toss back at him. He can't deny my logic.

"Fine, I'll show you. But it's not your room anymore. I'll have someone move your clothes to our bedroom." He leans back and paces across the room.

"No need." I have no intention of residing in his bedroom. He'll get bored of me eventually, especially once he realizes I'm not putting out.

He comes back and pulls me out of the chair. Then he throws his discarded jacket around my shoulders and pulls it tight. It swallows me but does its job in concealing my state of undress.

We march in silence. Dominic's face is neutral, but the way he ignores everyone we pass and growls at the ones who look at me, betray his fury.

He'll get over it.

We get to a bedroom, and I realize it truly is on the other side of the house. Why was he set on me having me away from him only to change his mind? What changed his mind?

Dominic opens the door and walks in. I trail behind him. He turns to face me and scowls.

Out of the corner of my eyes, I see a grey furball sneak its way towards Dominic. I open my mouth to warn him, then reconsider.

"What's so funny?" Dominic demands.

"What?" I ask innocently. Vova slowly crawls his way across the floor. Dominic is so focused on pouting that he doesn't notice the little furball approaching.

"What has you smiling?" he growls, and I can't help the giggle that escapes.

"Kateri– FUCK! WHAT IS THAT?" Dominic jumps so high he almost hit the ceiling.

I look at my precious cat and laugh.

"That's Vova, my cat!" I tell him through my laughs. I'm gasping for air as Dominic glares at him.

"Well, Vulva just pissed on my shoe!" I double over at his claim. I fucking love my cat. "This isn't funny. They're custom made in Italy!"

"Okay, diva. Calm down. He's just a cat." I crouch down and call him over. Vova runs into my arms and purrs. His kindness to me is the icing on the cake.

Dominic pulls his precious Italian shoes off with the tips of his fingers while glaring at Vova. He walks across the room and chunks them into the trash. Then he peels off his socks and does the same to them. The entire time, he's muttering curses.

"I wasn't informed of any animals. We'll have to keep him outside," Dominic muses. His frown lessens at his decision.

"No. He's my pet, and he's an indoor cat. He stays with me." This isn't up for debate. He's not going anywhere.

"He's a pest, and he sure as shit isn't staying in our bedroom." Dominic's fingers pull at the strands of his hair. That must be his tell when he's pissed. He does it quite often around me.

"Perfect. I'll stay in this bedroom with him." I grin at how well this is working out for me. I prance around the room looking at the boxes of my things.

"My wife isn't sleeping with her cat over me!" Dominic's raised voice betrays him. He's fucking pissed with me.

"Your wife didn't have a choice in marrying you. But she did have a choice in her cat. So, I'm choosing Vova." It makes perfect sense. Why can't he just let things go how they were supposed to?

"Vulva isn't an option! You don't get a choice!" Dominic marches towards me, then changes direction and starts pacing.

"His name is Vova. Short for Vladmir," I correct him.

"Vulva," Dominic repeats.

"No. Vova," I say it slowly so he can hear it.

"I'm saying the same thing as you. Vulva!" He stops his pacing to glare at me.

"I didn't name my cat after female genitalia. It's Vo-Va." I harden the pronunciation of each syllable.

"Whatever. Just figure out the damn cat and keep it away from me." Dominic looks at the furball in my arms one more time and sneers before storming out of the room.

I look down at Vova and tell him, "This is going to be interesting."

Chapter 20

Dominic

I didn't think anything could infuriate me more than my wife, but of course her fucking cat does.

I just finished showering his piss off my feet.

That bastard ruined my favorite pair of shoes. I don't have time to go to Florence anytime soon to get a new pair made. It's incredibly inconvenient.

I look in the mirror and curse at my scowling reflection. I've spent decades perfecting my stoic mask, only for it to be demolished in a few hours by my maddening wife and her horrid pet.

That stunt she pulled with Stefan had me close to shooting my friend. If he had let on for a single second that he was interested in her, I'd have killed him that instant.

The woman knows exactly how to get under my skin. And when it doesn't involve flirting with other men or cat piss, I might enjoy it a little. But today has given me premature greys. And it's only day one.

I roll my eyes at what I'm about to do but do it anyways because it seems to help my hotheaded brother.

I do the fucking breathing exercise his wife taught him.

After a few minutes, I actually feel better. Maybe he's onto something with box breathing. I slip back into my emotionless mask and make my way to my office.

I nod at the men I pass on the way there but can't stop my suspicions. Which one of them saw my wife so indecent? Did they stare? Did they want her? I know they were tempted. Despite being too thin and almost doll-like, she's beautiful.

I consider banning all Syndicate men from my house, then realize the absurdity of it. A lot of our work goes on here. I can't kick them out. I'll just have to ensure my wife is always decent.

I text Stefan to come back to my office, because we need to finish our earlier meeting. I try the breathing exercise again because I'm still unjustifiably furious at him. He touched my wife. I know he didn't choose to, but it doesn't change the fact that he did.

Stefan knocks, and I tell him to come in.

He walks in slowly, keeping his gaze locked on me.

"Boss, I didn't encourage it. I swear!" He's scared I brought him in here to punish him.

"I know. It was all Katerina. That woman is infuriating." I gesture him to sit down. I just want to get this over with, so I can sit in silence and mull over my next moves. My next moves with my wife. Not even with the Syndicate. Somehow this woman who was supposed to be nothing has now consumed my mind.

"So, we're good?" He hesitates, but when I nod, he sighs.

He starts unbuttoning his shirt, but before I can question it, I see the bullet-proof vest underneath it. He takes it off and places it on the chair next to him. As he's buttoning his shirt back on, Katerina's words about him being strong ring in my ears.

I'm stronger than him. I know I'm stronger than Stefan. And I need her to know it too. *Is there any way I can set up a fight in the ring with Stefan in the gym and have her watch me beat him?* She needs to know I'm strong too.

"Can never be too careful. She practically put a target on me." He chuckles as he glances at the bullet-proof vest. "She's a handful, and not at all the boring doll you described her as. You've got yourself a challenge. She might be more work than this was worth."

I feel a pang of anger at his implication. Katerina being this sexy, rebellious woman is the biggest perk of the alliance. I won't have him speaking ill of her.

"She's my wife. You will respect that," I growl at him. How dare he?

"Woah, calm down. I didn't mean any disrespect." Only because he's my second, do I let it slide.

"Don't let it happen again." My levity must be evident because he gulps and nods. "Let's just get this over with. In the past twenty-four hours, there haven't been any moves from the Bratva. Viktor seems to plan on holding up his end of the alliance."

"But do you trust that? I mean you have his daughter, so that's good leverage. But this is Viktor." Stefan seems just as conflicted as me.

"There's something off about their relationship. He handed her over too quickly, then at the wedding... I don't know. But I'm not banking on that bargaining chip." I'm still pissed at him for how he treated her. He doesn't deserve to be her father. "We're going to keep monitoring them. I'll call Bash and tell him to track them under the radar."

"What's Roman saying?" Stefan's referring to Roman's theory that the Bratva is up to something nefarious at the ports.

He's been the enforcer for years, but recently, before the war, he started catching many more Bratva men in our territory. Margot also accidentally uncovered that they're smuggling something into the docks. We don't know what it is, and Bash hasn't been able to find anything.

"He's still pushing his theory that they're doing something nefarious at the ports. I think we'd be fools to ignore it. But we can't let on that we don't trust them." In my gut, I believe Roman. He's been doing this a long time, and I trust his instincts. But I can't let on that I think they're up to something without proof.

"What do you want me to do?" Stefan's never been one to sit back and wait. He was actually one of the ones most involved in tracking my sisters-in-law in both incidents. Not that my brothers know that.

"Just keep an eye out. Let's make sure nothing nefarious is going on."

"Okay. Do you trust everyone here?" His question doesn't surprise me. Even though everyone in the Syndicate is thoroughly vetted and their loyalty has been tested, it can be disastrous to blindly trust them all.

"No. Not even everyone on the compound. Don't let on that anything's amiss. I don't know who's truly loyal." I tap my knuckles on the desk, and glance down at the *ding*. I don't even feel the gold band on my finger anymore, but it's there. It's a constant reminder of the change in my life. Of her.

"You can't trust her," Stefan says softly, as though that isn't apparent.

"Obviously." I barely refrain from rolling my eyes at the absurdity. But despite the reality of our situation, a small part of me is resentful of the chasm in our relationship.

"Just... be careful with her." His tone doesn't change.

"I can handle her. It's not like she could best me in a fight." His insinuation is ridiculous. I'm in no danger from her.

"That's not what I meant. It's just that you're... different with her. It'd be good to see you that way with a woman, but not with this one. Not with Viktor's daughter. I apologize if I'm overstepping." His clear eyes hold concern.

His words drench me in cold water. They shock my system. I'm not in love with her or weak around her. But he's not wrong. I'm different when I'm with her. I can't control my emotions. I can't focus on anything else. Her ability to distract me and snap my patience could be dangerous.

"Thank you for your honesty. You're dismissed." It's a curt end to our meeting. And I typically wouldn't speak to Stefan this way, but he's been on my bad side all day.

He nods and leaves.

And I mull over his words in the silence.

I can't let her get close to me. I may enjoy our banter, but she could be dangerous.

Chapter 21

Katerina

There's a knock on my bedroom door, and my heart skips a beat. Maybe it's Dominic. I scowl at my twinge of hope. I just want it to be him because it's fun to get under his skin, not because I'd be excited to see him.

"Yes?" I say, ready to set Vova loose on Dominic.

But it's Harold who pops his head in.

My shoulders sag.

"Dinner is ready and waiting on you. Mr. Montclair expects you to be in the dining room at seven p.m. each evening." Harold's disapproving stare makes me feel like I'm being scolded by Yelena again.

"I didn't know. I don't even know how to get to the dining room!" I know I'm whining, but I don't care. I don't want to be in trouble with Harold. And it's truly not my fault that no one's spoken to me today.

Harold just *tsks* and shakes his head.

He motions for me to follow him, so I pet Vova one more time, then leave the room.

After almost ten minutes of walking, we arrive at a set of ornate doors. He opens them, and steps aside. I walk into a room with a long table, a deep red Persian rug under it, and dark wooden seats. It's warm, but also dangerous.

The whole house has a better ambiance than Viktor's. It isn't tacky, even though everything is expensive.

"Sit," a voice says from the head of the table.

I turn to see husband dearest seated there. A place is set before him and one to his right. I'm tempted to sit at the other end of the table, but it'd feel too much like hiding from him. And one thing I'll never do is let him think I'd cower before him.

"Woof woof." I roll my eyes as I slowly make my way to my seat. If he wants to order me around like a dog, then he's going to get called out for it.

"I might like you better if you were an obedient dog." The smirk on his face negates the sting of his words.

"Liar." I wink as I sit down. "What's for dinner? I'm starving!"

"Open it and see for yourself. But it's probably cold since you weren't here for seven." Dominic tilts his head to the silver top covering my plate. I open it to reveal a ribeye with potatoes and brussels sprouts.

I couldn't have planned a better meal. It smells even better than it looks.

When Dominic reveals his plate, my smile drops.

"Ugh! You're just like Viktor." I slap my hand on the table, and the sound echoes around the room.

"Excuse me? What is your problem? I have the chefs make us a delicious meal, and you haven't even taken a bite before complaining." Dominic's already pulling his hair, but I don't give a damn about his feelings.

I glare down at his large serving, then my smaller one, then back at his.

"You won't let me eat a normal human serving because I'm supposed to be your trophy wife that you want to keep small and dainty! I won't have this happen again! Switch with me." I don't wait for his reply. I'm already grabbing his plate.

"Did Viktor purposely starve you to keep you skinny?" Dominic's cool tone sends shivers down my spine. It's thrilling when I get him so heated the mask drops, but this frigid tone feels like the arctic. It doesn't scare me, but it has me alert.

"It doesn't matter now." I change the topic quickly. "Here's yours."

I hand him my former plate with the much smaller steak. He glances down, then looks at the steak in front of me. His eyes narrow, and it seems he's taking it in for the first time.

Instead of bitching and demanding his steak back, he just picks up his knife and starts cutting into it.

I eye him with curiosity. Why is he okay with this? He should be angry.

He glances at me, then frowns.

"The food is already cooling down. Eat up before it gets to room temperature." His order would normally piss me off, but I'm hungry, and I can't shake that odd feeling.

It feels like every interaction we have just proves how different he is from Viktor. Even though they both lead criminal organizations, they're complete opposites.

I slowly cut my steak and take a bite. I have to pause to take in the flavor. It's exquisite. I start eating quicker, and by the time Dominic is finished with his small portion, I've already finished my large one.

Dominic looks at my plate and raises a brow.

"Looks like someone can put down a lot. You'll be gaining weight in no time," he muses.

I scoff.

"Did you just call me fat?" I'm beyond disbelief.

How dare he!

"No. You're far too skinny. I'm saying eating here will fatten you up. I'll make sure you get appropriate servings." The smile on his face insults me further.

"First, I'm fat, now I'm far too skinny. Make up your damn mind!" I'm bellowing at this point, but it's well deserved.

Someone chooses to walk in at this moment. A woman brings dessert to the table. I can't help but glance down. The crème brulé looks really good, but now, because of this fucker, I can't eat it.

"Go on. I won't judge you for wolfing it down like you did dinner." Dominic chuckles and picks up his fork. The woman's eyes widen, and she scurries out of the room.

"I swear to God, Dominic, if you say one more thing, I'm going to lose it!" I'm practically shaking at this point.

"I have no idea what has you so angry, little doll. The steaks were delicious, and so is dessert. We all know you can eat, so go for it." He gestures towards my dessert then takes another bite of his.

"What did you just call me?" I'm gripping my knife so hard my knuckles are white.

"Doll. Because you looked like a porcelain doll when we first met." He smirks, clearly enjoying my anger. "But maybe *'brat'* would be more accurate in this situation. Or would you respond to *'wife?'"*

"You motherfucking mudak!" My vision reddens. My hands shake. I'm breathing heavily.

"Now, now. None of that, *wife*. Be a good girl and eat, brat. Woof woof." He throws his head back and laughs.

With a roar, I raise my hand currently gripping my steak knife and thrust it down onto his leg. It slices into his thigh like butter.

To my surprise and annoyance, he only lets out a small curse.

He looks down at the knife hilt sticking out of his thigh in disbelief. Then back at me.

"You crazy woman." He grins as he says it, then laughs again.

I stare in horror, *and a little pride*, at what I've done.

I just stabbed my husband.

The head of the Syndicate.

In his house.

Filled with Syndicate soldiers.

I'm fucking dead.

I look at the door, not knowing what to do. I contemplate leaving, just to get away, but that seems cowardice. But do I need to find someone to help?

"No, no. You're going to sit right here and watch what you've done," Domonic commands.

I roll my eyes.

"I'll do as I damn well please. You had it coming." I look down at his thigh one last time and smirk. "You're a big boy. You can handle this yourself."

I wink at him, then skip out of the room. Not my problem.

Chapter 22

Dominic

The door swings shut behind my psychotic wife, and I stare in wonder.

She stabbed me.

My wife just fucking stabbed me.

I look down at the hilt of the steak knife sticking out of my thigh, and chuckle.

She's a firecracker. A fire spitting dragon. And it's exhilarating to experience the bite behind that bark. I can't believe I ever thought she was a boring, porcelain doll.

I truly didn't realize why she was getting upset at first. But when it dawned on me, I figured it was a good lesson on getting thicker skin. She needs to be tougher and learn how to handle criticism. Plus, I was only voicing her sentiment.

But once I figured it out, I might've continued taking jabs at her because that red face and the smoke spewing from her nose were fueling me.

I look down again and hiss out a breath. Fuck, it's starting to hurt. I assess the situation and note that a few stitches should fix this.

I take out my phone and call the Syndicate doctor, Dr. Anderson.

He picks up on the third ring.

"Can I help you with something?" he asks sassily. I swear him dating Matthias's maid, Dotty, has made him gutsy.

"I need some stitches in my thigh. Now." I'm not giving him an option, mostly because I need to make sure this doesn't get infected.

"It's Sunday evening. How the hell did you get injured enough to need stitches?" His sighs of exasperation annoy me. It isn't his place to question me.

"I pissed off the wrong person." Or maybe the right person. Because if anyone else stabbed me, they'd pay greatly. But my rebellious wife... I feel no need to avenge my thigh. I'm more amused than anything.

"Where are you?" The jingle of his car keys and the sound of a car door closing echo through the line. He's not far from here, so he shouldn't take long.

"At home. Meet me in the dining room." I'm not risking further injury by walking around.

"How did you get injured in your own home?" The question is understandable, but not excusable. It's none of his damn business.

"Just come over," I bark into the phone then end the call.

It takes him fifteen minutes to arrive, and in that time, I bask in my situation.

My sexy wife feels so passionately for me that she stabbed me. Yes, it may be feelings of anger right now, but that means I can turn them into lust.

Unfortunately, that train of thought leads me to a pretty uncomfortable position. My cock hardens at fantasy of her lusting over me. Of what we could do together. Of what we will do.

When Dr. Anderson arrives, I have to place my napkin on my lap to hide my issue. It doesn't last long though, because once he pulls the knife out, the pain overwhelms me. Thank God, because the last thing I'd want him to find as he demolishes my slacks is my boner.

He cleans the wound, and that shit hurts. A weaker man would be plotting his revenge, but I don't. I do wish she were here though. And not just because I want her to witness the consequences of her actions, she should have to do that.

But because she should be seated next to me and watching as Dr. Anderson stitches and glues me. I wouldn't even wince, and she'd be impressed by my endurance. She'd be here, by my side. When he starts sewing me up, she'd gasp and grab my hand.

Slap!

The sound echoes through the room before I can even feel the sting in my leg. What the fuck? Dr. Anderson just slapped my leg.

"Go shower off the blood once this dries." His eyes narrow in suspicion. "I'm only giving you pain medicine if you tell me what happened."

I chuckle.

"I don't want any pain killers. I can handle a little stab wound." I won't have my judgment impaired, not even for an injury. There's no one I fully trust enough to make sure everything remains well.

"Listen here, boy. I will go to your father and tell him something's amiss in your home if you don't open up." His threat holds levity. My dad may not be the boss anymore, but he's still my father. And the last thing I need is my family prying into my marriage.

"My wife stabbed me in the leg. But it was my fault." I'm quick to defend her actions because I can't have anyone questioning her. She didn't stab me because she's Bratva, she stabbed me because she's a woman, and I commented on her weight.

"Why?" Dr. Anderson's mouth purses.

"Because I said some things about her and eating and getting fat and being too skinny. You know…" I don't have an ending to that sentence because I'm pretty sure he does know that's the last thing you should tell a woman.

"I know that you're a fool! What's wrong with you? You're lucky she only hit fat and muscle." He doesn't seem upset on my behalf at all.

I scoff, offended that he called me fat. There isn't an ounce of fat on these thighs.

"I know I fucked up," I grit out at him.

"Yeah, you did." He stares at me for a hard moment, then packs his things. Right before he leaves, he looks me over, and sighs. "A word of advice. Find her and apologize. It's not her fault her husband's a jackass."

I scoff, but mull over his advice.

Maybe I should apologize.

…

I limp my way to my bedroom, only to pause when I find Katerina and that fucking cat on our bed. She's teasing him with a stuffed mouse on a string. She keeps moving it around and the dummy mindlessly chases it.

"Why is it in here?" I growl out, not wanting the pisser anywhere near where I sleep.

"He is the only reason I'm in here. He snuck out of my bedroom and came here. He likes playing on the bed." She doesn't take her attention away from the cat, and it annoys me.

I huff, but instead of taking the cue, she starts humming.

I throw my hands on my hips and glare at them.

"Well?" I almost shout at her.

"Well, what?" She finally turns to me, looking as exasperated as I feel. No. She doesn't get to be annoyed. I'm the one who was stabbed!

"Aren't you going to ask how my leg is?" I grit my teeth and raise a brow.

"Oh, that. Pfft, no." She turns back to the cat and waves me off dismissively.

I stalk towards her. She's in the middle of the bed, so I grab her ankle and pull her to the edge.

"You stabbed me. Then I told you to stay, and you left. And now, hours later, you don't even check on me!" I don't know why I'm so hung up on it. I don't know why her indifference bothers me. She wasn't indifferent hours ago when she stabbed me. Why is she now?

"You're clearly fine seeing as you just walked your happy ass in here. Your little boo-boo is not my problem." She rolls her eyes and tries to kick my hand off her ankle. I just squeeze tighter, not freeing her.

"Not your problem? You fucking stabbed me! If anyone else had done it, they'd be getting tortured right now!" I shake her leg, trying to knock some sense into her.

"What do you want me to do? Apologize? Thank you for your mercy?" She rolls her eyes. "It's not going to happen. I'm not sorry, and it's your choice not to punish me."

Thoughts of punishing her in a different way come to mind, and I have to concentrate on keeping my expression neutral.

"You'd do well to keep me happy. Pissing me off, injuring me, isn't smart." The threat's clearly empty seeing as I'm not retaliating after she stabbed me. But maybe she'll buy it.

Her eyes widen, then soften. Her lips tremble, and for a moment, I think she'll cry. Disgusting. She's too strong to cry over my stern voice.

She wiggles her way out of my hold and crawls across the mattress to me. She sits on her knees and faces me. She's so tall that we're almost at eye level.

"I'm sorry, mudak." Her voice quivers at the pet name, and I wonder what sweet thing she's calling me. Maybe it's *baby* or *sweetheart.* "What can I do to make you feel better?" She wraps her arms around my neck. "Maybe I can kiss it better?"

Her lips purse, and she brushes a light kiss on my neck. I can't hold back my groan. Her lips feel too good.

She slides her hand down my chest, passing over my hard muscles. I instinctively flex under her fingers, and her soft gasps shows how much she appreciates my time in the gym.

When she's inches away from my hard cock, she leans in, and her lips almost brush mine. I lean down to meet her, to finally get the kiss I'm owed. Her scent overwhelms me. It's vanilla and something. My arms wrap around her, one over her back, the other in her hair.

She finally finds my cock, and I can't help thrusting against her palm. I can feel the heat of her hand through my layers, and all I want is her skin on mine.

"I want to show you how I feel," she whispers against my lips. Her husky tone and those hooded eyes break my resolve.

"Then do it, wife." It comes out hoarsely.

She tightens her grip on my cock, then a jolt of pain has me hunched over.

She just slapped my wound! She just fucking slapped the spot where she stabbed me! This woman is psychotic!

She throws her head back and laughs.

"Does my big, bad husband really think I'm going to coddle him because he has a little boo-boo? That I'm going to kiss him better after he gets what he deserves?" She talks in an infuriating baby voice. The one people use when they mock others.

"Goddamn it, woman!" I chance one more glance at her, but the victorious gleam in her eyes has my blood boiling.

Pathetically, I limp my way into the bathroom, then slam the door shut. My ripped pants are thrown away. All the while, I'm cursing.

I turn the water freezing, trying to calm myself, but my dick won't deflate. I try to think of anything other than my insane wife to get it to go down. When what I crave is relief from this ache.

Wait, why am I letting her win? If she wants to toy with me and turn me on, then she is going to listen while I address it.

I switch the water to hot and let it calm me. Reaching for my body wash, I pause as a yellow bottle that isn't normally here catches my eye. I open it and sniff. Vanilla and something. I check the label. Milk and honey scented.

It smells fucking divine. It smells like my divine wife.

I pour a generous amount into my hand and lather it. The tantalizing smell fills the shower, and I inhale it. I bring my hand to my cock and stroke.

I can't hold back my groan.

One day with her and I'm jerking off in the shower.

My wife may be the death of me. And I might just enjoy it.

Chapter 23

Katerina

I hear a groan coming from the shower and pause.

Fuck, is he hurting? Did I seriously injure him?

I mean, I know I did. But is it worse that he let on? Then I slapped it. Fuck.

When I hear a second sound of pain, I climb off the bed and rush to the door separating us. At the third groan, I don't bother knocking, I just rip the door open.

I rush inside and make it halfway to the shower stall before my eyes connect with my brain.

Dominic has one hand propped against the wall, and the other... is stroking his cock. I inhale sharply, unsure what to do. The noise has his eyes flying open, and his hooded gaze lands on me.

"Katerina!" he growls my name, and I can't stop the shiver up my spine.

"I'm sorry!" I frantically say, avoiding eye contact.

"Why are you in here?" he growls.

"I thought..." I can't finish the sentence because my eyes drop. I follow the beads of water as they flow down his thick neck, across his massive shoulders and pecs, down his defined abs, veiny arms, to the hand that holds his rigid length.

The hand that is still gripping his cock.

Still stroking.

I can't concentrate on anything.

It's like I've short-circuited.

This is the first time I've ever seen a man naked. And it's hotter than I thought. Or maybe that's just the steam from the shower turning me red.

"Thought what?" he probes as he continues his slow strokes.

"I thought you were injured," I finally spit out. My whole body is reacting. I need to get out of here.

"I am injured. You injured me." His reminder has my gaze shifting to his thigh. The suture is bold and ugly. For a moment, I feel guilty.

"I'm just... I'm going to go." I point at the exit and turn on my heels, ready to make a run for it.

"You're running away? After everything we've been through, what scares you is my cock, little doll?" He laughs darkly, and his eyes challenge me.

"I'm not scared," I lie through my teeth. But he's right. The monster between his legs terrifies me. I'm in uncharted territory.

"Then stay and watch what you do to me." He raises a brow and grins. He knows he has me cornered.

"Fine," I say, then sit on the edge of the tub across from the shower. If I'm staying for the show, I might as well get a front row seat.

I'm hoping my presence will make him uncomfortable. I'm hoping that if I maintain eye contact, he'll feel guilty and stop.

But it seems to be doing the opposite.

His corded muscles flex as he grips his cock. His motions are controlled, just as I'd expect from him. His eyes never leave mine, and when he hisses out my name again, I realize my plan isn't working.

Something diabolical enters my mind. He's challenging me. But maybe I can challenge him back.

I'm emboldened by his nudity. If he can prance around exposed in front of me, then so can I.

I move my long hair out of the way over my shoulder and find the zipper at my back. He pauses when I stand.

"What are you doing?" His rushed question only spurs me on.

I just grin and wink at him.

I shrug off the hideous dress and let it pool at my feet. I'm left in a matching pink set. I wouldn't think boy shorts and a plain bra could be sexy, but the way his movements become erratic, the way he seems to lose his control, tells me otherwise.

"Fuck, Katerina. Take it off. All of it. Now!" Dominic's demand is hoarse. He sounds tortured.

I just smirk and sit back on the edge of the tub.

"I don't take orders from you, husband," I mock him as I spread my legs. Even though I'm covered, I feel so exposed. But I don't let him see my vulnerability.

"Take if off, wife," he growls. I can tell he's pissed, and my control over his normally composed demeanor floods me with power.

"No."

Instead of brooding like I thought he would, or maybe even begging, he does something much worse. He straightens and opens the shower door. Then he storms out and stalks towards me. He towers over my sitting frame. Water drips off him onto me.

"I can see the wet spot between your thighs. Your cunt weeps for me. You're just as turned on as I am. I can give you the relief you crave. You just have to listen to me." He's still fucking stroking himself.

"I'll pass. I can get my own relief. Thanks, though." I push him as hard as I can, and the only reason I get him to budge a few inches is because I catch him off guard.

Within seconds, I've distanced myself from him and am back in the bedroom.

I hear him growl, but that's as much as I get before I'm out of there too.

I call for Vova over my shoulder, and he follows me to my bedroom on the opposite side of the house. I change into pajamas, then hop in bed.

But I don't go to sleep. I just sit there and wait. I tell myself I don't know what I'm waiting for, but I do.

And sure enough, not twenty minutes later, my husband storms into my room.

Without even giving me the chance to argue, he pulls me out of bed and throws me over his shoulder.

Like a caveman, he carries me to our bedroom and throws me on the bed. He tucks me in tightly and gives me a sharp look.

"Try to get out of this bed, and I'll handcuff you to a bedpost." He growls then turns off the lights. I hear him get into bed and hiss in pain at the movement. I feel a slight pang in my chest knowing I fucked up his leg.

"Goodnight, husband," I whisper into the darkness.

He just huffs in response.

Chapter 24
Dominic

I shower first thing when I wake up. I can't help but take myself in my hand and chase a release. This fucking woman has me going crazy. After all the shit she did yesterday, that stunt in the bathroom was by far the worst. She's heartless treating me like that. And it makes me respect her even more.

I finish getting dressed and stick my feet in my shoes.

"FUCK!"

My shoes are wet. I pick one up and look inside. I can't make anything out because of the dark interior, but it reeks. That fucking cat pissed in my shoes!

I storm into my closet and check another pair before putting them on. Thank fuck they're dry.

I storm over to Katerina's side of the bed and shake her.

"Wake up, doll. It's time for breakfast." I don't actually care about having breakfast with her, I just want revenge for her cat ruining my wardrobe and her antic last night and fucking everything.

And maybe breakfast with her would be nice.

She glares at me then sits up. She wipes sleep from her eyes then pops out of bed. Her long legs in that damn nightgown tease me, but I ignore them.

"Coffee," is all she says as she walks towards the bedroom door.

"Stop!" I won't let her parade around the house in a fucking nightgown. I'm surprised when she listens, but I still hurry as I go to my closet.

I hand her the navy robe, and she laughs at it.

"Seriously?" she questions in a light voice.

"No one else gets to see my wife in her nightgown." No one else should see her period, but there's not much I can do about that.

She throws it on, and it swallows her. Even though she's not that much shorter than me, she's not nearly as muscular as I am.

She tries to leave with the robe open, but I grab her shoulders and stop her. I close the front all the way up to her neck, then tie the rope tightly. She rolls her eyes but lets me.

We make our way to the dining room, and she grabs the coffee pot. She pours herself a large mug and puts in a dash of sugar. She takes a sip and sighs.

"That's some damn good coffee," she says as she takes another gulp.

I try not to preen at the compliment. I didn't pick out the coffee. Hell, I don't even know what brand it is. But she likes my coffee, and that fills me with pride.

I make myself a cup and sip it.

We sit at our spots, and I have to hold back a chuckle when she notices it.

Her smile drops, her mouth left agape as she stares at her cutlery. Instead of a silver knife like I have, she has a dull plastic one accompanying the rest of her silverware. She slowly turns her glare on me, but I feign innocence.

She's out of her damn mind if she thinks I'm giving her weapons after she just stabbed me.

Instead of bitching about it, she huffs a breath and digs in. We both have three fried eggs, two slices of toast, and six pieces of bacon. On the side we have bowls of fruit and yogurt. Yesterday, I made sure Harold knew that she's to be served the same portion size as I am.

I was astounded yesterday by her outburst. I would never starve her to make her look a certain way. And she's too skinny anyway. It's not healthy. Hearing that it's because Viktor wouldn't let her eat enough made my blood boil. I already hated the man, but it wasn't personal before. Now, it is.

"What's your plan for the day?" I ask her. She can do whatever she wants. I'm not trying to control her. But I'm curious.

"What am I allowed to do?" she fires back sarcastically.

I frown at that. I made it clear she has freedom here. She doesn't have any limitations.

"You can do whatever you want. Go spoil yourself. Go shopping or something. I'll give you my card." I offer the only thing I can think of. Also, her dresses are hideous, and the more I get to know my wife, the less likely it seems that she chose them.

Her eyes narrow.

"What's my budget?" she counters, as though I care.

"There isn't one. The card doesn't have a limit." Matthias and Bash handle my finances, and they're damn good at it. She could buy out a mall, and it wouldn't make a dent.

"So, I can leave? Just like that?" She still sounds doubtful, and I wonder what kind of sheltered life she lived under Viktor's watch.

"Yes. You just need to let me know where you're going and have a security detail escorting you. These are just safety measures." It's true. But also, I want to make sure she isn't meeting up with any of those men from her past. *The ones with great dicks.* I grip my fork tightly as her words echo through my mind.

"Can Nik be my security detail?" She looks so hopeful that I can't deny her. But who the hell is Nik?

"Who?" I keep my voice even. Maybe it's one of her girlfriends.

"My guard. I think he moved in yesterday, but I'm not sure where." Her features soften as she talks about him, and I pray he's a sixty-year-old grandpa.

"Yeah, he can come. But I want one of my drivers to escort you." I don't trust a Bratva soldier with my wife.

I text Harold to get this Nik and bring him here. I want to meet the man who's in charge of protecting my wife. The man who brings such a smile to her face.

A few minutes later, a man walks in. A tall, muscular man. He's almost my size.

"Katya, baby! It's been too long." He speaks as though he has a claim to her. The nickname has my blood boiling. Who the fuck does he think he is?

I'm waiting for her to snap at him the way she would me, but to my utter horror, she flings out of her chair and runs into his open arms.

He holds her, and she climbs him like a fucking tree, wrapping her legs around his waist. When he's about to cup her ass, I growl.

He drops her and turns to me. He sends a look at my wife, and she blushes.

This is fucking unacceptable.

"Dominic Montclair, Katerina's *husband*." I enunciate *'husband'* very clearly, then march over and extend my hand for him to shake. I pull Katerina from his reach and into my side. She rolls her eyes and digs her heel into my toes, but I don't loosen my grip. This man needs to see that she's mine. I don't care what they were before she was my wife because they're nothing now. He works for me, and that's it.

I signed an agreement that he could remain her guard, but he's now going to have one of my guards watching him.

"Nikolai Markov, but my friends call me Nik. I've been Katya's guard for years. I'm grateful you've allowed me to continue in that role." He shakes my hand and there's no malice in it, but I don't believe he has pure intentions. "She's in great hands."

"Nikolai, she'll always be under my protection. The only hands she'll be in are mine. Be sure to remember that." I glare at him and tighten my grip on his hand. Instead of looking threatened, he just grins. This asshole doesn't believe me.

"Yes, sir." I don't like his tone, even though it's mild. I don't like his face either.

"Take her wherever she wants to go." I dig out my wallet and slap a black Amex with *Katerina Montclair* on it in his palm. "She has no limit. Text me every location you're at. I want updates every thirty minutes."

If he breaks a single rule of mine, I'll send him back to the Bratva immediately. As much as I'd love to do so, I can't break the treaty.

"Yes, sir." His serious expression reassures me that he'll keep her protected even if it's because he cares for her. "Come on, Katya. Time to get a new wardrobe!"

I hate his fucking nickname for her. I hate that he calls her something special. I hate that I can't.

"Bye, husband." My wife winks at me, then she's gone.

Her claiming me as her husband in front of that fucker soothes me. She doesn't like him the way she likes me. Even if she did give him that ridiculous hug.

For the rest of the day, I stew in my office. Every meeting is taken with a frown. And every five minutes I'm checking her location. I call my guard watching them every chance I have available.

It's a ridiculous distraction, but I can't help it.

Katerina Montclair is consuming my thoughts.

Chapter 25

Katerina

"Katya, what the hell is going on?" Nik whisper-yells at me in the backseat of the SUV. I knew he'd have questions after Dominic's strange behavior.

"What do you think is going on? I got married. Things change." I keep it vague, not because I'm hiding something from my best friend, but because I don't know what the hell is going on!

"I need details!" Nik's demands shouldn't catch me by surprise. He's always been nosy.

"We live together. That's it."

"That's not it. Girl, the way he was acting... That man's obsessed with you. He almost attacked me for hugging you!" His smile drops, and he crinkles his nose in disgust. "As if I'd ever think of you like that. You're like my little sister."

"No, he didn't, and he certainly isn't obsessed with me. But even if he were, a little jealousy is good for a man." I think I'm trying to convince myself too. He couldn't possibly be interested in me.

Nik just rolls his eyes.

"He isn't!" I'm more forceful this time, but it doesn't seem to be convincing anyone.

"And what makes you so sure?" His eyebrows raise as if he's certain he's gotten me this time.

"Maybe because I stabbed him yesterday. Only a crazy man would be obsessed with the woman that stabbed them!" The memory of the fucking plastic knife mocking me at breakfast has me rolling my eyes. I saw his expression. He thought he was so clever with that move.

"You did what?" Nik practically shouts at me. I elbow him to keep his voice down.

"He was being a dick at dinner, so I stabbed him in the thigh with my steak knife. Sue me!" Looking back with a clear head has me feeling less hesitant about my actions and, instead, proud of them.

"Are you fucking insane? How are you still alive?" Nik's still speaking too loudly, so I pinch his ear. "FUCK!" He flicks my hand off him and pinches my arm.

"He honestly didn't seem too pissed. He didn't even bring it up today." He's better than me because if my husband stabbed me at dinner, I'd slice off his dick while he slept. I'd slay that monster without hesitation.

"Exactly my point! He likes you." Nik's wide eyes and urgent tone beg me to agree. But I don't. I can't.

"This isn't third grade. He's grown man. He doesn't have a crush on me. He probably just doesn't believe in hitting women." I can't help the grin at that sentence. Dominic may fight with me, but I truly believe he'd never be violent towards me. Crazy how I trust my husband of two days more than my father of twenty-three years.

"So... he's not like Viktor," Nik states the obvious.

"No. Not at all." My heart clenches at the words.

"So, where does that leave us?" Nik's tone shifts to serious.

"Huh?"

"With Viktor. He wants us to spy on the Syndicate and help bring them down. What's our plan now?" Even though we're whispering, Nik switches to Russian. We know better than to be having this conversation in a language they can understand. The guards may act like they're not listening, but I don't believe it for a second.

I stay silent. I honestly hadn't thought of Viktor or the Bratva and my mission since coming here.

"Katya, if you like it here, then maybe we don't help Viktor." Nik's suggestion is uncomprehensible. I've never agreed with Viktor's beliefs or methods, but I've always done what he's demanded of me.

"What do you mean?" I whisper back in my native tongue.

"Dominic won't let anything happen to you. He'll protect you from Viktor. If you want to ignore Viktor, you could live a happy and free life here with your husband."

I mull it over in silence. Could it be possible? Could it be this simple? Could I actually be free from Viktor and live freely with Dominic?

"Just think about it. It wouldn't be a bad life with Dom Montclair."

His words echo in my mind for a while. He's right. There are far worse fates than being Dominic Montclair's wife.

After a few minutes of silence, I change the topic.

"Where are we going?" I had let Nik tell the drivers where to go since I don't go out much, and I've never shopped for my own clothes. "I want a whole new wardrobe."

"We're hitting up some boutiques, designer shops, and everything in between. We're getting a new wardrobe.

Everything from day clothes, cocktail attire, jewelry, pajamas, lingerie..." He winks with the last one.

But I'm not listening. Because there's something I want even more than that.

"Workout clothes. I want workout clothes," I tell him determinedly.

"Uh, sure. If that's what you want, we'll add it to the list." Nik doesn't understand, but that's fine.

"Train me." I don't ask, I demand. The new Katerina Montclair doesn't ask for permission, she demands obedience.

"Train you to do what?" Nik pulls out his phone and starts scrolling through something.

"To fight. Defend myself. Shoot a gun." He pauses his scrolling to look up and make a doubtful face. "I'm serious. I'm sick of having to rely on men for protection or being at their mercy. I need to be strong enough to command respect."

"We can ask your husband," Nik concedes after studying my face. I know my tone and expression convey how important this is to me.

"No. He said he doesn't care what I do. And there's a gym and range on the property. Let's start tomorrow!" The more I speak, the more excited I get.

"Huh. I'll think about it." I know Nik. I know what that means.

"Thank you!" I jump up in my seat and press a kiss to his cheek.

...

Hours later, we return home with the trunk full of bags and several more ordered to be delivered.

I climb out of the back seat and walk to the trunk, but the driver waves me off. I start up the stairs, but before I can reach the front door, it opens.

"Hey, Harold," I say as I push a strand of my now short hair out of my eyes.

We stopped by a salon, and I got a big chop. Viktor always wanted my hair to be long and feminine. Since this is my chance at freedom, I decided my closet makeover could include a me makeover.

I bought new makeup in darker colors. I contemplated darkening my hair, but I have Мама's hair, and it makes me feel connected to her. So, I chopped it into a bob that ends at my chin.

I fucking love it.

I feel like a new woman. A badass woman. But I haven't gotten used to it falling into my eyes yet.

"Not Harold," a deep voice purrs.

I pause halfway through the doorway and turn to face my husband.

But instead of meeting my gaze, his eyes roam over me. I hold my breath.

Viktor would have a heart attack if he saw me now. Not only is my hair short and my lips a deep burgundy, but I'm wearing black leggings and a matching black athletic jacket. I've fallen in love with the dark color. And I love pants so much that I'm not sure I'll ever wear a dress again.

Dominic's throat bobs as he swallows harshly. His eyes widen the further they roam, and by the time they're back to mine, his cheeks are tinted pink.

"Katerina," his voice comes out hoarse. He clears his throat then shakes his head. "You look different."

I can't tell if that's a good thing or not. Instead of letting myself go crazy wondering the meaning, I hold up a hand to pause us.

"Good or bad different?" I demand answers. My makeover gives me even more confidence.

"You finally look as fiery and sexy on the outside as you are on the inside. You're not a porcelain doll anymore." He grins as he says it, and I can see the spark in his eyes.

"I was never a porcelain doll," I counter, because fuck it, I wasn't.

"I'm starting to believe that," he muses with a grin.

"So, you'll stop calling me doll?" I'm so done with that nickname.

"Will you stop reacting when I do?" My answering scowl betrays me, and he chuckles.

I humph and walk past him through the door.

I call out behind me, "There are many more bags in the trunk. Why don't you go give the boys a hand and deliver them to my room?"

"Not a chance, tiger. They'll be going in *our* closet in *our* room. I made space for you today." The challenge in his voice is evident.

I don't turn to face him, needing to hide my smirk. I don't mind 'tiger.' And I'm not foolish enough to actually believe the clothes would actually end up in the other bedroom.

"You haven't seen how many clothes I bought. It might not all fit in your closet." His closet is huge. They will all fit. But I wouldn't be his tiger if I didn't fight back.

"Oh, it'll fit, tiger. You just have to want it enough."

I throw my head back and laugh at his poor innuendo.

I feel free.

And happy.

It's such a foreign feeling.

If this is the start to my new life, then I don't ever want to go back.

Chapter 26

Dominic

Ever since she came home looking like a new, sexy woman, Katerina has had a fire in her. Her attitude, while still feisty and rebellious, hasn't been vicious or paranoid. She's flourishing here.

She spends her days training for battle. Nikolai's been teaching her how to fight in the ring, to shoot a gun, a crossbow, knife fighting, knife throwing... If it's a way to be violent, she's studying it. But it's not just that.

She's been training in other ways. She's working out in the gym hours a day. And she runs around the compound every day. She's either really slow or building endurance because her runs are now at least an hour a day.

I don't know what I expected a wife to do. Maybe go shopping or bake or sew or garden? But not my wife. No, she's far too badass for that. That's why she's perfect for me.

I've been keeping tabs on her. I know her progress. She's turning into a damn good soldier. She used to be a terrible shot on every weapon. But her aim has tremendously improved. She lasts longer in the gym now too. I've even watched her in the ring on the security cameras. She's pinned Nikolai more than once. I've been across the house, ready to storm in there a few times when he didn't tap out quickly enough. It's not right that this man has felt my wife's body pressed to his when I haven't.

We still get into our tiffs, but for the most part, the water's been calm. Too damn calm. She's placed a damn boundary between us, and I want to tear it down. I want to touch my wife. I want to feel her skin. Her lips. Her cunt. I'm fucking desperate. I've gone crazy fantasizing about her. I jerk off in the shower every damn day.

There've been meetings I've zoned out because I'm picturing her naked. The closest I've ever seen was that first day in the shower when she stripped down to her bra and panties. They were plain, boring undergarments. But on her, it was the sexiest thing I'd ever seen.

I want to see more.

I want to feel more.

Fuck, she's driving me crazy. And I don't think she even means to anymore.

Chapter 27

Katerina

I didn't know peace like this was possible.

I feel free.

And alive.

Nik's been training me. I'm finally a threat. If anyone ever tries to hurt me again, I can not only stop them but can make them hurt. It's a euphoric feeling being strong.

I can shoot a gun. I can shoot a crossbow. I can fight hand-to-hand. I can fight with a knife. I can throw knives. I even know the basics of sword fighting.

I've been strength and endurance training as well. I run five to ten miles most days. On my rest days, I swim. Now, I'm comfortable with every piece of equipment in the gym. I've gained enough muscle to feel powerful.

But it's not just that. It's not just my own achievements.

It's him.

Dominic.

He gives me my space but doesn't at the same time.

I don't see him for hours while I'm training, but we have breakfast and dinner together every day. And we spend the evenings together.

He doesn't let us just sit in silence. He makes conversation. He commands my attention. He riles me up just to mess with me. And damn it, it's a little hot.

I hear him in the shower. I know he's loud on purpose, but I can't seem to leave the bedroom when he's in there. I've been tempted more than once to sneak in again, to finish what we started, but I've reasoned with myself every time.

I want my husband.

I want him so badly.

But I can't give in.

Giving in to him would feel like losing to him. I swore this marriage would be in name only, but now it feels like this marriage is real in every way except in its celibacy.

I didn't choose to marry him. I didn't choose him. And now I'm disappointed in myself for wanting him.

But he's so hot. Even when he's brooding or instigating a fight.

It's infuriating.

He's infuriating.

And I hate that I love it.

Chapter 28

Dominic

Katerina's doing some kind of outdoor workout circuit. It involves crunches, burpees, sprints, and even more intense exercises. I have no idea what possesses her to do it, but damn, it's been paying off. She's gotten so strong and muscular. Her body is driving me crazy, taunting me every day. And what's worse is I'm not the only one that notices.

She prances around in athletic wear so tantalizing, it's as if she's begging to be fucked. Right now, she's only wearing a sports bra and biker shorts. I've already spoken to her about dressing more modestly, especially around my men and *Nikolai*, but she ignores me.

Actually, she almost bit my head off with how pissed she was at me for that. Ever since then, she's been showing even more skin just to drive me crazy.

And it's working.

Like right now. I should be paying attention to this meeting. But I can't stop my gaze from drifting to the window. To the temptress outside luring me with her body.

"The Bratva's been abiding by the treaty. They're not a threat anymore. We should pop open that bottle of whiskey to celebrate," Alex says. He's not old blood Syndicate, but he's smart. I keep him in these weekly meetings to get another perspective. But lately he's been too blasé about the Bratva.

"The Bratva will always be a threat. And as soon as we drop our guard, they'll attack." Roman hasn't hidden his dislike for Alex. It's something I've taken into consideration.

And my brother is correct. The Bratva, despite any alliance we may have, will always be our biggest threat. They will never not hate us for the rules we enforce.

"You're cynical, Roman. You've spent too much time getting bloody with the enemy to see when violence is no longer needed." Alex smirks as though his retort is sound, but it just pisses me off. Why is he instigating a fight with Roman?

"What're you insinuating?" Roman straightens in his seat. His shoulders tense, and I can tell he's itching to hit Alex. It's been a while since he's gotten his hands dirty.

"I think he's saying that maybe the lack of interrogations is a good thing." Daniel tries to defuse the situation, but it clearly isn't working.

"I don't know why you're even in this meeting. Shouldn't you be with your pregnant wife? Isn't she a flight risk?" Alex crosses a line with that sentence. It takes effort to keep my expression blank. How dare he come for my family in front of me! I may be the head of the Syndicate, but my family holds my deepest allegiance.

"Watch yourself, Alex. You're picking a fight you can't win," Stefan chimes in. He knows the hierarchy in this room, and Alex definitely doesn't outrank a Montclair.

Roman's doing his breathing exercise, and I know it's the only reason he hasn't beaten Alex. I'm impressed by how much of a positive impact Cecilia has had on him.

"Just because I'm not Dom's brother doesn't mean I'm not right." Alex flicks his glare in Stefan's direction.

He's digging himself into a hole he can't get out of.

"Enough. Roman, we know about your stance and your suspicions. We aren't ignoring them." I can't let on that I agree with him. There's no proof. But I know in my gut he's right.

"They're not suspicions, Dom. You know they've been up to something since they kidnapped Margot. Something's going on at the docks. Why did they negotiate for port control? Why do they get shipments every other Saturday and pay in cash? What are they selling that's so bad they're hiding it from everyone? What could they possibly have that has them so bold that they were soliciting men outside our clubs?" Roman runs his fingers over his buzzed hair as he rambles. He's been mulling over this for a long time.

"I know, Roman. I know what you think. And we're keeping an eye on it. Besides the offshore accounts, Bash hasn't found anything." I'm trying to deter the conversation.

"There's something going on." Roman raises a brow at me, and I give him a look that says I believe him, but we need to move on.

"Alex, why do you think we can trust the Bratva?" I switch the direction of the conversation, needing to get it off Roman.

"It's been a month since the wedding and they haven't so much as come near our territory. And you have their precious princess. It's not like they'd risk that." My hands grip my armrest as he calls me wife '*that.*' I'm tempted to put him in his place, but I can't show my hand when it comes to her.

"She could be an ally," I muse softly. I don't know what possesses me to say something so controversial and ludicrous. Maybe it's hope that Katerina could be one of us? That I could finally have someone by my side?

"You think you can trust her? She's practically fucking her Bratva boyfriend right now." Alex scoffs as he points out the window.

The room silences.

I turn to see her doing leg pushdowns with Nikolai. She's lying at his feet and raising her legs to his hands, and he pushes them down. There's no lingering touch, but my blood boils.

How fucking dare he put his hands on her? How dare he touch my wife?

And how dare she be laughing and happy while doing so?

Who the fuck laughs while working out?

"See! That Russian whore's loyalty is nonexistent." Alex chuckles as if he's made his point.

I slowly turn towards him. My stoic mask disintegrates. Fury consumes me.

"What did you just call my wife?" My voice, while even, drops to a low timbre as I demand an answer.

"It was just a joke, Dom." Alex blanches as he says it, finally realizing his mistake. "I mean she's basically your Bratva mail-ordered bride." He forces a laugh as if it'll alleviate the tension.

I'm out of my chair in an instant. I round the table until I'm hunched over him. I have my knife pressed against his throat. He hisses as I draw blood.

"Don't ever speak about my wife that way. If you ever disrespect her again, I won't give you a chance to apologize." I say it loud enough for everyone in the room to hear. I need as many witnesses as possible so they spread it to everyone. My wife is off limits.

Alex just stares at me wide eyed. He looks close to passing out, and I realize if he's ever captured, he'll betray us in an instant to avoid pain.

Fucking pussy.

"Well?" I demand as I see the knife drawing a little more blood.

His eyes dart around the room as if anyone in here will save him from my wrath. They won't. They're smart enough not to insult the boss's wife.

"Apologize, dumbass," Roman spits out.

I know he's pissed on Katerina's behalf. I've kept her separate from my family because I don't want her to get close to them. I don't want them to fall for her only for her to betray us. But I also know they already view her as family. Which they've made known by the countless invites I've ignored.

"I'm sorry, Dom." Alex's eyes water, and I sneer when a tear drips down his cheek.

"Get out of my sight," I growl as I let him go. "All of you. Get out!"

I turn to face the window, glaring at my wife and her fucking guard. Why do they have to look so in love? Is Alex right? Is she fucking him?

I study their movements and note how familiar they seem with each other. They're comfortable in a way she and I aren't.

I can't stand it.

"Stefan, send my wife and her guard in here," I demand without turning my back.

I'm putting a stop to this.

Chapter 29

Katerina

A cough interrupts our workout. Stefan approaches us with hurried steps.

"Mrs. Montclair, your husband needs you in the conference room," he says in a formal tone.

He hasn't warmed up to me since our little flirting episode. I guess it's hard to forgive the woman who put your life in jeopardy.

"We only have ten more minutes. We'll come then," I pant out at I continue to hold my plank.

"No, he said immediately." Stefan averts his gaze, then looks over his shoulder hesitantly.

I follow his eyes and see my husband staring through the window at us. I wink at him and wave my fingers, but he just glares. I roll my eyes and stand up.

"I'll be back soon," I tell Nik as I head to the door.

"He wants both of you," Stefan says awkwardly.

I look back at Dominic questioningly, but he just continues to look at us with a hardness in his eyes I haven't seen before.

We walk silently to the conference room, and when we enter, Dominic turns to face us.

"What's going on?" I prop my hand on my hip as I ask sassily. But my tone doesn't bring a grin to his lips or a spark in his eyes like it normally does.

"I'm only going to ask once. And I will know if you're lying." Dominic's eyes bore into mine.

"Okay," I say hesitantly. I have absolutely no idea what he's going to ask, but it's making me nervous. What if he found out the alliance is a sham? What if he blames me?

"Are you having an affair?" Dominic hisses it out so sharply, spit flies from his mouth.

"What?" I tumble backwards into Nik. He catches me then quickly pushes me forward.

Dominic's gaze sharpens, and his face reddens. He runs his hand through his hair then clenches his fist by his side.

"With *him*?" Dominic seethes as he points at Nik.

I look at my best friend and note he doesn't seem amused like I am. I'm obviously not sleeping with him. But instead of finding humor in the situation, he's pale. He's so pale and stoic. None of his usual liveliness is there. He looks... scared.

"Nik?" I whisper and take a step towards him.

He quickly backs away from me but doesn't avert his gaze from Dominic.

"ARE YOU FUCKING HIM?" Dominic roars, capturing my attention.

"NO! I'M NOT FUCKING HIM!" I was amused until he raised his voice. Now I'm pissed too.

"YOU'RE LYING!" Dominic's eyes are wild as he stares at us. I see him grip his knife in his belt.

"I'M NOT LYING!" I yell back. I grab the first thing I see, a paperweight off the shelf, and throw it at him.

He catches it and slams it on the table, a loud roar echoes throughout the room.

"Your obstinance isn't attractive right now. You are my WIFE! I will not have you betraying me!"

"Sir, I am not sleeping with you wife. I swear on my honor." Nik thumps his fist to his chest in an oath, but it doesn't mean anything to Dominic.

"Silence from you!" Dominic stalks his way in our direction, but after three steps, he holds himself back. "Remember what I told you I'd do to any man that touches you!"

"I remember, you psycho. I haven't touched anyone!" I reach for a book to throw at him, but Nik tugs it out of my hands.

"He touches you every damn day when you train!" Dominic's on the verge of hysterics, and I realize I need to diffuse the situation. This isn't one of the times where our fights are fun. This time, he's serious.

"That's just exercise. It's not sexual in any way." I put up my hands in a calming motion and soften my tone.

"You expect me to believe that's all you are. I see how you act around him. How you look at him. You love him, don't you?" His voice cracks at the end. His shoulders slump, as if all the energy is drained from him.

"He's my best friend. Of course I love him. But I love him like a brother." I won't lie about who Nik is to me, but Dominic needs to understand it's platonic.

"He's not your brother! No red-blooded man would see you as their sister!" He's shaking with fury, but I preen at the compliment.

"Nik isn't attracted to me!" I finally spit out the truth that'll put this to rest.

"Katya!" Nik warns me with his tone.

"No, Nik. Let me tell him! He's clearly irrational," I reason with my best friend. I know his secret wasn't safe with the Bratva, but I think the Syndicate will be different. I think Dominic will be different.

"No, Katya. You can't. You swore." His voice shifts to begging, and it breaks my heart.

"Tell me what?" Dominic demands. I look at Nik, begging with my eyes. "Say it!"

"Nik isn't attracted to me because he's gay!"

I hear Nik exhaling next to me and turn to face him.

"I'm sorry," I whisper to him.

He just shakes his head.

"Is this true?" Dominic's voice turns skeptical.

"Yes, sir." Nik swallows, then continues. "I understand the consequences but know I would never betray Katya in any way nor let my sexuality ever get in the way of protecting her."

It breaks my heart that he thinks he has to defend himself. So what if he likes men? What's the big deal?

I search for Dominic's gaze to plead with him to be understanding. To be accepting. But his eyes never find mine.

After what feels like an eternity, Dominic's body releases its tension.

"This is wonderful!" He claps his hands together as a smile breaks across his face.

"What?" I'm dumbfounded. Surely, I couldn't be married to a man so brainless.

"I don't care that you're gay. All I care about is her protection." Dominic points at me as he says it.

I can't comprehend the emotions his words evoke in me. I feel special. Someone worth being cared for. Someone precious.

I've been guarded my whole life by Viktor, but it was never with my best interest at heart. The way Dominic says it... it's different with him. He cares.

"The same goes for me." Nik interrupts my spiral. I smile at him, knowing he means it. I've never had to question Nik's loyalty.

I walk over and give him a hug. He pulls me into his side and relaxes into me. After a moment, Dominic growls, and Nik pushes me away. Seems being gay isn't quite enough to warrant touching me. *What an idiot.*

"Who are you loyal to?" Dominic's question throws me off guard. But Nik seems to be expecting it.

"Katerina. Whether her last name is Sokolov or Montclair, she will always have my loyalty." Nik's voice is final.

I gasp and turn to him. Why wouldn't he lie and tell Dominic he's loyal to the Syndicate? What if Dominic sends him away?

But instead of being upset, Dominic's grin widens.

"This is perfect. Thank you!" I don't think I've ever heard my husband thank someone. It's out of character for him to be this cheery and excited.

He walks to Nik and holds out his hand. Nik grasps it, then Dominic pulls him in for one of those back pats men do.

"You are the only one I trust with her. More than even my men. Because they are loyal to me, not her. And your priority is Katerina." Dominic keeps his eyes level with Nik's when he says it, and Nik nods.

"She'll be safe with me," Nik swears.

"I know she will be, Nik." Dominic turns and freezes when he sees the window. "One other thing, when you train, try to do it away from my men. I trust there isn't anything inappropriate going on between you two, but I can't give them any reason to doubt us, and I'm not going to share your secret with them as explanation. That's your business."

"Yes, sir." Nik nods. "Time to finish our workout."

He starts walking towards the door, but I don't follow.

"Don't you think you're forgetting something, husband?" I hiss out.

"Huh?" Dominic looks around as if the room will give him the answer. "I don't think so."

"You're forgetting your apology! You just accused me, quite viciously, of cheating on you! Your little tantrum is completely unacceptable! I haven't done a damn thing to lose your trust! So, you owe me an apology." I try to keep my voice even but fail. My voice keeps rising until, by the end, I'm screaming at him.

Dominic looks like he's fighting a grin. He bites his lips to contain it. This fucker.

"I'm sorry, tiger. You're right. I shouldn't have yelled." Even though his words are what I wanted, they're not enough.

"Apology not accepted. I prefer my apologies in the form of twelve dozen roses, a ruby necklace, and a written apology."

He stares at me in amusement, but I don't give him time to respond.

I strut out of the room after giving my absurd list of requirements and laugh to myself knowing he'll never meet them.

...

Hours later, I walk into our bedroom and gasp at the sight.

Every surface holds vases of red roses. Beautiful, deep scarlet roses. On my nightstand lays a black velvet box and an envelope.

I open the box tentatively, but I should have known better. Of course, my husband has great taste. Inside hosts a beautiful diamond and ruby choker, fit for a queen. It's breathtaking. Something I'd pick up for myself. My fingers lightly dance over the cold stones, feeling the weight of it. Once I've gotten my fill, I move to the letter.

My dearest wife,

Let me offer you my sincerest apologies for my behavior earlier. I was out of line. However, you drive me insane, so you share the blame.

Nevertheless, I shouldn't have accused you, nor should I have yelled at you. That's not how a good husband behaves.

That being said, I present my full apology. Twelve dozen roses, a ruby necklace, and a handwritten apology. Worry not, I stocked up on fine jewels for my next fuck up.

Most sorrowfully,

Dominic Montclair

Husband to Katerina 'Tiger' Montclair

Chapter 30
Dominic

I wake at the crack of dawn with a yawn. I'm an early riser, but even for me, five a.m. is extreme. But it's not for my wife. She starts training at half past five every morning. And today, I'm joining her.

I used to work out in the mornings before she came, but for some reason, I've avoided being in the gym at the same time as her and have been going in the afternoons. But that's ridiculous. I don't want to avoid my wife anymore.

She turns off her watch alarm and hops out of bed. I do the same, but she isn't expecting it and shrieks. She practically jumps out of her skin.

"Sorry, tiger. I didn't realize you're so skittish in the mornings." The teasing tone in my voice has her relaxing. She's a vision with her short hair all tousled and her cheeks flushed from sleep.

"What're you doing up?" She squints her eyes at me as if I'm up to something nefarious.

Which I'm not. Well, not really. I am ambushing her workout, but that's not necessarily nefarious.

After my accusatory outburst yesterday, I want to make it up to her. I bought her the apology she wanted even though I knew it was a bullshit demand. She didn't think I could do it. But I can do anything. I'm fucking Dominic Montclair. So, every surface of the room is covered in vases of roses, a diamond and ruby chocker sits on her nightstands, along with a handwritten apology.

Harold looked at me like I was crazy when I demanded he retrieve everything she demanded. I would've gone myself if it weren't for meetings I had previously committed to. I picked out the thirty-grand necklace and even bought the matching earrings and bracelets for the next apology.

"Well?" She arches a brow at me expectantly.

I crack a smile at her cuteness. Even when she's questioning me, she's gorgeous. Her frosty eyes and white locks reflect the coldness inside me. She's my perfect ice queen. But I know the heat I can invoke in her when I ignite her fury.

"I'm joining you for your workout," I say in a calm tone. I turn to my closet, ready to get dressed.

"You weren't invited," she snaps at me, but I can see the glint in her eyes. She doesn't fully mean it.

"I'm not waiting for an invite. It's my gym," I throw back at her.

"I'm not starting in the gym today. I'm going on a run. You can come if you can keep up." Her tone tells me how much she doubts my endurance. There's no doubt in my mind that I can keep up with her. She's a woman, and I'm a man.

...

"How... much... longer?" I gasp out between pants.

I didn't realize my wife is Wonder Woman. Or the Greek goddess, Artemis. Because only Amazonian or godly women could have this stamina. This endurance.

At one point, I distracted myself by fantasizing what that means for her in bed. I bet she could go forever with stamina like this. But fuck, I'm too exhausted to even think of that.

"Oh darling, we're only halfway there. We've only run five point three miles." She doesn't even sound winded. This warrior isn't human. I cannot comprehend how my wife, no matter how trained and in-shape she is, can be this athletic. I know her long legs are helping her, but damn it, mine are longer!

"Perfect," I wheeze out. I can't tell if I'm being blinded by the sweat in my eyes or if I'm tearing up by this news.

We're only halfway there.

Fuck.

This can't be the same five miles I used to run. I've never run much more than this, but it was very doable back then.

It's not just that we've run five miles. It's the speed we're going. I can barely keep up with this Amazonian. I think we're running a sub-seven-minute mile pace. I feel pathetic that thirty-five minutes of running has me this nauseous. But I just can't compete with her. It's absolute torture.

And she knows it.

I see her grin when she thinks I'm not looking. When she sees my struggle. I hid it for a good twenty minutes, but now I can't. I've lost this one. But it's not my fault she's insanely athletic.

"Unless you need us to cut it short?" I can hear the laughter in her voice. She's making fun of me.

"No... I'm doing... great!" I gasp out. I can't let her win.

"Then you won't mind speeding up? I like a bit of a challenge." I look at this creature, and she raises a challenging brow at me.

What the fuck do you mean this isn't a challenge? Is she fucking insane? This is the hardest I've ever pushed my body. The most pain I've ever been in. And I've been stabbed and shot. By her! I've been stabbed by her, and yet, this is the most pain I've ever been in!

"Sure." I brace myself for the worst. I remind myself that running is mental. It's all about how you think. But fuck, I don't think I can do this.

She speeds up, and I focus on picking up my legs and keeping one in front of the other.

I'm blinded by my own sweat dripping into my eyes. My nose leaks like a faucet. My mouth is drier than the Sahara. My chest holds the weight of the world on it. My legs have thousand-pound weights holding them down.

"One more mile," an angelic voice says.

It takes me a moment to realize it's my beautiful wife. I'm in such a daze of pain and suffering that I forgot the outside world. I forgot she's the one causing my pain and suffering.

I look at her. Gaze upon my motivation to endure this suffering. My motivation to finish this. Not because she's my muse, but because I need to finish strong. I have to show her I'm not pathetic. That I can hold my own against her.

She's now coated in a sheen of sweat. And fuck her for looking that much sexier with it. Her cheeks are flushed, and it only adds to the vision. But her smile, that's what carries me through the last mile. Her joy in this masochistic torment distracts me enough so that I can finish.

And when we do finish, she checks her watch and smiles widely.

"Ten miles! Sixty-five minutes thirty-two seconds!" She sounds ecstatic, but I can't focus on anything.

My legs are jelly. I'm shaking all over. My stomach is twisted, and I'm nauseous. My heart is pounding from my head to my feet, and I feel lightheaded. I might pass out.

"My new PR!" She jumps into my arms, and I try to be strong for her, but I can't. I only manage to hold her for a few seconds before I drop her. My stomach twists.

Oh fuck.

I push her back. I barely make out her cursing me out as I turn and puke in the bushes. As I empty my stomach, I lean on a tree for support. I'm so weak from the run that I'll fall without it.

I feel her approaching, so I throw my hand out.

"Stay back," I croak. I know there's more about to come up, and I don't want her in the splash zone. Actually, I don't want her here at all. She shouldn't be seeing her husband so weak. She needs to always think of me as strong and able to protect her. "Go... away."

"Fuck off with that shit!" She swats my hand down and comes closer. She places a hand on my back and tentatively rubs it. "What kind of wife would I be if I ran you to the point of puking only to abandon you!"

Her referring to herself as my wife has my heart sputtering. But it's not enough to make me feel better.

"I don't want you to see me like this." I spit after I say it, trying to rid my mouth of the taste.

"Nonsense. I've puked from running multiple times in these woods. Nothing to be embarrassed about. Next time we'll just have to take it slower." She winks at me as she says it.

Next time?

Next time!

I can't tell if I'm appalled at the idea of ever having to do that again, or if I'm excited at the prospect of hanging out with my wife again.

"I think I'm done. Puking," I tell her hoarsely. I start to straighten but wince at the pain in every cell of my body.

"Come on, lean into me." Katerina hoists my arm over her shoulder. She takes on a majority of my weight as we walk towards the house. I can't help but revel in her nearness.

My brother's small wives would never be able to support them like mine can. Margot's too short, and Cecilia's too thin and weak. I grin cockily at how I lucked out. If we're ever in battle, I'd thrive with my Amazonian wife by my side. I can't say the same for them.

"Where do you want to go?" she asks lightly.

"Our bathroom." I turn my head away from her as I say it, so she doesn't get a whiff of vomit-breath.

"Sounds good." She finally sounds strained, but it pisses me off that it's because she's supporting me. I'm being a terrible husband.

She brings me to our bathroom and dumps me on the tub.

"You can take it from here. I'm not washing you. If I didn't see how horrible at running you are, I'd think you're doing this on purpose to get naked in front of me again." She winks as she says it teasingly, so I know she's joking. I just roll my eyes at her.

As she turns to leave, I grab her wrist.

"Thank you. For taking care of me. I'm sorry I let it get to this point." I stare into her blue orbs as I say it. I mean it with my full chest. I'm grateful to her.

"It's nothing. We'll just build you up to my runs." She laughs awkwardly then skips out of the bathroom.

When I'm left on my own, I stare at my hands and contemplate my life.

I have a wife. She sasses me and rebels and pushes me to my breaking point. And I love it. My wife has me excited. I'm living again.

And all because of a peace treaty.

Who would've thought?

Chapter 31

Dominic

There were pain relievers and a huge electrolyte drink on the nightstand when I got out of the shower. I don't even like the red drinks, but I drank it with a smile because she brought them for me.

At least we know my wife isn't trying to kill me. I thought it might be a possibility after our morning activity. Death by running. But she left out these to help me.

When I walk to my office, the door is ajar. I'm furious and ready to fire someone, until I step inside. Until I see who, or rather what, is inside.

Vova is sitting on my desk with a mischievous grin. Since when can cats open doors? What the fuck?

I look around the room for any shoes that could get pissed in since he's done it with every pair I leave out. He doesn't do it to Katerina's, so I know he's purposefully targeting me. It's unacceptable to have such disobedience towards me in my own home. But Katerina won't let me get rid of it, so I just endure silently. Well silently except when I bitch to her about it.

When I don't see any shoes, I take a deep breath. I approach my desk slowly, apprehensively. I don't want this day to get worse by having a cat attack me.

But he just looks at me cockily.

This little bastard did something in here. I'm certain of it.

I continue to survey my office, but nothing seems to be amiss. I finally take my seat, but only after patting it down for piss. I'm pleasantly surprised when there isn't any.

After only a few minutes, there's a knock on the door.

"Come in," I mindlessly say.

Stefan walks in, then smiles at the cat. He pets the damn creature behind his ears, and the motherfucking traitor purrs for him.

"You're such a sweet boy, Vova," Stefan coos at the fucking cat. And the cat preens. What a bastard. I'm the one who's giving him such a lavish lifestyle! Why doesn't he like me!

"What do you want?" I spit out at Stefan.

"I wanted to remind you that Viktor will be here in half an hour." Stefan's smile drops as he steps away from the cat.

"Fuck. I forgot." This day just went from bad to terrible. Viktor is the last person I want to see.

"You need to have this meeting. It should be a quick one. Just a post-treaty check in," Stefan reminds me.

"I know," I grumble.

"Does Katerina know he's coming?" Stefan asks after a moment.

I search his eyes for a deeper meaning. Why is he asking about my wife?

"Why would she know?" I'm skeptical of Stefan now.

"Because she may want to see her father?" Stefan gives me a confused look, probably trying to decipher my irritation.

"Oh." He's right. I should tell her. But something in me doesn't want to. We've gotten into a good rhythm, and I don't want Viktor messing that up. I don't want his presence to remind her that this all started because of a treaty.

My watch pings that Viktor's arriving early.

"Let's go," I tell Stefan as we walk to the front door.

I take a deep breath and put on my stoic mask. I can't let it crack. And I know I won't. Viktor doesn't have the power over me that his daughter does. She's the only one who can evoke my true feelings.

Harold opens the door and in walks Viktor. I approach with my hand out and shake his.

"My son-in-law. How's married life treating you?" His grin is laid back. There's no threat or concern in his words. It's like he doesn't even care about his daughter.

"We're doing well. Katerina's been," *perfect,* "more than I expected."

I keep my face neutral despite the smile threatening at the thought of my beautiful wife and just how unexpected she's been.

But Viktor's eyes darken. He doesn't seem happy with my response.

"If she's not behaving, I will talk to her. Sometimes she requires tough love for obedience. I can tame the wench." The glint in his eyes has my hackles raising. I know something's not right between them.

"That won't be necessary." I take a deep breath and unclench my fists before I'm tempted to meet his face with them. He called my wife a fucking *wench.* That's unacceptable.

But she's his daughter. I probably just don't understand a father-daughter relationship. But I just can't picture Roman ever speaking of his daughters in such a way.

"Hmm," he hums in acknowledgment.

I don't like that he didn't agree to leave her alone. I don't want him anywhere near her. But he's her father, so I won't stand between them. I just don't trust him. Not even with her.

"Let's go into my office." I lead us there.

When I open the door, the cat jumps out with a fierce battle cry. I sidestep, but it's unnecessary. He's not coming after me. He launches himself at Viktor viciously. He's biting and scratching. My good boy.

"This mudak!" Viktor curses, trying to get free.

I guess when she calls me that it isn't a compliment. I almost smile at my wife's crude, Russian nickname for me when Viktor kicks the cat.

Vova shrieks and runs behind my legs.

"Don't touch my cat," I bark at Viktor. I'm oddly protective of the feline. I bend down and pick him up. He curls into my chest, but keeps his eyes pinned on Viktor.

Viktor sneers at him as he brushes off his suit.

"I'm relieved to be rid of that pest. Get it out of here!" Viktor marches into *my* office after ordering *me* around.

I pet the good boy behind his ears a few times until the hair on his back lays down, then I place him on the ground.

"Go find Katerina. She'll take care of you," I tell him softly, then stand.

I follow Stefan into my office and offer Viktor a drink. Unfortunately, he accepts, so I pour three glasses.

I offer his guard one, but he remains stationed outside the door, so I hand the third to Stefan.

"Let's talk business, son," Viktor says in a condescending tone.

"Dom will do," I tell him through gritted teeth. I am not his son, no matter my relationship with his daughter.

"Alright. Dominic, I–" Viktor starts, but I cut him off.

"Dom," I correct him sharply.

The only person who calls me *Dominic* is my wife. I don't think she even realizes it. I didn't mean to introduce myself with my full name when we met, but I'm glad I did. Now the name is reserved for her.

"*Dom,*" he hisses out, "I wanted to meet in person as a sign of good faith. We've upheld our end perfectly. I'm glad this alliance has been mutually beneficial."

"We've noticed your behavior, and we appreciate it." I nod my head in agreement.

As we discuss trivial details, I notice Viktor become more tense. His eyes keep darting to the window as if he's looking for something... or someone.

"Is there something wrong?" I ask him.

"I must confess, I had an ulterior motive in coming here. I wish to see my daughter." His eyes bear into mine in a challenge.

I'm not going to say no, but something about it bothers me. While it's a normal request, it's odd. Katerina is free to leave whenever she'd like. She's free to meet her father. So why is he sneaking his way into our home just to see her? Maybe she doesn't realize she's allowed to?

"Of course. I'll call her in here now." I tell him through gritted teeth. I don't like being fooled. I knew this meeting was a farce. I knew when he insisted I host that it was a trap. But I didn't listen to my instincts.

"I'd like to speak to her privately. You know, father-to-daughter." His sleezy grin makes me uneasy.

I nod in agreement, then tell Stefan to go get her. He shoots me a worried look, and it concerns me that he feels hesitant too.

A few long minutes later, my beautiful wife walks through the office doors. I shoot her a smile, but it drops at her expression. She's a few shades too pale, and her posture is ramrod straight. She seems worried. No, she seems like the weak, timid porcelain doll she used to be.

"Hello, Katya." Viktor's tone may be endearing, but his eyes are hard. "Why don't you give us the room?"

"Of course." I sneak a glance at Katerina and almost call this all off and demand he leaves. She looks like a shell of herself.

I lightly touch her back on my way out, a silent show of support, and her demeanor changes.

I see her shoulders pull back as her fists clench. I see her become the fighter I respect. It fills me with relief. She'll be just fine in there.

But just in case she needs me, I'm standing outside the door listening the whole time.

Chapter 32

Katerina

Fuck.

This is my karma for torturing Dominic this morning.

Because of my ill intent, Viktor's here to torture me.

Dominic shuts the door behind him, and the sound echoes throughout the room. I refuse to feel fear because of his absence. I don't need a man to protect me. I'm strong now. I don't need to fall into the silent Bratva Princess role. I can be the fierce Syndicate Wife I've become.

I meet Viktor's sharp gaze and return it with a glare of my own. I cross my arms over my chest in a defiant stance that I know will piss him off.

He looks me over for a minute, sneering the whole time, then throws his head back and laughs.

"Look at you. With your masculine haircut and clothes. I bet you think this makes you tough. I bet you think this makes you fierce. But you're not. You just look ugly and pathetic," he spits out in Russian. He laughs again as if my new me is something unthreatening.

I look over my black cropped leggings and grey hoodie. Thankfully I threw it over my sports bra. Viktor would probably beat me for parading around so inappropriately.

"You don't know anything!" I spit at him, still in our native tongue. I know my husband well enough to know that he's listening through that door right now. We don't need to give him any reason to storm in here.

"I know you've been screening my calls and ignoring my texts. But you can't shut me out. You can't get rid of me. You were sent here on a mission, and you're failing it. It's your job to help us. Remember who your family is, brat." Viktor's sharp eyes meet mine in a challenge.

"What if I don't want to do your mission?" I throw back at him. I remember my conversation with Nik. This is my chance to put him in his place.

Viktor storms the few steps between us and grips my arms tightly. He shakes me furiously, as if trying to knock some sense into me.

"I don't give a shit about what you want. You belong to me. You will do as I say." Viktor's voice is somehow a low whisper while still yelling. His face reddens with rage as spit flies from his mouth.

"I won't do it! I won't betray him!" I use a defense maneuver to get out of his grip and push his chest hard. "I'll tell him everything. I'll tell him this truce is a farce!"

"Oh, I see how it is. You like him. But let me assure you of something, the only thing he likes about you is that cunt. You're just business with a side of pleasure. All he cares about is the treaty. And if the treaty is void, he doesn't need you anymore. If he casts you aside like the useless trash you are, life will be so much worse than just marrying Sergey when you come back to us, little traitor." Viktor's eyes light up as he speaks of my impending misfortune. He's a sick bastard.

I hear Vova scratching the door, trying to get in. I hear my husband pick up my cat and sooth him. And that's when I know he cares for me.

"It isn't like that." I shove him again. "I'm not just some slut to him!" I can't be. We haven't even done anything sexual.

"So, you think he'll protect you? You're Bratva! It'd be a betrayal to his people if he did. You're just something that warms his bed. You stupid, naïve girl. You don't understand this world." He points a shaky finger at me as he speaks.

I slap it away.

"I don't need him to protect me. I can protect myself!" I push him hard enough for him to stumble backwards. I raise my fist to hit him, but he intercepts it.

He leans over me and stares me down. He pushes me, but I won't fall. He glances at the door, then steps back.

"This is not the place for your tantrum. I'll be reaching out soon, and you will answer. Get close to him. Find their weaknesses. Exploit them. I will kill him and you if you tell him anything. I'll kill them all. I'll drop a bomb on this fucking compound. Do not test me!"

With that, he steps back and brushes himself off. He heads to the door with the threat hanging over my head. It's a horrible thought, but I know it's something he's capable of. If the Syndicate thinks they're safe because I'm here, they're sorely mistaken.

"Fix yourself! You look terrible." Viktor spits at me then walks to the door. He gives me a minute, then opens it.

I don't hear what happens out there. I don't hear what he says or Dominic's responses. I don't hear anything as his words echo in my mind.

I stand there in a trance as time stands still, contemplating my next move.

Suddenly, there are hands on my shoulders. I instinctively swipe them off and get in an attack stance.

"Woah, easy there, tiger. It's just me," a familiar voice says.

I blink a few times to clear my head. When I open my eyes, I find my husband looking at me with concern.

"What happened?" he asks softly.

"Nothing." I avert my gaze, not needing him to catch my lie.

"You can tell me, tiger." No, I can't. And damn him for caring.

"It's nothing." I try to sound nonchalant.

"It's not nothing. You look like you've seen a ghost. You're pale and shaking. What did he say to you?" Dominic's voice rises and becomes agitated.

"No!" I fight back.

"TELL ME NOW!" he bellows.

"It's none of your damn business!" I bite at him.

"What happens in *my* house with *my* wife will always be *my* business!" He raises a hand as though to grip my arms like Viktor fucking does, and I storm out.

"FUCK YOU! You possessive mudak!" I storm out of the room, but I only make it to the hallway before he's on me and grabbing my shoulders, turning me to face him.

"Don't you ever speak to me that way in front of my men!" His eyes are wild as he says it. I can tell this is more about the *in front of his men* part.

"Ooh big bad boss is embarrassed by a woman standing up to him," I fuss out in a condescending baby voice that I know he hates.

"*You* listen to *me!* You are *my* wife, and you'll do as *I* say!" His ownership of me is my last straw.

I reel back to punch him, but my wrist gets trapped.

We both turn and see one of his guards holding my wrist.

In an instant, Dominic is on him. Despite his rage, he's gentle as he pries my wrist from the guard's grip.

"How dare you lay a finger on my wife?" His tone is so icy, it's menacing.

The guard gulps as his eyes widen. "But, sir..."

"NO! DON'T EVER FUCKING TOUCH MY WIFE! DON'T EVER COME BETWEEN US!" Dominic roars at him.

"But she was trying to hit you," the guard explains nervously.

"What my wife does to me is our business!" Dominic must tighten his grip on the guard's wrist because he flinches. Then Dominic throws his wrist down. "Get out of my sight. All of you!"

The hallway clears instantly, until it's just the two of us. Dominic turns to me and rage morphs into concern.

"Are you okay?" He lifts my wrist to inspect it.

I pull myself from his grasp and flick his forehead.

"He grabbed my wrist. Of course I'm fine. I've taken much worse beatings than that." I roll my eyes.

"EXCUSE ME?" Dominic interrupts me, his face morphing in fury.

He's ridiculous. I'm sure this man has been through so much worse than being grabbed. Then realization hits me.

"This is because I'm a woman! I don't need to defend me! I can take care of myself. Or do you not remember me kicking your ass this morning on the trails?" I pull away and start making my way down the hallway only for him to grab the back of my neck and turn me with a flick of his wrist. He pins me against the wall with a hand on my throat.

"I will always defend my wife. I know you can do it, but it's my job. So, you're going to be a good little wife and let me." He smirks with a dare in his eyes.

"There's no fucking chance. I don't need you," I bite back at him, noticing our proximity for the first time.

He leans in closer.

"Yes, you do."

His breath teases my lips.

"For what? What could I possibly need you for?" It comes out breathy.

He closes the distance between us.

"There are many things I can do for you." His eyes light up as he says it.

He presses his hardness into me.

I moan instinctively.

"I can do that on my own," I gasp out.

I tilt my head towards him.

"Not as well as with me."

He hovers his lips over mine.

"Maybe it's you who needs me."

I bite his bottom lip.

He growls.

"Fuck it!"

His lips crash into mine.

I lean into him. Finally tasting my husband. I wrap my arms around his neck. Leaning in–

RRRRINGGG!

Dominic ignores the call as he parts my lips with his tongue. He doesn't ask for permission, he just takes.

RRRRINGGG!

The phone rings again.

"FUCK!" Dominic curses as he pulls back slightly.

He pulls out his phone and answers without checking.

"WHAT?" he yells at the receiver.

I can't make out what the other person says, but Dominic looks sheepish.

"Sorry, Mom. What can I do for you?" he says in a way only a scolded son could sound.

After a few moments, Dominic looks at me, then down at our entangled bodies.

"I'm sorry, but we can't make it. We're... er... preoccupied," Dominic starts to flush, and I pray she doesn't ask what he's doing.

"Yes, ma'am," he says stubbornly.

After a few moments, there's another, "yes, ma'am."

He removes his hand from my throat to run it through his hair.

"We'll see you then." He hangs up and puts his phone away.

He looks at me longingly for a moment, then pulls himself off me.

"You have fifteen minutes to get ready. We're going to my parents' house for family dinner." He sounds exactly how I feel.

Nervous and unprepared.

Chapter 33
Katerina

I rush to put on a charcoal jumpsuit and black pumps. Gazing at my reflection in the mirror, I debate whether it's good enough.

"Stunning," my husband's husky voice tickles my ear.

I meet his eyes in the mirror as he crowds behind me.

"But it's missing something." As he says it, he lifts his hands and I see a glint of sparkle. He puts the ruby and diamond apology choker around my neck and clasps it.

I shake my head.

"Dominic, it's too much for family dinner." I lift my arms to take it off, but he swats them away.

"If you can't wear my hands and lips around your neck, then you'll wear my necklace," he muses. "Later, we're finishing what we started," he promises darkly.

All I can do is roll my eyes because as much as his words send a shiver down my spine, I can't admit my feelings.

He takes a step back, and I notice he's wearing a suit the exact color of my jumpsuit. There's no way he matched on purpose, right? But the ruby cufflinks and red tie argue that he did.

I barely have time to put on lipstick and brush my hair before he's ushering us out the door with a hand on the small of my back. I try not to lean into it, but the warmth of his palm is so comforting.

We ride in silence. I can't think of what to say. I want to ask about his family, but he hasn't been open about them. They've been off limits. I didn't expect to be invited over. I figured they didn't want anything to do with his pretend wife.

There's a foreign feeling in me as we sit in silence. It's anxiety. Which is crazy because I don't get nervous. Why do I even care?

But there's so much unknown. Why did they invite me? What if it was only to drive a wedge between Dominic and me? What if they don't approve of me and want me gone?

They were nice when we met at the wedding, but I was cold and distant. Definitely not a warm and welcoming addition to the family.

My husband doesn't seem to share my unease though. He drives casually, weaving through traffic. I survey him, trying to find any sign of concern. His fingers grip the steering wheel a little too tight; his knuckles are a little too white. *Good. I don't want to be alone in my anxiety.*

It relieves me that he's in the same boat as me. I know he's a master of hiding his emotions, but not from me. I can see through his act. And I can see his discomfort.

"Relax. I'm not going to stab any of them." I break the silence with a joke.

He turns his head towards me and shoots me a glare.

"Too soon to joke about, then?" I tease him. He cracks a smile and lets out a small chuckle. It feels like winning the Stanley Cup to make him laugh.

"You barely stabbed me." He rolls his eyes as he dismisses my claim to fame.

I gasp.

"How dare you! You needed the doctor to come stitch you up!" I swat his leg jokingly, but since it's his left one, when I pull back, I accidentally brush over *it*.

And *it* is hard.

And big.

And firm.

I freeze with my hand resting on his steel pipe.

He coughs and starts to laugh.

"Either start getting to work or let me go, but don't just hold my cock," he says through a chuckle.

I tighten my grip, and he hisses, then I pull back quickly.

"Why are you hard? We're about to be with your family!" I try to sound disgusted, but I'm not sure I succeed.

"After our little encounter in the hallway, you can't expect me to be anything but hard. Fuck, tiger. My blood just stopped boiling." He runs his hand through his hair, messing it up.

"That's unfortunate for you," I muse, sounding unaffected. I keep my attention focused on my manicured fingernails instead of meeting his gaze. I can't let him see that I've been just as affected.

"You're telling me you feel nothing after that kiss? Hottest damn minute of my life. Cut too damn short." He sounds so exasperated that I can't help but grin. I love getting on his nerves.

"Honestly, wouldn't even rank it top five hottest kisses for me," I say nonchalantly.

"Bullshit," he grits out. I see his fingers tighten on the steering wheel and can't help but push him further.

"Well let's see." I start counting on my fingers. "There was Zeke in junior high. You never forget your first kiss. Then there was Gabriel at prom. Oh, that was a prom night I'll never forget." I chuckle at the fake memory, and it makes Dominic growl. I'm lying through my teeth. Half these kisses didn't happen, and the ones that did, they didn't come close to our kiss. "Skipping to college, there was Danny at the frat party. Now, he knew how to kiss... everywhere. Oh, I can't forget Anton! He might deserve first place. I've never had dick like—"

"ENOUGH!" Dominic roars, cutting me off.

"Don't raise your voice at me!" I reprimand him sharply. I reach over and squeeze his arm, digging my nails into it. Then I pat it condescendingly. "Yours deserves an honorable mention."

"You're such a fucking brat," he mutters through clenched teeth.

"But I'm your bratty wife." I tease him, and it has the opposite effect that I expect. Instead of scowling, he grins.

"Damn straight. And every fucking man better remember it," he threatens the nonexistent men in our car.

"A big, fat diamond ring on my finger would make that known. Too bad none of them will see I'm taken." I sigh as I look at my lonely wedding band.

He just rolls his eyes.

"We're here." He points out the window towards a beautiful mansion. It looks ethereal with its character.

We park, and he hops out of the car, but I sit and wait. I'll be damned if my husband doesn't treat me like a lady. If he isn't a gentleman yet, I'll train him to be. Because if you're as stubborn as I am, you can teach an old dog new tricks.

My husband makes it halfway up the front steps before realizing I'm not by his side. He looks around confused then storms towards me. He shoots me a questioning look, but I just raise my eyebrow at him.

He opens my door and inspects it.

"Is there something wrong with the door?" He sounds genuinely concerned.

"There's something wrong with my husband," I throw at him.

He stumbles back.

"What the hell did I do wrong this time, crazy woman?" He looks a mix between shocked and amused.

"I'm a lady. A lady doesn't open her own door. You're supposed to be my gentleman," I scold him.

He just laughs.

"Tiger, you're so far from a lady it's not even funny. I watched you kick Nik's ass in the ring yesterday."

"I can be a lady and still be a badass. Now help me out, jackass." I stick my hand out of the car, and he grips it tightly. He pulls me out and once I stand, he shuts the door and leads us to the house.

But he never drops my hand.

He lifts his key, ready to unlock the door, but I stop him and knock.

"This is my parents' place. I can let myself in," he grumbles.

"Dear God, it's like you've never been taught any etiquette. I can't just barge into the house of someone I don't know." I pull my hand from his.

When I hear footsteps, I nervously step away from Dominic. I don't want them to think there's anything going on between us. He immediately grips my waist and pulls me into him. He tucks me into his side with a fierce grip, and I unsuccessfully try to wiggle free.

"Smile, tiger. It's time for you to behave like a lady," he whispers in my ear.

I scoff and stomp on his foot. He hisses out a breath and squeezes me tighter.

"You little mudak! I swear–" I start to curse him out, but the door swings open, shutting me up.

I paste on my brightest, fakest smile as a middle-aged couple I barely recognize greets us.

"I'm so glad you guys could make it!" Dominic's stunning mother says as if she didn't demand we come mere hours ago.

"Thank you for having us, Mr. and Mrs. Montclair." I hold out my hand, ready to shake theirs, but it's ignored.

His mother pulls me in for an unexpected hug. Dominic doesn't loosen his hold so it's awkward when she can only put one arm around me.

"Please, dear, call us Damien and Evelyn. We're thrilled our newest member of the family could finally make it to dinner," Damien tells me with a grin and leads us inside. "It's a mandatory weekly event, Sunday family dinners. We know your lives have been busy, but we want to see you more."

"Katerina, we're having steak and vegetable medley for dinner. I apologize for not checking earlier if you had any food allergies or preferences. If this doesn't meet your needs, please let us know." Evelyn looks distraught at the idea that I could possibly not be able to eat their dinner.

"Oh, she'll eat anything! Don't worry about that, Mom," Dominic says with a chuckle.

I dig my fingers into his back until he hisses.

"Young man, Katerina can speak for herself. And she can do it a whole lot better than you can. I raised you better than this!"

Evelyn uses such a motherly-scolding tone it almost brings tears to my eyes.

"Steak sounds lovely. Thank you," I tell Evelyn with a sweet smile, when what I really want to do is applaud her for putting Dominic in his place.

"Everyone's in the sitting room," Damien says as he ushers us down the hallway.

I look around and note just how homey everything feels. How homey the house feels. How homey this family feels. How full of love it is. I've never experienced anything like this.

"Did you grow up here?" I whisper to Dominic.

"Yes. My parents' have lived here since they got married." He says it like it's no big deal, but he isn't seeing what I am.

I may have grown up in a big mansion too, but it was never like this. I push past my envy to excitement. They're treating me like one of their own. Maybe I'm actually welcome in this family.

We walk into the living room, and I finally see people I recognize. Margot and Matthias, Cecilia and her husband whose name I can't remember, and Bash.

"Kat! I'm so glad you're here!" Margot jumps up from her spot next to Matthias and gives me a hug. I hug her back awkwardly, still not used to any form of affection. Cecilia waves at me from her spot practically in her husband's lap. She's showing even more than when I saw her at the wedding. I can't imagine what it's like being pregnant with triplets.

"Hey, Margot! What've you been up to?" I ask to be polite. She jumps into a story about the wild alien romance book she's narrating. It sounds... interesting.

Once she's told her story, it becomes almost a Q&A for me. I'm fielding questions about myself. They don't seem judgmental, just curious. Dominic gets scolded more than once for interrupting me, correcting me, or refuting my answers. He's taken to just sulking next to me.

Everyone has been more than welcoming, and by the time Evelyn rises and ushers us to dinner, my nerves have dissipated.

I realize I love the Montclair family, and I love being a Montclair.

Chapter 34
Katerina

Damien sits at one head of the table and Dominic beelines to the other. I try not to roll my eyes at the patriarchal seating.

I stand behind the seat next to my husband as he pulls out his chair obliviously. I kick his foot to grab his attention. His head snaps in my direction, and he looks at me questioningly. I gesture to my chair, but his eyebrows scrunch in confusion.

"Pull out my chair, husband," I hiss under my breath and nod at the other husbands doing it for their wives.

"Of course, my lady," he says sarcastically and pulls out my chair.

I flash him a wide smile as I take my seat.

I look down and smirk at my utensils. For the first time since I stabbed him, I have a real knife instead of a plastic one.

My smirk isn't long lasting though. It falls when a large hand confiscates my steak knife and replaces it with one of those damn fake silver plastic ones.

I glare at my husband as he pockets my real knife. He smirks at me and pats his jacket.

"Safety measure. You understand," he whispers mockingly.

"Don't trust that false sense of security. I will make this plastic knife hurt just as much as a real one," I promise quietly with a sweet smile on my face, so his family doesn't suspect anything.

A few servers enter and place our meals in front of us, and my stomach drops.

Steak.

We're eating steak.

We're eating steak and all I have is a fucking plastic knife to cut it with.

I glare at my husband, and he looks at me so innocently that if it weren't for the smile he's biting back, I'd believe he was unaware of the situation.

"Is there a problem?" He says loud enough, the whole table looks at me.

"No problem. Thank you for checking, *husband*," I grip his leg that I stabbed under the table in a silent threat.

I scoot my chair away from him, wanting to put space between us. But he doesn't let me get far before pulling me by my seat even closer to him than I was before. Even through the suit, I can see his huge bicep bulge as he moves me. He catches me staring and smirks. *Damn him.*

I ignore him and start on my vegetables. Once my plate is cleared except the slab of meat, I slowly pick up my plastic knife and get to work. I saw and saw and saw the steak, but it's almost futile.

It takes me a full minute to cut one bite. By the time I'm on my third bite, I've given up.

"Give it back!" I demand under my breath.

"No," he whispers back.

"Give it back, or I'll fucking stab you with this one too!" I threaten.

"Steak seems to make you violent. It would be a hazard to give you anything sharp." He pauses, then looks at me concerned. "Do you want me to help you?"

I eye him skeptically.

"I don't want your help. I want my knife." I don't trust that caring look on his face. He's up to something.

"Too bad." He pulls my plate closer to him and starts cutting up my steak for me. I glare at him as he does it. I notice from the corner of my eye that we've caught some attention. Thankfully, it's only Bash and Cecilia. Margot would definitely be asking questions.

Once a piece of my steak is cut, Dominic stabs it with his fork, and I hiss at him.

"Don't fucking think about eating my steak!" I point my plastic knife at him, so he knows I'm serious.

"It's for you," he says lightly.

I stare at his fork in horror as he brings it to my lips. He's out of his fucking mind if he thinks I'm letting him feed me in front of his family.

"Absolutely not!" I hiss.

"It's the only way you're eating this steak, doll." He brings the fork closer to my mouth. I swat his hand away.

"Fuck you!" I stab him with the plastic knife, but it doesn't penetrate his slacks. It must irritate the last wound though because he lets out a gasp.

He grabs my hand and stands so quickly his chair almost topples over. In a swift move, he pulls me up beside him.

"Excuse us. We'll be back in a minute." His stoic tone takes me by surprise. Somehow, he has that mask back in place for his family.

I take in their shocked expressions and smile assuredly. The last thing I need them to think is that I can't hold my own against my husband.

He drags me out of the room and pushes me up against the wall before the door even slams shut.

"You got steak juice on my suit, tiger!" He sounds appalled at the state of his suit. I look down and see it's only a few drops. I roll my eyes.

"Take it to the fucking dry cleaners, you misogynistic asshole!" I bite back at him.

He crowds me against the wall, arms on either side of my head, caging me in. It's not often I feel small, but beneath this behemoth of a man, I do.

"You say a lot for a pretty little lady. What would daddy think?" He mocks me with the worst thing possible.

My vision reddens. How dare he bring Viktor into this! I reach into his jacket pocket and before he can react, I'm holding my steak knife against his neck.

"You mudak," I hiss. I press the knife against him but not hard enough to draw blood.

"Careful, tiger. I don't think your claws are as sharp as you think." He chuckles harshly then moves quicker than a bear. He has his hand wrapped around the front of my neck, lightly chocking me. Fuck him for manhandling me. But fuck me for liking it.

"You have no idea what I'm capable of." Everyone miscalculates me, but one day, they'll see.

"The stitches on my thigh disagree. But you're no murderer," he muses. Even with a knife to his throat, he doesn't deem me a threat. But I can tell it's not because he underestimates me, but because he knows he's safe from me. But not everyone can claim that.

"I'd do whatever it takes to get revenge." One person in particular comes to mind.

"But you wouldn't kill your husband," he challenges me. He knows me well enough to trust me. I deliberate if I would kill him if I had to, and then something horrible dawns on me. I don't know if I could.

"Not unless you give me a reason to," I lie.

"Would you do it in front of them?" He raises a brow and points to the door with the hand not around my neck.

The distance he puts between us with the move leaves me cold. Without a thought, I wrap my leg around his and pull him into me. He immediately grips my ass and pulls me up until my core rests against his hardness.

"If I didn't know better, I'd think you enjoy being threatened," I muse as I grind up against him.

"Fuck, tiger," he moans. "I only enjoy it when it's my wife threatening me."

"I wish I could say I only enjoy threatening my husband, but that'd be a lie." It comes out husky. I can't stop teasing him, but this one isn't a lie. I do love my violence.

"You better not be threatening any other man like this." He thrusts against me as he growls it out.

I moan at the contact and chase him with my hips, seeking more.

"Quiet, tiger. You wouldn't want your in-laws hearing you're not a good girl." The mockery in his tone pisses me off just as much as his movements arouse me.

I bring my mouth close to his.

"They don't need to know it, but I'll never be a good girl for you," I promise him. He just grins in response.

He brings his lips so close I can feel his exhales mingle with my own.

"I can make you my good girl. Just wait and see," he says confidently. Such misplaced confidence.

I bite his lip then push him back creating distance between us. His shocked expression fills me with pleasure.

"You'll be waiting a long time, darling." I laugh as I say it.

He pulls me by my neck into him until our lips brush.

"Fight me all you want but know who you belong to." His dark tone sends shivers down my spine.

He brings his lips down to mine. My eyes shut, and I bask in his touch. The kiss is heat and passion and need. It's all the pent-up fire we've been fighting.

But all too quickly, it's over. His abrupt absence leaves me cold and needy. I groan as my eyes fly open to a nightmarish scene.

Bash is standing behind a confused Dominic with such fury, he's shaking. He must have pulled my husband off of me. I can't imagine the scene he walked in on nor the conclusions he came to.

"DON'T EVER LAY A HAND ON YOUR WIFE AGAIN!" Bash shouts at my husband.

Dominic's confusion morphs into fury. He turns to face his brother, and somehow, stands so tall, he seems even bigger and more intimidating.

"DON'T EVER COME BETWEEN US!" Dominic yells back.

Bash doesn't back down. Bash launches his fist at Dominic, catching him in the eye. I gasp at the move, completely caught off guard. I pegged Roman as the hothead, not Bash. He seemed too sweet and nerdy.

"What the fuck happened to you?" Bash seethes. "You're not the brother I once knew!"

I step towards Dominic, needing to check on my husband. Bash hears me and starts to make his way to me. He doesn't drop his gaze from the furious Dominic though.

"Are you okay, Katerina?" His voice drops and is filled with genuine concern. It fills me with such guilt.

Oh no. We've worried sweet Bash to the point of hitting his brother. But I fear telling him the truth will only scar him. I hide the knife behind my back before he can spot it.

"I'm okay, Bash. Thank you for stepping in, but it's not what it looked like," I try to assure him, but he doesn't believe me.

"You don't have to cover for him." His concern is endearing but so misplaced. "Why don't you go finish your dinner. I need to talk to my brother."

For the first time since meeting him, Bash doesn't look like a boy, but instead a strong man. I believe behind those glasses lies someone formidable.

I look at Dominic questioningly. I don't want to abandon him with his brother like this, but I also cannot be here if he tells him the sordid truth. I'll die from mortification.

Dominic looks me over, his searing gaze setting me on fire from within. When his eyes land on my mine, he nods. I thank Bash and head inside.

At least with my steak knife, I can finish my dinner.

Chapter 35

Dominic

I keep my eyes on my sexy wife until the door shuts behind her then I turn my attention on my baby brother.

"What is wrong with you!" Bash demands incredulously. His eyes widen, then he pulls his glasses off and rubs the bridge of his nose.

"Calm down. It wasn't what it looked like," I try to assure him. Despite my instinct of ordering him to back off, I know I need to explain it to him.

"It looked like you were choking your wife while threatening her!" Bash points at me accusingly with his glasses, then sighs and puts them on his face.

"What you didn't see was her threatening me with a knife to my throat." It comes out heated. I won't have anyone thinking my wife is weak or needs someone to defend her. She's more than capable of taking care of herself.

"No?" He gasps in disbelief.

I pull down my collar and reveal the red markings of the blade.

"Dom, is she a threat to you? To the Syndicate? Do we need to find a way out of this marriage?" Despite it coming from a good place, his insinuation of taking Katerina from me enrages me.

I stalk toward him until I'm towering over him. He's only a couple inches shorter than me, but he's leaner and younger. I glare at him.

"No one can take her away from me. I'll kill anyone that tries," I promise. He needs to know. She's mine. No one can change that.

Instead of looking scared, Bash looks confused.

"But... she was trying to kill you? She had a knife against your throat." He looks so innocent when he says it. I tread lightly, knowing he's too pure to understand the appeal of her passion.

"She wasn't trying to kill me. If she was, I'd be dead. She was just putting me in my place. She's incredibly passionate, and it's thrilling." I can't hide my grin as I say it. She was so fucking sexy, threatening me. My sexy tiger has so much bite behind her bark.

Bash looks between me and the door she just went through and back at me a few times before shaking his head.

"You guys are freaks. I'm glad you found each other." His nose scrunches, and his lips curl. "Blah! I won't interfere again. Just don't do your little freak shit in the hallway. I don't want to walk in on it again."

I smirk and nod. "We'll keep it PG for you."

He throws his hands in the air then storms down the hallway to the bathroom.

I return to my seat at the table to see my plate has been cleared and a flourless chocolate torte is in its place. I gaze upon my wife as I dig in. The sight of her, the feeling on her nails digging into my thigh, and the taste of chocolate seduce me.

Conversation goes on around me, but I don't pay any attention. My entire focus is on the temptress next to me. She catches my gaze and raises a brow. I blow her a kiss, and she rolls her eyes then turns her back to me. But she can't hide the flush on her cheeks.

"Guys, why don't we meet in Dad's office?" Bash suggests.

It takes me by surprise. I'm always the one pushing for Syndicate meetings after dinner, but tonight, I don't want to. I don't want to leave my wife. And not because I think she'll stab anyone in my family without my supervision, although they'd probably deserve it, but because I simply don't want to leave her side.

Roman and Matthias look just as reluctant to leave their wives. For the first time in my life, I consider cancelling a Syndicate meeting. I look at Katerina in question, but she just ushers me away.

"Go talk business. Your dad's going to show me his knife collection." She sounds excited at the prospect, and my gaze flies to my dad. He looks just as giddy as she does. None of us have taken an interest in his more unusual hobbies, but it looks like my wife has.

"Have fun," I tell her then kiss the top of her head.

I freeze as she tenses. What the fuck did I just do? Just because we barely kissed doesn't give me the right to kiss her whenever. Or does it? I mean I am her husband. But we don't have that kind of relationship.

I rush out of the room without looking back. I walk quickly into Dad's office and lean against a bookshelf.

As my brothers trinkle in, I maintain a mask of indifference. Far too many people have seen me emote because of my damn wife. No one needs to know what I'm feeling... except her. She brings it out of me.

"I see married life has been treating you well," Matthias says with a smirk. When I shoot him a glare, he wiggles his eyebrows at me.

Bash coughs in discomfort, but we ignore him.

"I never thought I'd see the day Dominic Montclair was smitten for a woman. I bet she leads you around by your cock." Roman adds unhelpfully.

Bash chokes and turns red.

"My relationship is not up for discussion!"

"We're just messing with you. It's good to see you happy." Matthias's words make me wonder if I seemed unhappy before Katerina.

"Let's get on task. What did we need to discuss?" I ask, ready to put an end to the conversation.

My brothers look at me in shock.

"What?" I demand.

"You don't have something planned? You always want to talk about work." Roman sounds confused, but then he smiles. "Oh, I get it. Something else is on your mind now."

He wiggles his brows suggestively, so I reach over and punch him. He just laughs harder.

"Fuck off. If no one has anything to say, then meeting dismissed." I straighten my stance and head to the door, ready to get back to my wife.

"Oh, I have a lot to say," Roman starts.

"Me too!" Matthias continues, and they high five.

I ignore their jabs as I make my way to the family room. Sure enough, Dad has multiple sets of knives laid out and is explaining the history and use of each one to Katerina. She's actively engaged in the conversation, eagerly taking in the information.

I hang back by the doorway and just watch her. I can't put words to the feeling in my chest at watching her with my family. There's just something so right about it.

My mom is the first to see me and beckons me into the room. I come in and sit next to her. Katerina looks up at me and winks, then makes a small stabbing motion with one of the knives in my general direction. A laugh erupts from my chest at my psychotic wife and her stabbing tendencies.

"You don't know what it does to a mother to see her child so happy. I'm grateful for Katerina. She's brought you such lightness. She's such a marvelous young lady." Mom grabs my hand in hers and squeezes.

My chest hurts at containing the laugh at Katerina being referred to as a lady after our conversations, but I know my mom is being serious, so I won't mock her.

"She's great, Mom. She's strong, fierce, and stubborn in the best way. She doesn't let me get away with anything. I thought she was this weak, boring woman when we met, but she's been full of great surprises." I smile softly as I tell my mom about my wife.

"She's a great addition to the family," Mom says sweetly, then her eyes harden. "You're not allowed to miss anymore family dinners. And don't forget, your brother's vow renewals are next weekend."

I try to remember anything about the vow renewals but can't.

"We'll be there... Which brother is it?" I try to keep my voice light, but wince anyways, knowing the slap on the back of my head is coming.

"Roman and Cecilia's vow renewal. They didn't have a wedding, remember?" She sighs as she scolds me.

I honestly didn't remember. I can't be bothered with the details of my brothers' love lives. I have more important things to worry about.

Before I can respond, Roman and Cecilia are on their feet.

"It's time for us to go," Roman says, ushering his wife out the door.

"Let me say goodbye!" She stops him. "He has me on a strict prenatal routine." Even as she rolls her eyes, she lets out a sweet giggle and lets him pull her in for a hug.

Matthias and Margot stand and start saying their goodbyes.

I make my way to my wife and help her to her feet. I gently pry to karambit knife out of her hand and place it on the table.

"Let's go home," I tell her.

She stands and gives my dad a hug. I feel a pang of emotion in my chest. I've never seen her hug Viktor. It's nice to see her receiving parental love.

After Dad releases her, he pulls me in for a hug. Before I let go, he whispers in my ears.

"She's a good woman. You treat her well." I nod. It's the kind of fatherly threat Viktor should've given me. I hate that it didn't come from her father. "You chose a good queen for the Syndicate. She'll be a great asset."

He pulls back, and I try to shake off my astonishment. He can't mean for me to include her in Syndicate affairs. She's Bratva. She's a woman. There's no place for her in the Syndicate.

The rest of the evening is spent mulling over his words. Katerina is fierce for sure, but I'd break so much tradition bringing her in.

Chapter 36

Katerina

The guards seated on either side of me ignore the glares I'm shooting at them. But then it dawns on me who's actually to blame, and I redirect my fury to my infuriating husband standing by his brothers at the altar. He meets my gaze and smirks. Of course he finds this situation humorous, he's the one that orchestrated it.

Instead of sitting next to Margot and his parents at Roman and Cecilia's vow renewal, Dominic has me seated a row behind them flanked by Syndicate guards. And all because I had a few choice words for him this morning.

I tried to holster a gun and knife under my dress, but Dominic scoffed. When he insisted I leave them behind, I may have threatened to sneak them in and use them on him during the wedding. Not my finest moment. He dramatically declared me a threat that needed constant supervision. So that's how I ended up here.

The ceremony passes in a blur. The emotional vows made me uncomfortable. Promises of forever love and lots of babies had my skin crawling. But there was also a pit in my stomach. Would I still find it so troubling if Dominic wanted it with me?

I love my life here. I like the rhythm we've gotten into, but there's still so much in our way. We fight constantly, even if it's lighthearted, and that can't be good for a relationship. He doesn't trust me. I'm the enemy's daughter, so I get it. But I doubt I could ever earn that trust. I don't even know if I could trust him. Despite proving to me countless times that he's nothing like Viktor, how can I be sure? Moves like today, not letting me bring weapons, are point enough.

Roman and Cecilia look at each other so adoringly, and I realize how different this is from my wedding. Mine was cold and formal, nothing like this. I wonder if we had it now, now that Dominic and I know each other, how different it would be. Our vows would have small jabs at each other, and we'd be smirking the whole time. He'd probably bring up in his toast the time I stabbed him. I'd bring up the time he vomited after a run.

My eyes wander to my husband's, and I find his already on me with a faraway look. I don't know what he's thinking, but I wonder how close it is to what's in my head. I keep my attention on him until the ceremony ends, and the happy couple retreats down the aisle.

Margot turns to me as people pour out of their seats and looks worriedly at the guards flanking me.

"What's with the security?" She lowers her voice. "Is there a threat here?"

I almost laugh at the absurdity of her statement, but then I realize the fear in her eyes and the tremble in her voice are real. She's actually worried. It's so unlike her normal gregarious demeanor, that it stuns me.

"No, not at all. This is just Dominic messing with me for pushing his buttons earlier. There's nothing to worry about." I gently hold her hand, trying to assure her.

She relaxes then laughs.

"What'd you do to him? I know the rest of the family thinks you're all innocent, but I know a fighter when I see one. You drive him crazy, don't you?" Her eyes shine with pride as she says it. I nod slowly, not wanting to get myself in trouble. "I did the same with Matty when he first took me. I think it's what made him fall in love with me. Men like them need someone to keep them in line!"

I follow her gaze to our husbands heading towards us. Both have their gazes set on their wives as they march through the crowd. Matthias looks dotingly upon his, whereas my husband looks calculated and cunning. Something tells me Margot's little fights with Matthias weren't quite as... bloody as ours.

Matthias grabs Margot and pulls her into his side. He places a kiss on her head and wraps an arm around her. She giggles which brings a soft smile to his face. I don't catch what she whispers in his ear, because, suddenly, there are hands on my waist pulling me back.

I stomp on my assailant's foot then pull my elbow into their stomach. I reel back, ready for more of a fight, when a husky voice fills my ears.

"Tiger, as much as I'd love to pin you down and prove how much stronger I am than you, now's not the time."

I take a step back until my back is flushed against his chest. I can feel his exhale. Then his hands trail closer together until they're intertwined on my abs. My breath gets caught in my throat. We haven't been this close since family dinner on Sunday. I'm so caught up in the feeling of him that I don't register the church emptying until I hear a snicker.

Margot and Matthias are watching us. Margot looks at me knowingly, but Matthias stares at his brother like a puzzle he's trying to solve. Margot wiggles her brows suggestively, and my cheeks flush. I step forward, breaking our contact.

"Shouldn't we go to the reception now?" My voice is higher than normal as I try to collect myself.

Dominic nods and leads me out of the church with his palm on the small of my back. I try not to overthink the gesture. He's just treating his wife as a husband should in public. This doesn't mean he wants to touch me.

We drive to the reception with Margot and Matthias. I'm thankful for the company keeping us distracted. Margot dominates the conversation, but I don't mind. Her voice becomes background noise to my thoughts.

When we arrive at the reception, Dominic walks around the car and opens my door for me without being prompted. I grin at him, pleased that I've trained him well.

"Looks like I can teach an old dog new tricks," I whisper gleefully in his ear.

"I don't know if I should be more offended by being called old or being compared to a dog?" he rumbles back. I just smirk and elbow him teasingly.

The reception goes smoothly for a few hours. I notice the Montclair brothers and the Syndicate guards checking the entrances occasionally. I realize Margot might've had reason to suspect the guards were here for our safety.

"Hey bellissima, can I get you a drink?" I turn to see a guy close to my age standing behind me. I look around, surprised to see he's talking to me.

"Oh, no thank you." I decline in a sweet voice.

"What's your name?" he relents. He seems like a nice guy, but unfortunately for him, my husband isn't one.

"I'm Katerina Montclair, Roman's sister-in-law." I offer him my hand to shake, obviously displaying my wedding band. Dominic needs to get me a loud engagement ring to avoid these situations.

"I'm Mateo, Cecilia's cousin on her mother's side. It's a pleasure to meet you." He steps back, a clear sign that he's no longer hitting on me. I release my breath and smile at him. "It's such a nice event. The Montclair family seems so kind."

The Montclairs being described as kind instead of ruthless makes my lips twitch. I fight to contain my laugh. This poor man has no idea what his cousin married into.

"I'm blessed to be married into such a good family." There's more truth in that statement than I expected.

"They put on a great party. I mean, did you see the cake?" He points to where it stands tall next to us. He seems so excited, and I realize he must not go to many events like these often.

"It looks really good–" My words get stuck in my throat as I'm yanked back into a hard chest. I see Mateo's eyes widening as he takes a few more steps back, and I instantly know who's holding me.

"Mateo, meet Dominic Montclair my–"

"Her *husband.* If I ever find you flirting with my wife again, I won't stop until you're begging for death's sweet escape." Dominic's voice is lethal as it slices through the air.

Mateo visibly pales, then scurries across the room.

I roll my eyes and grit my teeth as I break free from Dominic.

"How dare you treat me like property! I'm allowed to converse with other men!" I seethe at him.

"How dare *me?* How dare *you* flirt with some guy as though you aren't *my wife!* Don't make me remind you of what I'll do to any man that tries to get your attention." Dominic's shaking in his fury. His ears are red, as are his cheeks.

"You don't get to control me! I don't listen to you. Haven't you learned that yet?" My fury matches his own as his eyes narrow.

"What I've learned is that you're a brat. What you need to learn is that you're mine. My wife! And no other man gets any part of you!" He points his finger at me accusingly when he calls me a brat, then he points it back at himself, violently jerking it towards himself every time he claims me as his.

I look around and my eyes catch on the sharp silver cake knife. I smirk as I whip my hand out to grab it. He seems to listen a lot better when I have something to fight back with. But all too quickly, my hand is grasped in his, and he uses it to pull me into him.

"Not so fast, tiger. Now isn't an appropriate time to showcase your weaponry skill." He chuckles darkly as he pulls me even closer.

I huff and roll my eyes. I hate that he knows me so well. I push against him, but he effortlessly pulls me right back in. I struggle against his hold trying to recall how Nik taught me to get out of this one.

"You're going to cause a scene," I hiss at him when I realize how we look.

He looks around, then back at me. With my heels on, we're almost eye level. He lifts me slightly off the ground and carries me to the dance floor. I refuse to be impressed by his strength.

"What are you doing?" I mutter at him.

He ignores me and readjusts us until we look like we're a normal, non-matricidal couple dancing. He spins me around the floor, and with each turn, the distance between us diminishes. Until we're chest to chest. Until our lips are mere centimeters apart.

"I'm enjoying a dance with my exasperating, infuriating, captivating wife." Even though I can feel the anger hanging in the air, there's something else in his eyes. A different kind of heat.

Lust.

And I smile because I can use that to my advantage. I soften my features, matching his passion. It's easy because I'm feeling it too. I'm just stronger at fighting it. Glancing at his lips, then back at his eyes, I lift my chin slightly towards his mouth. His eyes widen, then a wicked grin takes over. His hand travels up my back pulling me in. He tilts his head, and when our lips are a breath apart, I pull back and laugh. It sounds almost maniacal. But I can't help it. This man brings me to the brink of insanity.

"Darling, I won't be the one to crack first. You'll have to be on your hands and knees begging for me before I give in." I pull back as I say it and meet his steel eyes.

His hand snaps up my back and grasps the back of my neck. He uses it to pull me back into him. But instead of going for the kiss, he hovers.

"Maybe you're right, tiger. Maybe I need to show you why you're mine, so you stop fighting it." His features change, and suddenly, I'm looking at man who's at peace. And that terrifies me.

"What... what do you mean?" I ask warily. For the first time, I feel unsure. I don't know what his next move is. He diverted from the script. He wasn't supposed to agree with me.

"Come," he muses then untangles himself from me. He steps back, breaking all contact except the hand gripping the back of my neck.

And then he marches me out of the ballroom. Through the hotel. To the front desk. Then up the elevator. Until we're in front of a door to a hotel room.

He unlocks it.

Turns the handle.

Then looks at me.

"Get inside. You're never going to question whose wife you are again."

Chapter 37

Katerina

Instead of walking into the room, I remain in the hallway with my hands on my hips.

"'Never question whose wife I am?'" I hiss his words back at him. "You brought me to a hotel room to what, fuck some obedience into me? To show me who's boss? Well guess what, I'm not your wife. Not really. All of this is fake. Don't forget that."

Blackness consumes his irises. His entire body tenses. He grips the back of my neck again and leads me into the bedroom. The door slamming shut echoes throughout the silent room.

"This isn't fake, and you damn well know it." His voice is lethal. He doesn't beg for my understanding; he demands my affirmation.

"Dominic, this is a business agreement. We're not really married. It's not real!" I push him. I'm trying to remind myself too. When he agrees with me, when he backs down, I'll finally be able to let this go.

"IT'S FUCKING REAL! IT'S ALWAYS BEEN REAL!
WE'VE BEEN MARRIED SINCE OUR FIRST FIGHT AT
OUR RECEPTION! I'VE BEEN YOUR HUSBAND SINCE
YOU STABBED ME IN THE LEG! YOU ARE MY WIFE!
AND I'LL BE DAMNED IF ANYONE, ESPECIALLY YOU,
QUESTIONS OUR MARRIAGE!"

His raised voice sends shivers down my spine.

"I didn't know. I–" I stammer over my words.

"I hate how much I want you. I hate what a distraction you
are. You're always on my fucking mind. I can't get you out of
my fucking head. I crave you!" He stalks towards me, but I stand
my ground. Even when we're only a breath apart. "You are my
wife. And it's time I start treating you like it, Katerina."

"Dom–" I breathe out.

"Shh. Stop talking. Stop fighting. For one goddamn minute,
just listen–" He runs his hand through his hair as he shuts me
up, and fuck him for thinking he can. So, I cut him off.

I grab his lapels and pull him into me. My lips attack his. I
don't start slowly. I'm not nice about it. Our teeth clash. Our
tongues duel for dominance. There's hair pulling, and clothes
tearing. We're a blur of motion. Of passion.

His hands land on my waist, and he lifts me then tosses me
on the bed. He shoves at his suit jacket, throws his tie off, shreds
his shirt. I stare at his torso covered in tattoos. I saw him naked
once, that time in the shower, but this is different. This time, I
get to touch him. This time, he's mine.

I crawl to the edge of the bed and start to stand. Ready to
study my husband's art.

"Stay on the bed, tiger," he commands in a strong tone.

"No." I roll my eyes and hop off.

He instantly scoops me up, but this time, instead of tossing
me on the bed, he carries me onto it and straddles me.

"You wouldn't be my Katerina if you weren't obstinate." He laughs as he says it. "But in here, in bed, you listen to me."

He lays on me, so I can feel his hardness. He leans down and starts kissing my neck. His mistake is leaving himself vulnerable.

I wrap myself around him and flip us over so I'm on top.

"Now, I wouldn't be your Katerina if I listened to you in bed." I grin, then slowly drag my dress up my body, then over my head. I'm left in only a thong.

Dominic's greedy eyes devour me. He stares for a full moment in awe, and I've never felt more beautiful. He slowly lifts his hands and places them on my waist. They deliberately travel over my torso, across my abs, up until they hover over my breasts.

"My wife is fucking unreal," he breathes out.

He doesn't give me a chance to react to his words before he's palming my breasts. One in each hand. He squeezes them then runs his thumbs over my peaked nipples. I gasp at the unfamiliar sensation and arch my back, chasing the contact.

"Tell me what you like," he demands.

With my lack of experience, I don't know what I like. I just know I like his touch. In any way it comes.

"Just don't stop touching me." It comes out more of a command than a request. He smirks and continues his assault.

Leaning down, I capture his lips with mine. I bite his bottom lip and tug on it before moving down his scruff. I kiss and suck my way down his neck in a way that's sure to leave my mark. When I get to his shoulder, I bite down hard. He jerks back and hisses. I follow him and do it again.

"Fuck, tiger. If you want rough, you better be prepared to take it just as hard." His threat has me pooling with arousal. I want him to be rough. I want him to be unleashed.

"I can handle you." I whisper in his ear then bite the lobe. I nibble my way up it, and when he pinches one of my nipples, I moan into his ear.

"Tiger, your little noises are so fucking sexy. Let's see how loud you get with me inside of you." His voice is husky. He's breathing heavily. I know he's on edge, and so am I.

Instead of fucking me with his dick, he slides a finger over my damp panties. I freeze, waiting for his next move. He flicks them to the side and slides his fingers through my wetness. It feels so good that I follow his finger when he tries to pull away.

"Such a needy girl. I bet I can make you come on my fingers with just a few touches." He raises a brow at me in challenge.

"You can try, but I'm not confident in your abilities," I lie through my teeth.

He smirks at me then slowly slips a finger inside. It's a tight fit, and for the first time, I get nervous. If one of his fingers feels this tight, then there's no way I can take his monster cock.

All thoughts vanish when his thumb finds my clit. He starts rubbing in slow circles at the perfect pace. I lose myself in the feeling. I start meeting his thrusts, and soon enough, he's added a second finger. There's a pinch of pain, but it's not enough to stop me.

He flicks his fingers against a spot in me I didn't know existed at the same time he pushes down on my clit. I immediately shriek as my body starts to tremble. I lose myself in the sensation. I'm falling forward into his chest, and his other arm wraps around me, holding me to him.

"I've got you, Katerina. I'll always have you," Dominic murmurs under his breath as he rubs my back.

His fingers don't stop their assault until my orgasm ends. I lay against him for a few minutes, trying to compose myself. I've never experienced anything so powerful.

I've never experienced anything like my husband.

Chapter 38

Dominic

Katerina relaxes against me as I hold her tightly. I can feel her breath tickling my shoulder, but I don't move. As much I need to be inside her, I won't be the one to break this connection. I finally have her in my arms; I can't let her go.

She eventually pulls back and looks me in the eyes. The flush on her cheeks distracts me. She's lethal in her beauty on a normal day, but right now... I understand why there've been so many wars fought over women.

"We're not done, right? I thought teaching me to never question whose wife I am constituted for a little more than a finger bang?" Even though her words are sharp, her tone is breathy and light. She may be taunting me, but it's because she wants me to fuck her.

"That was your warmup, tiger. Now I'm going to fuck my wife. Maybe I can fuck some sense into you." I roll us over as I tell her, so I'm back on top. As much as I say I want to be in charge, I love it when she fights me for it.

I shimmy off my pants and underwear, then kneel before her in all my glory. The look of awe and shock on her face at my size has me biting back a grin.

"It's alright. It'll fit," I boast, teasing her.

"It won't hurt, will it?" She sounds genuinely worried, and it has me pausing.

"Since when have you been afraid of pain?" I throw back at her. I know the best way to get my wife over her fear is to throw it in her face. And like I knew she would, her eyes harden at the challenge, and she reaches down to shimmy off her panties.

I grab them and pull them the rest of the way down her toned, muscular legs. Her strong body has me hard as a rock. I have to squeeze the base of my cock to ground myself. I'm already leaking precum, I can't lose my control like a teenager.

I line myself up at her entrance then freeze. I know she's my wife, but I don't want kids right now. I honestly don't know if I ever will.

"Katerina, are you on the pill?" I close my eyes and pinch the bridge of my nose because I know she's not. She doesn't take any medications. And I didn't expect that I'd be enjoying my wife tonight, so I didn't pack any condoms.

"I have the implant. There's no risk of pregnancy," she assures me, and an odd look crosses her face.

She shakes it off then leans down and grabs my cock. She squeezes it, then strokes up and down my length. I twitch in her grasp. Inhaling sharply, I pry her sinful fingers off me. I line myself up, and ease my head in.

I'm surrounded by the feeling of her. Nothing has ever felt so good. I try to slowly inch myself in, but I can't hold back. I thrust the rest of the way, until I'm seated inside her.

But my euphoria comes crashing down at her cry. My eyes fly open, and I see something horrific. My wife's eyes well with tears. She's about to cry. Fuck! A single tear runs down her cheek, and I quickly swipe it away.

"Katerina, what's wrong? Did I hurt you?" I'm freaking out. I'm tempted to pull out in case I'm still hurting her, but I'm too scared to move. What if I hurt her even more? This is a fucking nightmare. And the worst part is it still feels good for me. How can something that hurts her so much feel this fucking euphoric for me? It's so wrong.

"No, no, it's fine. I'm fine. I just didn't expect it to hurt so much. But you got excited." She chuckles as she pushes the words out.

"Do you want me to stop?" I don't even care about my own pleasure right now. I refuse to move a muscle, not until she tells me what she wants.

"Fuck me, Dominic. I need my husband," she orders me. She wraps her legs around my waist, and fuck, it feels even better. Then she uses those strong legs to pull me in further. I didn't realize I'd slipped out some.

The move feels so good, but I'm still hesitant. When she glares at me, I know I have my Katerina back.

"Either you fuck me, or I'll go find someone else who will," she growls, then pinches my ear.

My vision reddens. It takes everything in me to stop myself from brutally taking her. I know she's goading me to get what she wants, but how dare she bring up another man while I'm inside her.

"Don't ever talk about another man." I pull back and freeze with only my head inside her. "Especially not when I'm inside you." I thrust back in hard, driving her into the bed. She moans, and I know she's not listening. "You are my wife." I pull back out, then quickly thrust in again. "No one touches you."

I start thrusting in a quick pace. If I slow down, she uses her legs to pull me in harder. She's a needy, impatient woman.

"Who's your husband?" I growl out, needing her affirmation.

Her eyes twinkle, and for a sick second, I think she's going to deny it.

"You are. Dominic Montclair is my husband," she cries out, then continues to meet my thrusts.

Then, she takes me by surprise. She flips us over, so she's on top of me. I stare at my wife in awe. There's no one sexier than her.

"Remember who your wife is." Her eyes bare into mine in challenge. She lifts her hips then pushes down on my cock. And fuck if it isn't the hottest thing I've ever witnessed. "I am your wife. No other women get you."

She freezes, not moving an inch.

"The only woman for me is Katerina Montclair," I promise her.

She grins then fucks me again. Hard and fast. And I realize she's claiming me. She wants me just as much as I want her. It's fucking perfect.

I run my fingers through her hair at the base of her skull, then tug her head back. My lips find her breasts now on display, and I attack them. She's moaning and groaning, withering against me. I have to use my other hand to guide her hips back up and down and meet her thrusts.

"Dom," she moans.

I freeze and pull back. She whimpers, but I ignore it. I hold her against me when she tries to grind down.

"It's Dominic to you. Always Dominic." I growl at her. Everyone else calls me Dom. Except her. My wife calls me Dominic, and that's the only thing she's allowed to call me.

"Dominic," she corrects herself.

I nod then continue my assault. She's writhing, close to the edge. I'm right there with her. I adjust my grip on her hips enough, so my thumb reaches her bundle of nerves. I press down hard, and that's all it takes.

She lets out an earth-shattering scream, and I follow right behind her.

I'm seeing stars.

I'm having an out of body experience.

This woman is unreal with the way she feels. The way she milks every ounce out of me.

When we come down from our high, I pull her into my chest and lay us down. She rests on me with my cock still inside her. I rub her back lightly, and soon enough, she's snoring softly.

Her little snores are adorable. I don't think she even knows about them, but sometimes I wake up in the middle of the night and listen to her until I fall back asleep.

When I know she's passed out, I pull out and roll her off of me. She curls in a ball, and I sneak out of bed to the bathroom. When I get in there, I look down and chuckle.

The red tinge on my cock exposes her lies. My wife never had a string of men before me. She was a virgin. And the infuriating woman lied to me to rile me up. And it worked every single time. At least now I know it won't hurt her again.

I clean myself, then bring in a rag and clean her. I hop into bed and pull her into me. I've wanted to sleep with her in my arms for so long, and now I will every night.

Tonight changes everything. Now she believes she's my wife. And that this marriage is real. No one will ever question it again. Especially not her.

Chapter 39

Katerina

I wake up wrapped in a warm blanket. I cuddle deeper, until it rises and a snore sounds in the air. A snore I recognize. I open my eyes to see my husband curled around me. Then I feel it. I feel his bare cock resting against my ass. Naked. We're both still naked from last night.

Last night was a whirlwind. I'm terrified he regrets it. Or that he doesn't mean what he said. Because I meant it. Every moment was what I've been craving. I didn't even realize I needed him, but I did. I needed my husband to be real with me and to claim me as his wife.

"Good morning, tiger," the sexy man behind me coos.

I slowly wiggle my way out of his grip. He doesn't seem eager to let me go but eventually relents. I keep myself covered by the sheets as I untangle myself. I don't know how to act after last night. I don't want things to change, but what if he has new expectations now.

"Is this morning the gym or a run?" he asks casually. I turn to see him crawling out of bed, his full body on display. He doesn't seem shy at all. But besides the nudity, he's acting normal.

"Today's the gym, then artillery." I avert my eyes, wanting to give him privacy, but as soon as I get out of bed, his eyes are glued to me. So, I stop being shy. I prance past him into the bathroom.

He follows behind me.

"Perfect. I'll hit the gym with you. I don't have any major meetings, so I'll go shooting as well." I smile at his plans and realize nothing important has changed.

I turn on the water and adjust it to a warm setting. I step into the shower, only for my bear-sized husband to climb in behind me. I keep my back to him, not giving him any attention, but when I reach for the shampoo, he swats my hand away.

"Hey now!" I snap at him.

He just laughs and squirts some of the shampoo in his hand. When he puts it back, I go to try to get some but stop when he lathers it into my hair. I stand there dumbfounded as my husband washes my hair. It feels so good, but I know what he's doing.

"I'm not having sex with you in this shower. I'm sore from last night, and it's far too small in here." I all but stomp my foot.

"Stop talking. I'm helping my wife get clean. I have no intentions of fucking you until you're ready. I know women can be sore after their first time." His words aren't boastful, but I gasp at them.

He knows. He knows I lied and that I'm a virgin. Or, well, that I was. I wait for him to tease me or berate me for lying to him. But to my surprise, he stays silent.

He rinses out my hair then lathers it in conditioner. I don't bother telling him he doesn't need to put it on my scalp. I don't really care if it leaves my hair greasy. He's being so kind, and it's melting my resolve. I didn't know Dominic was capable of acting this way.

He starts washing my body, and I let him. He's meticulous, making sure every inch of me is clean. While his movements aren't sexual, his heated gaze lights me on fire.

When he finishes cleaning me, I swat his hand from the shampoo. I gather some in my hand and clean his hair. I appreciate my height at the moment since I don't have to get on my tiptoes to reach him.

When I'm done cleaning him, he gets out and grabs us towels. We dry off and get dressed. I tell myself putting on my dirty clothes is fine because I'll change into workout gear when we get home, and after the workout, I'll shower again.

We head home, and conversation flows as normal. We change into workout gear and head to the gym. I like working out with him because he challenges me to be better. Later we go to the shooting range. He gives me a few helpful tips but overall seems impressed by my skills.

I can't help the pride that flushes through me when he compliments my stance. Nor the victorious feeling when I hit the target every time.

And the whole afternoon, even though we're acting normal, something's different. It's the way he looks at me. There's something in his gaze that I can't describe. An emotion I'm not familiar with.

The man who looked at me with contempt and disappointment all those months ago is long gone. And in his place is a man who cares for his wife in ways I don't understand.

Chapter 40

Katerina

"Pick up your knees!" I not-so-gently remind my husband. "You're dragging your feet. We ran this route two days ago!"

He's red-faced and panting. That's fine, but I won't let him injure himself due to poor form.

"Goddamn it, tiger. You're gonna kill me." Despite his words, a grin overtakes his features. I know he enjoys our runs, even if they do leave him exhausted.

"We're almost at five miles. Only two more minutes." We're looping back to the beginning of this trail so his run can end. I'll rerun the route to get my full run in. We've learned since our first run that he can't do my full workouts.

He nods and speeds up. I pick up my pace. He's ready to finish, and I'm excited to keep going. I can't help but notice how much more enjoyment I get from running with him by my side.

"Done!" I tell him, and he immediately halts. He dramatically throws himself onto the ground. "Get up, drama king, or your men will think you're weak."

I lightly kick his side, and he reaches out to grab my foot. I leap out of his reach and circle him.

"I'm going to finish my run," I tell him as I make my way back into the woods.

"You've got this, tiger. If you beat our time, I'll give you a treat." His husky tone has me picking up my pace. I'm sure as fuck getting that treat.

I've only been running alone for about five minutes when I hear footsteps behind me. I laugh and pick up my pace.

"You need to be careful, darling. Remember what happened last time you tried to keep up with me!" I laugh knowing Dominic will only last a few minutes at this pace.

But instead of responding, the footsteps gain on me, then I'm tackled. I let out a shriek as I meet the ground. I whip my head around, but instead of being greeted by my husband's dark eyes, I'm met with blue ones. Cold, angry, blue ones.

I recognize his blond hair instantly. It's Alex, one of the Syndicate men that's made his feeling of me clear. He doesn't trust the *Russian scum*. I've always tried to be more overbearing when he's around just to frustrate him.

He grabs my wrists and forces them behind me, pushing me into the dirt. *This fucking bastard thinks he can overpower me.* I kick my leg around him, then twist my wrists. I'm able to push into his grasp then break his hold on me. I roll us over to where I'm on top of him.

"What the fuck are you doing?" I yell at him because he's clearly lost his damn mind.

"I don't trust you, you bitch. You're a distraction we can't have. So, I'm going to eliminate the distraction." He grins sadistically, and his eyes gleam with a sickening light.

I'm caught so off guard by his words, that I'm a moment too slow when he flips us back over. He hits me in the face once, and

I immediately feel blood start to pour out of my nose. He tries to hit me again, but I block and redirect it. All the training I've been doing makes the muscle memory easy, so I use his arm to throw him off me. I jump to my feet and swipe at his legs. He steps back just in time. He lunges at me again, but I dodge him. I lunge at him, and this time, I tackle him to the ground. I reel back my fist and hit him twice in the face.

"You fucking psycho!" I yell at him as I hit him again and again.

He fights against me, but he's no match for my fury. I don't stop until I'm physically being pulled off of him. I turn to fight the second guy, only to be pulled into his chest. I lift my leg to stomp on his foot but freeze when he speaks.

"Katerina, it's me. Are you okay? What happened?" Dominic's urgency has me halting. He pulls me in tighter as he stares daggers over my shoulder.

"I'm fine. But this fucker won't be if you let me get back to him," I growl out. I'm still fucking furious.

"Tell me what happened." Dominic's tone turns lethal.

I stall for a moment, worried he won't believe me. I know we've come a long way, but Alex is Syndicate. And I'm Bratva by blood.

"This crazy bitch started attacking me! She's a wild animal. All I did was try to defend myself," Alex cries out from where he's still lying on the ground.

"I didn't ask you," Dominic spits out. His entire demeanor changes when Alex starts talking. Relief floods me. He's going to listen. "What happened, Katerina?" His words are soft when he addresses me.

"I was running then he tackled me to the ground. He said I was a distraction, that he was going to get rid of. This psycho was trying to kill me. But I kicked his ass." I can't help the smugness in my tone towards the end.

"She's lying!" Alex's voice pierces through my calm. I try to jerk out of Dominic's arms, but he pulls me in.

"Stay put. You've done enough damage," he whispers in my ears. Then he raises his voice. "I don't think she is lying."

"You're going to believe this Russian whore over your own men. She must have a cunt of gold." Alex spits after he says it, and blood flings out of his mouth.

Dominic releases me instantly, but before I can launch myself at Alex, Dominic's already on top of him. My husband has my attacker pinned to the ground with his knees and is choking him.

"If you ever speak about my wife like that again, I'll kill you." Dominic's calm tone makes it even more terrifying. "You made my wife bleed, and for that, you'll pay severely. If she weren't such an Amazonian warrior, I'd be beating you now. But she's damaged you enough for the both of us, you insipid worm."

Alex struggles against his hold, until he's gurgling. Dominic tightens his grips until Alex pales significantly, and eventually, his eyes roll to the back of his head.

Dominic pulls out his phone and dials someone.

"Roman, I have someone for you. I want him to pay." There's a moment of silence then. "He's one of ours. We need to make it hurt. He came after my wife." He growls out the last two words, his claim on me does something to me. "He's going to beg for mercy at our hands."

When I realize what he's ordering I step forward and place my hand on his shoulder.

"I want to be a part of it." I don't ask, I demand.

"Kat–" he starts.

"No, Dominic! I want to make him pay! He tried to kill me." I keep my voice even, so he knows this isn't just my adrenaline talking. "I've trained for this."

He hesitates for a moment, then nods his head.

"Scratch that. We don't need you. Go hang out with your wife." Without giving Roman a chance to respond, he ends the call.

Dominic stands and stares at me for a moment. An indiscernible look crosses his face. I call a soft smile to my lips to convey that I'm fine but wince with the movement.

Within seconds, Dominic is cupping my face with both of his hands and tilts it up for him to inspect. He gently prods around. I jerk back when he touches my nose, and he curses.

"Your nose is broken. I can't believe that bastard," Dominic seethes. He closes his eyes for a moment, then opens full of emotion. "Katerina, when I heard your scream... I've never been more terrified. I sprinted faster than I ever have. I had to get to you."

"Oh... uh... Thank you." I'm still not used to this vulnerability from him.

He cracks a smile as he stares into my eyes. His shine with pride.

"But I should've known you can take care of yourself. I mean, by the time I got here, I had to save him from you." He scowls at the mention of Alex. "Not that he deserves saving."

I grin at him, loving his praise. I lean forward and kiss him. It's soft and slow, unlike any of our others. He groans and pulls me into him. When I finally pull back to catch my breath, he sighs in exasperation.

I step out of his embrace and look over his shoulder.

"What now?" I ask him.

"Let's get him to the basement. When he wakes up, we'll deal with him." The dark look crosses his face again.

"Are we going to kill him?" It's not that I have a problem with it, I'm just wondering about the protocol.

"That's up to you, wife." He doesn't even hesitate in answering.

"There isn't protocol for this?" I'm skeptical of his answer.

"Fuck the protocol! He tried to *kill* you. You get to decide his fate." Dominic doesn't seem like the kind of person to ever stray from protocol. I'm glowing on the inside that he's doing it for me.

He walks over and throws Alex's unconscious body over his shoulder, and we start the trek inside.

Chapter 41

Dominic

My wife inspects the basement cells I've been hiding from her. I know she was oblivious to them, but she wanted to be involved. I get why. If someone tried to kill me, I'd want to torture them too. We're more alike than I realized. Somehow that makes her even sexier to me.

"I didn't know our basement was a torture chamber," she muses as she inspects the table full of weapons and instruments of pain. "I guess this must be standard for criminal organizations. I used to hear screams coming from Viktor's basement. I never went down there, but I knew what was going on."

Her face doesn't reveal her emotions. I can't tell what she's thinking, but I know any comparison to her father is bad. And I didn't miss that she called him Viktor, not any term of endearment.

Despite having the same basement as him, it infuriates me that Katerina had to grow up in a home with one. Was she scared when she heard men being tortured? Was she a young girl terrified in her own home? I vow to myself that if we ever have children, these rooms won't be used. I won't have our kids living in fear.

Alex moans from where he's hanging by his arms from the ceiling. He starts to wake up, and when he realizes what state he's in, he starts fighting against his restraints. It's futile with the hold the chains have on him.

"You're wasting your energy." I warn him in an even, calm tone. I'm not feeling either of those things, but I won't let him in on it. I may not get my hands dirty as often as Roman has to, but I know the nuances of an interrogation. Showing any emotion is a weakness they can exploit.

My wife, however, doesn't know this.

"Listen here, you bastard. We have some questions for you, and you're going to answer them. Fight it all you want, but we're getting our answers." She pauses, then a sinister grin overtakes her feature. "In fact, if you fight it, I might enjoy it even more. I'm not satisfied from the beating I gave you earlier."

She points the knife she pulled from the table at him. Her manic demeanor placates me. I'd rather her crazy and bloodthirsty than sobbing and inconsolable. My wife's strength is unmatched. Not even being attacked fazes her.

But Alex, the dumbass, just laughs.

"You don't scare me. What's the Bratva Princess going to do with a little knife?" he taunts her.

He's so fucking stupid testing her. She has more fight in her than any of my men. He underestimates her because she's a woman, and that's his mistake. I guess he didn't learn from his earlier beating.

Katerina just laughs. She throws her head back and lets out a crazed cackle. Then she flicks her wrist. Before I can track it,

Alex is mewling in pain. I see the hilt of the knife sticking out of his shoulder, right under his collarbone.

I'm beyond impressed by my wife's aim. And more than a little turned on. But she doesn't stop there. She pulls out another knife and spins it. The control she has over the blade as it dances through her long, elegant fingers has me instantly hard. There's something about her intensity that has me entranced.

"Alex, are you ready to answer some questions now?" Her voice no longer rings with fury, instead carries a sweet tone. It's menacing in this context but still causes my blood to boil at the thought of her using it at other times.

"You're batshit!" he shouts at her. Tears well in his eyes, and when she takes a step toward him, he blanches. "Dom, you have to stop her! Get your psycho wife on a leash! You can't let her do this to Syndicate members!"

I open my mouth, ready to respond, but am cut off by my enchanting wife.

"No, no, Alex. We're talking right now. Just you and me." She pouts, and for a moment, I'm filled with envy. How come he gets her sweet tone and sexy pouts? Her attention should be all mine.

But then she slashes her knife down his cheek making a gash that looks like he's been mauled by an animal. By a tiger. *My* tiger.

Yeah, maybe I don't want her to treat me like him. A thigh stabbing every now and then is one thing, but I don't want my face marred.

Alex howls in pain as tears mingle with blood. He thrashes in his chains, begging for release. But his cries land on deaf ears.

"You can't see it, Dom, but she's destroying the Syndicate from within. I'm loyal to you and look at what she's doing to me. Soon it'll be other members." His high-pitched justification makes my blood boil.

"She's done nothing of the sort. You earned her wrath in all its glory." I'm transfixed by the scene folding out before me. My warrior wife removes the knife from his shoulder, causing blood to gush out. Only to stab it back in just as aggressively. "Look at her." I can't help the awe in my voice. "She'd be a valuable asset to the Syndicate. Maybe she'll be the one to fill your spot."

He roars in fury, but I ignore it. The words that started as a taunt, now make so much sense. Of course she'll be the one to replace him. Except she won't be as low-leveled as he was. She's going to rule by my side. Become my Syndicate Queen.

She looks at me in question, all her attention directed at me. I nod and grin at her. This is the perfect resolution. And it'll stop any of my men from going after her. She'll truly be one of us.

Alex breaks our connection by blubbering. His reaction seals his fate. If he can never accept my wife, then he doesn't belong with us.

"Are you done with him? Take your time, if not." I don't want to rush her, but I have other plans for us.

She stabs his other shoulder with a smile on her face. Even blood-splattered with a sweat-sheen, she's breathtaking. Her fury and violence when aimed at someone else is sexy as hell. She's ruthless, my queen. Irresistible.

"I'm done with him." Her eyes sparkle in an excited way. Her hips sashay as she stalks towards me. I ache to touch her.

"Do you want to kill him?" It comes out huskily. I don't care about Alex anymore. All I want is my sinful wife.

"No. But he can't ever come near me again. Because not only will I protect myself, but my big, sexy husband will too." When she reaches me, she presses her soft lips on mine.

I instantly pull her into me. My arms tangle around her back and through her short locks. Her taste overpowers my senses as I lose myself in her. She wraps one leg around my waist and pulls me in closer. I grip her thigh and use it to place her heat over my hardness. She grinds onto me, moaning against my mouth.

I trail my lips lower down her neck, tasting her. I grip her roots and pull her head back revealing more skin. I suck and lick, enjoying her noises.

"Be my Syndicate Queen." Between nibbles on her neck, I ask it. I say it loud enough so our audience can hear.

"Of course, my husband. My king." Her husky voice rings through the air.

She claws at my shirt, trying to undress me. As much as I love her enthusiasm, there's something I need to take care of before we tango.

No one gets to see my wife. And no one lives if they attack her. I changed my mind. I don't care if she lets him live because I won't let him. He doesn't deserve life after attacking my wife.

Without untangling from her, I reach into my waistband and pull out my gun. I don't even pull my lips from her as I fire the headshot. The bang fills the room, causing her to look behind her. As she turns, I keep my lips locked on her throat.

"Damn, darling. You got him right between the eyes. I'm impressed." Startled, I pull back and see her eyes shimmering. Her grin is downright salacious. "That was so sexy," she breathes out at she pulls my shirt off of me.

I carry her to the table and place her on it. We're frenzied as we undress, ready to find our releases in one another.

"Flip over. I'm taking you from behind. You'll love it." Knowing I get to teach her everything, that I get to experience all her first, is an unmatched feeling.

She obeys immediately, turning to face the table. I kick her legs apart, then gently push her down onto the table. She lifts her hips and the sight of her from behind is lethal. From her muscular back to her glistening opening, she's perfection.

I line myself up, then push inside. She gasps at the sensation, immediately feeling how much deeper I can be inside her in this position. We haven't tried this one yet, but I know my wife.

I take her hard and fast as we chase our releases. She's meeting my thrusts pushing against me. The entire time, my eyes remain on her. I can't look away from her beauty.

"My Syndicate Queen... My wife.... My queen," I chant over and over again. I'm obsessed with her and with whom she's become to me.

She's my everything.

And now she'll rule by my side. Where she belongs.

Chapter 42

Katerina

Dominic has me seated next to him at his desk. He's actually replaced his old desk with a new one that has openings for two chairs. He's deemed it our office. I do think the replacement was also prompted by the cat scratches and destruction done by Vova on his desk. But I appreciate the gesture.

Stefan and a few other Syndicate higher ups enter the office, including my brothers-in-law. Their expressions vary from curiosity to anger at the sight of me. I know we are gathering to officially induct me into the Syndicate, but it appears they weren't told that.

As they stand on the other side of the desk, they murmur amongst themselves. There's clear distress between them. Dominic clears his throat, and they quiet.

"I had you come today to welcome my wife into the Syndicate. It's time she gets her place, and with the vacancy Alex has left, it's the perfect opportunity." The pride in his voice has me stroking his thigh under the table. I try to convey my gratitude with the contact. His hand sneaks down and squeezes mine.

"Er... Dom. Is this the best idea?" Stefan seems the only one brave enough to question the big, bad boss.

"Are you questioning my decision?" Dominic's voice, while calm, holds a sharp threat.

"No, sir. I trust you. I'm just wondering what makes you believe she is... ready? She hasn't gone through the training required of a Syndicate member." Stefan looks less confident the more he speaks. He fidgets with his fingers.

"Katerina has been training extensively since she's been here. Her weaponry skills rival even my own. She just proved herself by taking out a traitor among us." Dominic's grip on me tightens as he mentions Alex. I know even death hasn't absolved his sins in Dominic's mind.

The men become enraged at the mention of a traitor. It's not something anyone takes lightly, especially in the underworld.

"Who?" Stefan demands.

"Alex. He attacked my wife because of her heritage. She bested him, and we took care of him." He stands and places his hands on his desk. "Let it be known, anyone who comes for my wife, faces not only my wrath, but also hers. And I can assure you; you'll be begging for mine when you're in her reach. Don't be fooled by her beautiful face, she might be one of our most lethal weapons."

The men stare at me with expressions ranging from fascination to disbelief. I make note of which ones seem to view this arrangement the most negatively. I won't let my guard down, even in the compound anymore.

"What will be her position? Will she replace Alex?" Stefan seems doubtful of my ability to fulfill Alex's role.

"No, she's far too important to waste in such a way." Dominic looks around the room, waiting for someone to interject, but they remain silent. "She will be the Queen of the Syndicate. She'll rule by my side."

The room erupts into chaos. Men are commenting on how it's not a real role, some even mention that they won't take orders from a woman. That this is no world for women.

But my dear brothers-in-law stand there with grins on their faces. They look at my husband with a knowing look, and I feel left out of an inside joke. Dominic just shakes his head at them.

When the volume of the room and words hurled reach an unacceptable level, I fly to my feet and bang my fist on the desk.

"SILENCE!" The room immediately quiets. "I am loyal to my husband. I will rule by his side. I have the Syndicate's best interest at heart. But make no mistake, should any of you cross me, I will rain hellfire upon you."

I glare around the room, daring anyone to test me.

"If any of you question my loyalty because of my heritage, know I was never involved in Bratva affairs, and I loathe them more than any of you do in this room. If you question my competences because I'm a woman, then I challenge you in the ring." I pause, needing them to soak it in. "Know this, I am not one to be underestimated. Alex did, and that was his fatal mistake. Heed my warnings."

To my surprise, the men in the room nod at me in respect. Some come forward to shake my hand. The Montclair brothers welcome me and voice loudly that they will follow my command.

Dominic clears the room, and when the last one leaves, he turns to me.

"Tiger, you did so well. You demanded their respect." His stoic demeanor dissolves into a grin as he pulls me into him. He cups my cheeks as he stares into my eyes.

"Well, I learned it from you. That's how you lead these men." I turn to him and note the heat in his gaze. "And my husband is the big, bad Syndicate boss."

His eyes darken at my words.

"Seeing you up there, commanding the room... Fuck, tiger. I was hard as a rock. I had to hide my cock behind my chair. But my strong wife, leading a room of my men was too much to handle."

He bites my bottom lip and tugs on it.

"It's time I worship my queen."

He picks me up and sits me on the edge of our desk. His hands pull down my pants, taking my thong with them. My shoes are thrown over his shoulder, then my bottoms follow. Once I'm bare from the waist-down, he kneels before me.

"I've dreamt of doing this. I don't know how I've gone so long without tasting you." He inhales deeply then attacks.

His tongue collects my wetness as he devours me. He isn't gentle or patient. No, not my husband. He's ruthless and relentless as he inhales me. His need for me overpowers him. It's noisy and messy and fucking euphoric.

All too soon, I'm tipping over the edge. I expect reprieve, but my husband's never gone easy on me before, and he doesn't go easy on me now. He continues his feast as he demands more orgasms from me.

I can't help but revel in my life. The arranged marriage to the enemy has turned into this.

Chapter 43

Katerina

The dentist's office door swings shut behind me as I walk down the street towards the parking lot. Nik brought me to my semiannual cleaning. It's been a long time since I've left the compound, so I'm not used to walking around, which is why I'm not alert when a black car with tinted windows pulls up in front of me.

Not until the doors open, and armed men flood out. They move synchronously as they ambush me. One grabs me from behind. As I try to escape his grasp, another grabs my legs. Despite my struggle, they're able to throw me into the backseat of the car and slam the door shut. I lunge for the door, but the child lock is on.

"Quit your dramatics, Katya. This is not how I raised you to act," an all too familiar voice says.

Chills run down my spine. My head whips to the person on the other side of the backseat until I'm facing Viktor. I fight the urge to launch myself at him. Even though I don't have any of my weapons on me, I know I could land a few strikes. But attacking him won't do me any good with his guards surrounding us.

"What do you want?" I grit out. I'm done pretending for him. I'm not the Bratva princess he gave to Dominic. I have become a strong woman capable of defending herself.

"I want your cooperation, damn it! You haven't responded to any of my calls or messages. Tell me what you've discovered!" Viktor doesn't even pretend to be composed. But his fury doesn't deter me.

"No."

Even the narrowing of his eyes, a clear indicator of abuse to come, doesn't compel me to comply. I won't betray my husband. I won't betray my Syndicate.

"Oh, so you think you're special. You think he cares for you." He throws back his head and lets out a bone chilling cackle. "Naïve girl. All your worth is your cunt. And even that's replaceable."

"Maybe to you, but not to Dominic!" My fists clench at my side. Unlike Dominic, if I hit him, he'll hit me back. But it would be worth it.

"Bullshit. What could he possibly have done to convince you of that?" His disbelief is written all over his face. He thinks I'm so naïve that I'd believe anything. But he's wrong.

"He inducted me into the Syndicate!" As soon as the words leave my mouth, I know they're a mistake. Him possessing that knowledge can only mean trouble.

"Ah, so you have been following my mission. And here I thought you were useless." He's testing me with his words. He doesn't expect me to deny them; the Bratva Princess never would've. But I'm not her anymore.

"No, I won't do your bidding. I'm not your little doll that you control anymore. I'm the Syndicate Queen." Words that sounded so fierce in my head fall flat.

Viktor laughs darkly, actually taking amusement in them.

"'*The Syndicate Queen!*'" He cackles, mocking me. "You stupid whore. You were barely able to be the Bratva Princess, and all that demanded was being pretty and silent."

"You don't know who I've become! I'm capable of leading by his side!" I all but shout the words at him. I'm losing control, grasping at straws. This isn't how I foresaw our confrontation going.

"You think he could ever trust my progeny? You'll never be anything but Bratva in his eyes." There's curiosity in his, and I can't tell if he's confident in his words.

"He doesn't see me that way. He knows I was never involved with your little organization. That's why he trusts me enough to be in the Syndicate." The words are closer to a plea than a statement.

"You truly believe when he finds out you were sent to betray him, he'll understand? That he'll forgive you?"

A pit forms in my stomach.

"He's never going to know. I never did anything to betray him. And I never will." But despite my best efforts, his words fill me with self-doubt.

"He'll throw you on the streets, and you'll come crying home to me. If that's the choice you make, instead of coming home a valued member of the family, you'll be a reject. A disappointment. Even Sergey will frown upon you."

"I would never come crawling home to you, pidor!" I spit in his face to jab the ultimate disrespect.

I feel the sting of my cheek before I even register the hit. I should've seen it coming, but in my rage, I wasn't paying attention.

I lunge forward, punching him in the nose, reveling in the sound of it crunching beneath my hand. He pushes me off him and returns a punch, which I block. His next one lands on my nose. My hands wrap around his neck in a vise grip. Rage fuels me. Which keeps me blind to the hit to my side. The wind is ripped out of me, and I'm left gasping for air.

Viktor shouts to his men, and the car jerks to a stop. The backseat door is jerked open, hands grab me, and I'm thrown from the car.

"When you're ready to come home, you better have valuable information, or your life will be hell. You'll be begging for Sergey when I'm through with you." Viktor's words are the last I hear before the door closes, and the car speeds away.

They dispose of me in the parking lot, so I hobble to Nik's car. The gasp he lets out at the sight of me is all the indicator I need of how fucked I am. There's no chance I can hide this from Dominic.

"Fuck, Katya! What the hell happened?" Nik surveys the lot, looking for the threat. His gun is unsheathed, ready to make someone pay.

"Viktor happened," I confess glumly. I'm ashamed I let him even get one hit on me, much less two.

"Where is he?" Nik's voice is merely a growl, but I can't let him out of the car.

"Just drive us home. I'll tell you later," I mutter before closing my eyes.

Five minutes pass of him barraging me with questions before he finally resigns to my silence. My shame won't let me open up to him.

I check my reflection in the overhead mirror and note that my nose is bleeding, and my eyes are forming black circles under them. I lift the hem of my shirt to reveal a giant green and yellow bruise forming. Fuck. There's truly no way I can hide this from Dominic.

When we get home, I sneak inside. I make it halfway to my old room when I hear my husband approaching. The familiar pattern of his footsteps taunts me as I pick up my pace.

"Where are you going, tiger?" His jovial voice causes me to flinch. I know the moment I turn around, that cheery demeanor will vanish.

"I'm going to my room. I need some alone time." My even voice doesn't betray my lie.

"That's not your room," he growls from right over my shoulder.

He wraps his arms around my middle and lifts me in the air. The howl of pain I let out causes him to halt. He tenses and gently places me on the ground.

"Katerina, what's wrong—" His words transform into a snarl when he turns me around.

"It looks worse than it is." I try to alleviate his worries, but my words only seem to anger him more.

"Who did this to you?" His voice is so dark and low that it sends shivers down my spine.

To anyone else, it'd be terrifying. But to me, his wife, it's almost arousing. Because his anger is in defense of me.

"Katerina, who touched you. Who hurt you." His words aren't a question, they're a demand. He needs answers. He needs to make them pay. But unfortunately, he can't touch my assailant.

"Don't worry about it, darling. You should see the other guy." I aim for teasing, but it comes out rough.

"I don't give a damn about the condition of the other guy. His life is coming to an end." His eyes are fully black now as his fists clench at his side. He's bloodthirsty to avenge me.

"You can't kill him." I press a hand to his chest, trying to calm him. He immediately wraps my hand in his large one and forces it closer to him.

"There's not a single force on this earth that could stop me from killing the person who hurt my wife." He tilts my face into the light as he inspects my injuries. His gentle touches contrast with his furious words. He's my personal angel of death.

He carefully lifts my shirt up to inspect my midsection where he touched earlier. When he sees the bruise, he lets out a sound of anguish doused with fury.

"You can't kill Viktor Sokolov." My teeth grit together as I tell him.

His head snaps up in shock at my words. His mouth opens then shuts, before his eyes narrow, and he composes himself.

"Your father did this to you?" His words are calm, as though we're speaking of the weather. It's the calm hiding the hurricane of wrath within him.

"He stopped being my father a long time ago." I need him to know that. I need him to know that I don't relate to Viktor. That I don't claim him.

"Because of this? He's done this before?" That same even tone is used as he inspects my wounds. But the tremble of his hands betrays his façade.

"Yes," I murmur, transfixed by him. My husband cares for me. I know he does. Viktor is wrong.

"When did it start?" I hiss when he lightly touches my nose, and he quickly jerks his fingers back.

"After Мама died. I was seven." For the first time ever, I'm allowed to feel the pain and hurt. I'm allowing myself to feel what he's done to me. My own father.

A small tear trickles down my cheek, but before I can wipe it away, I'm crushed against my husband's large chest. One hand holds my head against his shoulder, while the other rubs my back. He's not gentle with his comfort, despite his best efforts, but it's what I need. I need his overbearing aggressive reassurance.

"I'm so fucking sorry, Katerina. That fucker doesn't deserve to even be on the same planet as you. He will never touch you again. No one will. I swear on my life." The confidence in his promise fills me with relief. Despite the reality of the situation, I believe him. He won't ever let me get hurt again.

After a few minutes, he calls the Syndicate doctor to come check on me. I assure him I'm fine, but he won't be dissuaded. When the doctor confirms a broken nose and rib, Dominic curses and paces furiously.

We have a calm evening, then head to bed. Despite my attempt, there's no fun time. I know he's scared of hurting me. When I assure him that I've been in worse pain before, it sets him off again, and he leaves to calm down. Eventually he returns and holds me until I fall asleep.

Chapter 44

Dominic

My watch notifies me of a text from Bash confirming the preparation. With one last glance at my sleeping wife, I sneak out of bed.

I know my actions are about to break the treaty. But in my eyes, he broke it first when he hurt a member of the Syndicate. The most important member. And for that, he must pay.

Unfortunately, I can't kill him without causing a war. It's the only thing keeping me from doing so.

Finding out about her childhood, of the hell he put her through, his own daughter, almost destroyed me. I was so consumed by anger that I had to lock it up. I had to put on my mask of composure, so I didn't scare my wife. I was murderous, bloodthirsty. I still am, but now I'm rational.

After a quick debate between tactical wear or a suit, I land on the latter. I'm a man of business; I can threaten while still dressing with class.

It takes all my effort to drive the speed limit on the way to the ostentatious mansion my wife was raised and abused in.

How many memories does she have of those halls that are full of pain? Does she even have any good memories? My heart clenches at the realization.

The gate opens as my car approaches thanks to Bash's hacking skills. When I'm parked close to the front door, I exit and storm the stairs.

The banging of my fists on the wooden door echoes through the night. I don't stop my pounding until it opens, then I push inside. I storm pass the furious woman who shouts at me in Russian.

"VIKTOR! COME OUT!" I bellow, storming down the hallway.

I make it halfway to his office when he slips out the door. To my dismay, he doesn't look rattled. He doesn't even look surprised. It's as if he was expecting me. His lazy, sinister grin adds gasoline to my fury.

The only condolence I have is that his nose is broken. There are even red marks around his neck. At least my strong, fighting wife was able to land some blows. She was able to fight back just as hard. She didn't revert back to the scared, small porcelain doll she was under his reign.

I storm towards him and when he's in arms reach, I throw him against the wall. His neck is trapped by my hand, pinning him. My other arm punches his torso repeatedly. I don't stop until I feel the crunches of ribs. If my wife has broken ribs by him, then he'll have broken ones by me.

I lean into him until my face is a breath away from his. I ignore the sick smirk on his face. The look in his eyes as if he knows something I don't.

"Let me make one thing clear, Viktor. Treaty be damned, if you ever lay a finger on my wife again, I'll kill you. I don't give a damn about the consequences and fall outs. She is mine. And you will not touch her." My voice is so low I barely recognize it. I punctuate my threat by clenching my fist even tighter as I choke him.

He tries to speak but can't get words out with my tight grip. I loosen my fists only enough to allow him the air to speak.

"Is that so? So, she's betrayed me? She's confessed everything to you? I guess the jig is up." He raises a questioning brow at me. "And Yelena, calm down! No need to sound up a storm. He can't kill me."

I ignore his directions to his maid, who's been yelling for help. I'll be gone before the soldiers arrive anyways.

"She told me of your abuse, you sick fuck!" I punch his broken ribs, the reminder fueling my fury.

"Well, I had to train her to be the perfect Bratva soldier. The perfect honeypot. And boy did she do a good job. I mean, just look at you." His eyes gleam with delight.

Despite sensing the trap, I have to ask. I have to push. All logic tells me to leave it alone, to not trust a thing this man tells me, but my curiosity is my downfall.

"She was never involved in the Bratva. And she'd never be a honeypot!" I snap at him. He's lying.

"Oh yes, that's what she told you when you inducted her into your little Syndicate. She swore her loyalty to you. Spilled all her secrets of betrayal. The plans of your demise she entered the marriage with. It's sad to see such a valuable asset get turned." His disappointed words throw me for a loop.

"You're lying!"

"Ask her yourself." The confidence in his words, in his grin, guts me.

"Why would you tell me this? Why would you betray your spy in the Syndicate?" The bitter words fly from my mouth. This is it. This is where I catch him in his lie.

"She betrayed me first when she attacked me. She plays only for herself. She'll take down anyone in her path. She'll stab you in the back just as she did me at the first opportunity." Viktor's calm flickers to fury only for a moment before he sighs. "Inducted into two families, loyal to none."

Alex's face appears in my mind, but I push it away. There's no way she attacked and killed him because he doubted her. His accusations were false. They had to be. I know my wife. I know her. I know her loyalty to me... *Right?*

My eyes remain on his a moment longer, trying to decipher his honesty. But I can't tell truth from lie. It muddles my mind.

I hear cars pulling up to the house and take that as my cue. With one last threatening look, I drop him and retreat back to my car.

The entire drive home is spent convincing myself of her loyalty. The walk through the house is spent questioning everything. Her peaceful, sleeping form mocks me in our bed, and I can't seem to join her. Instead, I shower, and as I do, I recollect every encounter we've had. I try to puzzle it all together.

And when I go to sleep, on the opposite side of the bed as her, the distance between us is insurmountable. She sleeps soundly as I wage within myself, wondering if I even know my beautiful, elusive wife.

Chapter 45
Katerina

A ringing sound wakes me. Groggily, I reach for my phone. A gasp of surprise pulls from me when I see its Petya, my brother.

"Hello?" I whisper, confused. Petya hasn't reached out in months. The last time I saw him was at my wedding, and he was only around for a few minutes.

"Katya, I need to see you today." The words are not only rushed but also spoken in our native language. This is urgent and secret.

"What's going on, Petya? You're stressing me out." It'd feel nice to be speaking Russian after so long, if it weren't for the direness of the situation.

"I can't tell you over the phone. But I need you to meet with me. Today." His agitation is evident in his tone. And I don't miss how he didn't alleviate my concern.

"Where?"

He rattles off a park far from Viktor's home, and I agree that it'll work. Right before we end the call, he calls out, "Don't tell your husband. Come alone."

My eyes wander to my husband. He sleeps soundly as I plot with my brother in my native language. My gaze remains on him, curiously eyeing the space between us. Since the vow renewals, I've woken in his arms every morning. I guess it's lucky that we didn't today, so I could take the call.

It feels wrong to hide something from him, but this is Petya. This is my brother. My only family. He's not like Viktor. If he's asking me to meet with him secretly, I'll do it, and if it warrants telling Dominic, then I will. Afterwards.

"Okay. Nik will drive me." Petya trusts Nik. I know this in my bones.

"Nikolai can come. But no one else." Without waiting for a response, he ends the call.

Silently, I slide out of bed and make my way to the closet. The black set I put on is perfect for the park. I tiptoe into the bathroom and do my usual routine. As I'm sneaking through our bedroom, Dominic sits up in bed.

"Where are you going?" I'm thrown aback by his tone. It's gruff and almost accusatory.

"The park." It's only a lie if you count it by omission.

"Sounds fun. I'll come with you." He raises a brow, as if challenging me. I internally curse my brother. Why did he have to ask me to lie to my husband? I hate this.

"I actually want some alone time and fresh air. How about we do lunch afterwards?" Over lunch I'm going to come clean to him, I decide. I won't lie to my husband, at least not for long.

His eyes narrow as he looks me over. It's like he can sense my dishonesty, but maybe it's just guilt corroding my perception.

"Fine," he grunts out, then turns his back to me.

His flippancy hurts me. I walk to his side of the bed and lean down to kiss his lips. He returns the kiss, but it feels cold and distant. There's none of our usual passion. It worries me.

There's a pit in my stomach as I leave the house.

...

Petya meets me on a park bench, sitting down nonchalantly. He's the perfect picture of ease. None of his earlier worry to be seen.

"What's going on?" I ask, needing answers. A large part of me is hoping he's here to tell me Viktor died.

"How are things going with your husband?" He's speaking in Russian again, and as I look around, I realize neither of us have any guards with us. It's a dangerous thing to do.

His question registers and confuses me. Why does he care about my marriage?

"We're doing well. Why do you ask?" My response is said in Russian as I realize we're trying to be inconspicuous and not understood.

"How well?" he pries.

"What do you mean? What do you want to know?" I start to feel defensive of my husband. Why is my brother asking about him? What is he planning?

"Does he trust you?" Petya continues to dig, asking odd, invasive questions.

"Of course. He's my husband." Petya nods and looks content with the answer, but I'm skeptical of his reaction. "I won't betray him. Not even for you. Petya. So, don't ask it of me."

This is where I draw the line. I'm loyal to my brother, but not as much as to my husband. I won't let him ruin my marriage. No matter what.

"None of that. I need your help. And Montclair's." Petya leans back against his seat and looks around as if he's birdwatching. It's ridiculous to see him acting so calm while in such a serious conversation.

"Help with what?" There's bite in my tone, but only because I'm defensive. What does he want from us?

"Taking over the Bratva." He finally looks at me, and despite his sunglasses, I can see the urgency in his eyes. He needs us.

"I don't understand." Petya has always been next in line, but only after Viktor steps down. Why is he no longer waiting for that to happen?

"Viktor is no longer fit to be Pakhan. He's gone too far. It will be difficult. His men are just as corrupt and are willing to die for their greed. But it must be done." A torn look crosses my brother's face. He doesn't want to betray his father, but whatever Viktor did, it's unforgivable.

"What'd he do?" It's the first time I've ever seen Petya have ill feelings towards Viktor. It agitates me. What could Viktor have done that's so bad that his perfect son has turned against him?

"It's bad, Katya. It's better you don't know." I scoff at his treatment of me. Because I'm a woman, he thinks he has to hide the worst of the trade from me.

"Tell me or I won't involve Dominic." It's leverage I don't have, but I'll use anyways.

"Отец's not the man you think he is." Petya grips my hand, his eyes full of regret. "He's been selling girls from the motherland here. His men have been working out of the ports. There are hundreds of women he's brought over. All to be sold for sex. It's unimaginable. I know it's hard to believe, but it's true. I only just found out. He hid it well, but there were numbers that weren't adding up. Katya, I just can't believe it."

I always knew he had no regard for women. Look at how he treated his wife and daughter. But this... this is unconceivable. Hundreds of women, forced into sexual slavery because of his greed. Fury I've never felt before consumes me. How fucking dare he?

"You understand why I must do what needs to be done? Why I must kill him?" My brother sounds destroyed. He never saw the worst of Viktor. He's only known the respectable Pakhan. I try to put myself in his shoes, but I can't. I can't unsee Viktor as the monster I know him to be.

"You're next in line. With him gone, you become Pakhan." I state numbly.

"Yes. I need your husband's help." I can tell he doesn't want to ask it. They're sworn enemies. But if it means ridding the world of Viktor, especially after yesterday, I'm pretty sure my husband will support it.

"How can we help you?"

"I can only trust a handful of my own men. There's too big a risk someone will tell Viktor. I need the Syndicate to help me. When it's done, I'll guarantee a peace alliance with no strings attached." He's desperate, but he's also a good man. I know his word is a promise.

"I'll talk to him. But under one condition." This is my opportunity. "I'm the one to kill Viktor."

His head whips back. He stares at me in bewilderment. "You? Why?"

"Petya, he beat me for years, and Мама before that. He has no regard for women. Even before knowing what he atrocities he's been committing, I swore I'd be the one to end him. Don't take this from me."

My brother's face drops. His eyes fill with regret. His back hunches as he sucks in a breath.

"Katusha, I didn't know. I... I'm sorry I abandoned you. I am so sorry." He grips my hand and squeezes it, trying to comfort me.

"It's fine." I don't want to make a big deal of it. I didn't tell him to make him feel bad. I just need him to know why I hate Viktor. Why I deserve to be the one to end him.

"Will you be able to follow through with it? Can you physically kill your father?" He's not trying to accuse me. He's making sure the mission can be fulfilled.

"He's no father to me. I've been training for this day." I promise him. Then I smirk. "And I'm not a stranger to violence. I stabbed my husband once because he called me fat."

Petya barks out a laugh. "That's my Katya. I always knew you were a fighter." He ruffles my hair, and I punch his arm. I'm satisfied when he flinches in pain.

Petya's phone rings. He checks it, squeezes my hand, then leaves, answering the call. I know this isn't the end of this, but it is for now.

As Nik drives us home, I brainstorm how to tell my husband. I know he'll help my brother. I just know it. My husband will be here for us.

Chapter 46

Dominic

Vova glares at me as I pace back and forth. Even looking at the damn cat makes me furious. How could I have been so blind? How could I have been so foolish? I fell for the oldest trick in the book! The enemy sent me a siren, and I welcomed her with open arms.

I couldn't sleep. Not with all the space between Katerina and me. Not with all the questions swirling in my mind.

My plan was to confront her about everything this morning. In my heart, I was certain there was a rational answer. One that didn't involve lies. Because my tiger would never. She may stab me, but she'd never betray me.

I was waiting for her to wake up when her phone rang. As soon as she switched to Russian, whispering in a language I don't understand, I knew in my gut. I knew he was right. She isn't loyal to me. She never has been.

I didn't believe for a minute she was going to the park. I know she was going to meet with someone. When my men following her confirmed she was at the park, the relief I felt was immense. I rejoiced in happiness.

Until I got a second call moments later, informing me of her brother's presence. Pyotr Sokolov. The Second-in-Command of the Bratva. It was a knife to the heart. Worse than any wound I've ever endured. Agony like no other.

I would've rather anyone else betray me over her. Because I'm not only losing a soldier, but also my wife. My one true source of happiness. Ripped from me. To learn it was all a lie was more than I could endure.

My watch informs me that Nikolai and Katerina are pulling through the gate. With my stoic mask in place, I storm to the front door.

When they walk through, my wife smiles at me. It only worsens the pain. She puts her arms around me in a hug, and I bask in her deceptive passion for one more moment. Then I place my arms around her, restraining her against me.

"Dominic, we need to talk." Her sweet voice is daggers in me. Each word puncturing me. Paining me. "It's important."

"More of your lies, I'd presume?" My harsh words cause her to pull back, but my grip is unrelenting. She's not getting out of my hold.

"What the fuck, Dominic?" She hisses and stomps on my foot. I don't even feel it, not over the pain in my chest.

"Detain them in the basement," I order the waiting soldiers.

It takes three to get Nik and just as many for my... Katerina. Just as many for Katerina. I refuse to be impressed by her fight. It can no longer amuse me. She's not mine to be proud of.

"DOMINIC! ARE YOU FUCKING CRAZY? WHAT ARE YOU DOING?" Katerina's yells go unanswered, but that doesn't stop her from shouting and fighting all through the house.

I return to my office but remain in the doorway. I can't even find reprieve in here. Her spot next to mine mocks me. The desk which holds what used to be a fond memory turns sour in my mind.

No longer able to endure the reminders, I leave. I can't find a single room in my house that doesn't remind me of her. I end up sitting in my pantry on a chair I dragged in from the kitchen. Because even the kitchen, a room I never entered before her, holds memories of feeding her blueberries for a late-night snack.

My mind is a jumbled mess. I'm so lost, I don't even know where to begin. The best move would be to call Bash and have him do a sweep of everything to see what's been compromised. But I don't have it in me. At least not yet. When it comes back showing all she's done, all her disloyalty, it'll only crush me further. So, for now, I sit in my misery with only expired chips to keep me company.

My phone ringing interrupts my pity. The unknown caller ID sends a shiver down my spine.

I answer the call but don't say anything.

"Dominic Montclair. It is Pyotr Sokolov, your brother-in-law," a deep voice says from the other end. I recognize it, and it pisses me off. How dare he call me after conspiring with my... Katerina!

"What do you want?" I grind out.

"Erm... have you not spoken to Katya yet?" His tone changes to one of confusion. "I thought I gave you enough time."

"Yes, I have." I pretend to understand. I want to know what trap they're planning for me. If I feign ignorance of her betrayal, then I can find what's really going on.

"What is your decision? Will you help?"

"With what exactly?" I'm truly lost.

"With overthrowing Viktor." He says it like it's obvious, but I stagger back.

I suck in a breath. "What?"

"Are you sure you spoke with Katerina? She met with me this morning to discuss the Syndicate's aid in overthrowing Viktor. He's gone too far this time and must be stopped." Fury makes way for confusion. I don't understand their angle.

"Why should I be interested in Bratva politics?"

"Because he's breaking your rules." He says it slowly, as though he's talking to a child. Clearly, he doesn't think I understand what's going on... which I don't.

"What's he done?" I need to know. This is imperative. If Viktor's broken our rules, then the treaty is void, and I can go after him. I can kill him for touching my... Oh.

"He's human trafficking women from the motherland and turning them into forced sex slaves by the ports." Pyotr disgust matches my own.

It all clicks into place.

What Roman's been suspicious of for two years.

What Margot inadvertently stumbled upon.

Their surplus of cash.

Their new merchandise 'we can't compete with.'

Their need for more fucking ports.

They're human trafficking.

I'm sick to my stomach. He's been doing this for years right in front of us. Countless women have suffered when we could've intervened. If I hadn't told Roman and Bash to pull back from digging, we would've found this so much sooner.

"How many?" I grit out.

"Hundreds of women. So many have died. Either from overdosing on the drugs they have them addicted to or... There's no limit to the number of women in Russia. He'll never stop unless we stop him."

My stomach churns. Hundreds of women suffering because of our inaction. It is our duty to those women to step in.

"The Syndicate will aid in any way. Should we reach out to Lorenzo?" The Mafia would never allow this sort of thing and would gladly help overthrow Viktor.

"No! There are few men I trust. Only a handful of my own. I only reached out to the Syndicate because of your connection with my sister. She's clearly loyal to you. She even threatened me if I tried to harm you or come between you. I'm grateful she met with me today at all." He lets out a chuckle as if the idea of his sister threatening him on her husband's behalf is sweet. He doesn't know the war machine that she is.

"Why did you meet with her?" I demand as dread settles in.

"So she could convince you to help. I figured it would be easier for me to convince my sister than you, and you'd believe your wife over me, so that's the route I chose."

The breath is knocked out of me. This means she didn't betray me. She isn't disloyal. She's truly my wife. She always has been. And Viktor was just trying to separate us.

She needed to talk to me! That's what she said. She needed to talk about this. She was helping.

Fuck. Fuck fuck fuck!

I have her locked in the basement like a criminal. Like the enemy. I'm treating my wife like a prisoner in her own home.

I'm sick to my stomach.

I treated her like trash. I casted her aside. I didn't even give her a chance to defend herself. I acted as though she meant nothing to me when really, she's my light. My fire. When I thought it was all a lie, when I thought I had to end the life I built with her, there was no other life worth living. There is no happiness without her.

"I have to go!" I abruptly say.

"You will help?" he rushes out.

"Yeah. The Syndicate will help."

I hang up, and race to my wife to beg for her forgiveness.

Chapter 47

Katerina

These basement walls mock me. Memories of our tryst down here haunt me. What once was a sacred space, becomes another prison.

My heart aches, but I refuse to let any tears escape. I won't cry over another man. He's not Viktor, I know this, but this imprisonment feels too similar.

I'm not foolish. I know why he did this. He had me followed to meet Petya. He knows I lied to him about going alone and now doubts my loyalty.

But what I don't know is how long this seed of distrust has been in him. Has he always questioned my loyalty? Has he been pretending this whole time?

But that doesn't make sense. Why would he believe me over Alex? Why would he induct me into the Syndicate? If he didn't trust me, why would he invite me into the most sacred aspects of his life?

My next move is to prove my loyalty, but I fear he won't listen. If he's already made up his mind about me, if he's already lost his trust in me, it'll be hard to convince him. But he has to listen. Not just for our marriage, but for all those women suffering because of Viktor. It's our duty to help them. I have to make him understand that.

The basement door swings open, and in rushes Dominic. His eyes are wild, and his hair is untamed. He looks like a wreck.

He rushes into the cell I'm locked in and rips it open. Standing before me, he appears smaller than ever. Less intimidating.

We stand in silence, each waiting for the other to speak. Needing to hear his thoughts, I keep my mouth shut. He doesn't seem furious; he seems distressed.

"Katerina, I was wrong. Your loyalty was questioned, and instead of coming to you, I reacted poorly.

"Reacted poorly? You locked me in the basement where you kill enemies!"

"I know. I'm sorry. Trusting has always been difficult for me. As the head of the Syndicate, trust is a commodity I can't give freely. Your relation to the Bratva made you someone I couldn't let close. You never were supposed to become anything to me. Much less my wife and leader of the Syndicate. When knowledge of your betrayal came to light, I resorted to my old ways and pushed you out."

"But haven't I proved myself to you? Shouldn't I have been given the benefit of the doubt, or at least deserved a conversation? You threw me out like I was nothing." My fury doesn't hide my hurt.

"I'm sorry. You have to believe me," he begs.

I take a step back. "No."

He drops to his knees.

"I'll write you all the apologies you want. I'll gift you all the flowers out there. Just please forgive me. Trust doesn't come easily. And after what Viktor said–"

"You spoke to Viktor?" I pull him up, needing to see his eyes.

"Last night. I went to his house and threatened him if he ever touched you again." I open my mouth, but he talks over me. "I don't care about the consequences. He hurt you, and that's unacceptable. He made me question your loyalty. He spoke of how you spied for him and then betrayed him."

"That's not true. I never spied for him, not even when he demanded it from me. That's why he went after me." I fight back, needing him to understand.

"I know that now. He was trying to drive a wedge between us. Then this morning, you started speaking in Russian and wanted to go to the park alone. I knew you were lying. I had one of my men follow you. When I saw you with your brother, I jumped to conclusions. I thought you were selling us out. I should've known. You're my wife, my tiger. You deserve better."

"What made you see reason?" I ask, hoping sense came to him on his own, but doubting it.

"Pyotr called. He explained everything." He runs his hand through his hair. "Fuck, Katerina! He's been trafficking women! He's a fucking monster. We have to stop him."

"This we agree on. He can't get away with it."

"He won't. The Syndicate will work with your brother and his men. We're going to figure this out," he assures me.

"We?"

"You, me, our men, and his. You're Syndicate too." His eyes plead with me to accept him.

I stare at him doubtfully. "If I were truly Syndicate, you wouldn't have doubted me so quickly. You wouldn't have been so easily persuaded."

He looks tormented. "It's not like that."

"Yes, it is."

We just stare at each other for a long moment, the chasm between us growing even wider.

"Let's start planning what we'll do," I eventually say.

...

After hours on the phone with Petya, we've come up with a rough idea of what will happen. Petya and his men will already be inside. They'll lax security enough to let us slip in. The Syndicate will handle the men loyal to Viktor, while Petya blocks off Viktor. He won't suspect his son of being in on it. Only once Dominic can escort me to his office will Petya reveal his disloyalty. Then I'll be given the opportunity to kill him.

I can tell Petya doesn't think I can do it. But he doesn't know the real me. Dominic knows I can do it, but he's silent during that part of the plan. He's pensive, as if there's something he's keeping to himself.

During dinner we were out of step. He pretended everything was normal in hopes that it will be. Whereas I was pretending to ease his worries. I need him to trust me enough to drop his guard.

They have a complicated plan, but I know an easier, less risky way to go about it. Where the only one in harm's way is me. I can't risk Petya's few men or the Syndicate, including Dominic, for a job I was always meant to do alone. This is my journey.

When my watch shows it's one in the morning, it's time to go. In the silence of the night, I sneak out of bed. Tiptoeing through the room, I pack a bag. In it, I put a few workout outfits, one of my old dresses, toiletries, and a wad of cash taken from the safe. Enough to last me a few days.

When my phone alerts me that the Uber is ten minutes away, I unlock a window in the den. I hesitate before opening it, trying to recall if windows alert Dominic's phone when opened. After a few moments, I decide it doesn't matter. If he gets an alert that the window is open, he won't see it until the morning, and I'll already be long gone.

I hold my breath as I open the window, but no alarm goes off. Checking through my bag one final time, I ensure everything I need is packed. I pull out a stun gun since I can't risk one of his men finding me but also won't kill them. I heft my bag over my shoulder and lift one leg out of the window.

"FREEZE," a voice booms.

My heart stops, as does the rest of me. Half inside, the other half out the window, I look up. Through the darkness, I can barely make out the outline of a furious man, gun raised at the ready. My husband looms in the darkness, a force to be reckoned with.

Our eyes lock, and a silent battle ensues. His gaze is full of questions, asking me why I'm leaving. Mine is pleading, begging him to let me go.

Well, most of me pleads. There's a small part of me that begs him to ask me to stay. To say, 'don't go.' That forbids me to leave.

But in the silence, the only move made is him lowering his gun. His sorrowful eyes devour me one last time, before he takes a step back. He nods at me solemnly.

Disappointment battles relief as they flood through me. He's letting me go. It's a double-edged sword.

I slowly duck through the window, and with one last glance back at him, I pull my other leg through, and sprint into the night, taking with me the essentials I need to carry out my plan, but leaving behind my heart.

Even though he didn't ask me to stay, I hope he knows I wanted to. And when this is all over, he knows I sacrificed myself for him.

Chapter 48

Dominic

I watch the silhouette of my wife race through the property, heading towards the gate. With each step, my heart is carried further and further from me.

Despite how much I longed for her to stay, I know she needs to leave. I betrayed her, and now she needs to deal with it in her own way. Without me.

Even though she doesn't want me, I won't leave her unprotected. Dropping my gun, I call the only person I know who can track her from afar.

After grumbling about his brothers constantly interrupting his sleep to find their women, Bash agrees to surveil her. Contrary to what I had predicted, my morally-sound baby brother didn't put up a fight or even scold me for stalking my woman. I worry that we've been a bad influence on him.

After that's settled, I sit in the chair facing the window and stare out of it. Despite knowing the improbability of her returning, I don't close it in the hope that she does. All through the night, I watch the window. And when the sun rises, I head to my office.

At the sight of Vova on my desk, my heart beats again. For the first time since finding my wife halfway out the window, I can breathe. Because if she left her cat, then surely, she's returning.

I drop in my seat, cat in hand, and pull up all the info Bash sends me. It's time to see what my tiger is planning.

Chapter 49

Katerina

It takes three days to organize my plan. Three long, lonely days. Three days in a seedy motel, plotting endlessly.

There's one last step I need to do before I'm ready to kill Viktor. I need to acquire a weapon.

I could easily go to a store and buy a gun. But I want it to be personal. Because this is personal.

Calling the only man who I know will help me, but keep it a secret, we agree to meet in a nearby park. He doesn't question why I'm desperate for a blade, nor why I refuse to tell his son.

Damien Montclair meets me on the walking trail with a kind smile. He pulls me in for a quick hug, then releases me.

"Should I ask why you secretly need a karambit knife?" His caring tone encircles my heart and squeezes it. This is how a father should talk to his daughter. With care, tease, and slight worry.

The real reason I asked him for a knife instead of buying one is because I wanted some parental love with me to give me strength. Having my father-in-law, who loves me like a daughter more than my actual father, having his blade with me would be symbolic. A father's love being the weapon that kills a father's hate.

"It's better you don't know." I can't risk him telling Dominic. If Damien knew I was risking myself, he'd intervene.

"You're not going to kill your husband, right? Because you know I can't let you do that." He chuckles teasingly.

"It's not that. This is something I need to do on my own. It's been a long time coming." I can't laugh with him at the image of killing Dominic. It's too horrific to imagine.

He slows his walking and turns to me. "Do you need to talk about it?"

After a moment, I realize I do. I need someone to know.

"My mother was a wonderful woman. Fierce and bold. Мама protected me with her life. After a while, it all became too much for her. I never blamed her for her choice because I know who's really responsible. The promise of avenging her is what pushed me through some of my hardest days. Now that Viktor has crossed a line, it's time. I know what I need to do."

"Be careful, dear. This is a tough fight," he warns.

"I will be," I lie. I know there's no coming out of that mansion alive. "This is something I have to do alone."

He chuckles and puts an arm around me.

"You're not alone, dear," he reassures me.

"I know. You guys support me." I try not to roll my eyes at the cliché.

"No, I mean we do, but no. I mean you're literally not alone. You've been tailed this entire walk." He points behind us.

"What?" I whip my head around and, sure enough, see a man I vaguely recognize further back on the trail.

"I see the way my son looks at you during family dinners. He loves you fiercely. He may have let you go, but he's not going to stop protecting you. I can assure you; he's known your every move and has had men tailing you the entire time. I wouldn't be surprised if Bash was helping too."

I'm stunned silent. His words make sense, but I never even considered it.

"He's not going to risk you, Katerina. You may have plans to kill your father but know that you're not doing it alone." He squeezes my shoulder. "If you were, I'd never arm you for it. I'd get you someplace safe. Because we love you. You are our family. And we won't let you get hurt. No matter how noble the sacrifice."

His words shock me. I didn't realize he knew what I was planning. I didn't think any of them did.

"He's trafficking women," I whisper.

He tenses, then lets out a curse. I've never heard him so much as utter a foul word, so it takes me by surprise.

"He's never been a good man. He always puts profit over morals. There's no redemption for him. But that doesn't mean it's your burden to bear."

My steps falter, taken aback. I never considered that he knew Viktor. It's hard to match this cheery man with a crime family leader.

"I have to do this. For my mother," I plead with him to understand.

"Then give them a signal of when you're going. Make sure your backup is prepared. Don't go in recklessly." His words are firm. He's not ordering me around as a power trip, he's trying to protect me.

This goes against everything I planned. The whole reason I left was so no one else would get hurt. If I kill Viktor on my own, then Petya and Dominic never break the rules. Their disloyalty will never see the light.

But if what Damien says is true, then I can't stop them. But I can at least make it easier for them.

"I'll let them know." He nods in approval, and for some reason, it fills me with certainty. "Be careful with this." He hands me the blade.

"I won't lose it," I promise him.

"I don't care about the knife; I care about my daughter. I want her coming home safely." He stops walking and turns to me.

I give him a hug, holding on tightly. The feeling of a father's love is something foreign to me. Something I never thought I'd have. I cherish it.

"Thank you," I mumble into his jacket.

He pats my back soothingly. After a moment, he releases me and steps back.

"Go on, dear. Do what you need to do. And remember, you're not alone anymore. You never will be."

Chapter 50

Dominic

The empty seat next to me in my office mocks me. The place where my wife should be seated, safe and protected. Instead, she prowls around town, sleeping in a damn, disgusting motel.

It took me all morning the first day she was gone to realize why she left. Part of it is due to my accusations, but I believe most is out of protection for her brother and me. She believes that if she kills Viktor on her own, she protects us from taking the fall.

We won't let that happen.

Pyotr is up to date on her moves. We've adjusted our plan slightly. Pyotr and his men have been staying near Viktor's mansion, so he can swoop in when Katerina arrives and be there to protect her. Once she goes in, the Syndicate will invade and finish the job.

It'd be a good plan if it didn't put my wife in danger. I know she can look after herself, that she's strong and capable, but it doesn't stop the sick feeling I get every time I picture her alone in that mansion.

But this is the route she chose, so it's the one we'll take. I have to trust her. I have to trust that she knows what she's doing. It makes me laser focused on every step of our plan. The need to execute this perfectly overwhelms me. Because one misstep, and she's the one who pays.

I looped my brothers in first. What Viktor's doing is so horrific that Roman didn't even gloat about being right. We never imagined he would go this far, do something so despicable. Even Matthias is stepping in to help.

We have a plan. We know what comes next. But the wait is killing me. My patience has disintegrated. The man who could sit in silence for hours, plot things months in advance, can't wait a few days to takedown the enemy.

The tail I have on Katerina has been updating me religiously. A moment hasn't gone by that she hasn't had trained professionals guarding her. I may have let her go, but she'll never be out of my sight. She'll never be left unprotected.

When I check my text from Mark, the man currently following her, I hiss out a curse. What the fuck in my dad doing with my wife? Why didn't he tell me he was meeting with her?

I pull out my phone and dial his number. When it goes to voicemail, I dial again. On the first ring of the third call, he picks up.

"You need to learn patience, my boy," he says through a chuckle, but I don't find anything about this funny. "Why do you call?"

"You know damn well why I'm calling," I hiss out.

"Ah, yes. The lovely Katerina. You want to know why we met and what we discussed." His knowing tone irritates me. I've always respected my father, always saw him as a strong leader and mentor, but right now, I want to throttle him.

"Well?" I demand.

"That's between her and me," he vows.

I pull at my dark strands so hard my head stings.

"Absolutely not. Tell me now!" I demand.

"No. She has entrusted me with her secrets, and I won't betray her." He doesn't understand.

"She ran away! She's planning on putting herself in danger!"

"I'm aware." What? He knows, and he still won't tell me?

"Then you understand why I need to know," I push. This isn't up for debate. I must know.

"I understand why you *want* to know. However, I will not break her trust." The finality in his voice makes my blood boil. Because I get my stubbornness from him, I know it's a lost cause. He won't tell me if he's made up his mind. But I'm not going to give up.

"SHE'S MY WIFE!"

"She's my daughter," he counters.

"Agh! Goddamnit, Dad! You need to tell me what you told her. What she told you. I have to know how to protect her." I'm close to begging, but I don't care. My only objective is protecting my wife.

"I told her you had someone tailing her," he offers as if that helps at all.

"WHY WOULD YOU DO THAT?"

"It's funny to see my carefully curated, stoic son become so enraged over his wife," he muses.

"Of course I'm enraged! My own father won't help me protect my wife. Do you want her to die?" He doesn't understand the situation. He doesn't realize what's at risk. My whole world is in danger. And if he knows something that can protect her, he has to tell me.

"Don't be dense. Of course I don't. But this is a fight she has to do on her own. I told her to give you notice before she made her move so you could be there to protect her. I only gave her the knife once she agreed."

"KNIFE?" My wife is going into the enemy's lair with only a knife to protect her?

"You know, she really is the perfect match for you. She's strong and intelligent. Fierce and bold. She'll do well at your side."

"You think I don't know this? She's the perfect woman for me! Which is why you should have told her to come home to me where it's safe," I growl.

"She wouldn't have listened." Obviously, she wouldn't have. But I wouldn't have taken no as an answer.

"I don't care. You should have dragged her back to me, kicking and screaming!"

"I've aged in retirement. Your wife is a fighter, a soldier. I couldn't best her." I truly don't know whether that's the case or if he's bullshitting. He still works out religiously, but so does she.

"AGH! Damn it, Dad! I need to go."

"Be wise in how you handle things, son. Remember who she is, and what this means to her. She was never meant to be yours, but you've been gifted her anyway. Don't risk losing her."

I hang up.

'She was never meant to be yours.' And look how I've fucked things up. I accused her to the point of making her flee, and now she's putting her life in jeopardy.

I haven't been a good husband.

Before I can dwell on it, my phone rings again.

"The target approached my car," Mark tells me.

I grit my teeth at the name.

"It's Mrs. Montclair to you; not the target," I correct him.

"Yes, sir." He coughs, then continues. "She told me she's going in tonight." Mark's words send a chill down my spine.

"I'll prepare the men. Stay on her, but don't go in after her." I hate the words as I say them, but I have to follow the plan.

It's time to end this.

Chapter 51

Katerina

The entrance to the prison where I was tormented for most of my life stares back at me. Feelings of inferiority and weakness threaten to surface, but I push them down. This time when I step through the door, it'll be with a strength I never possessed before.

This is where it all ends. It's down to him and me. A fight to the death. Because despite what my husband and brother have planned, this doesn't end until Viktor dies, or I go down trying.

Mustering a look of distraught, I gear up to play the part of heartbroken daughter. I'm back in one of those hideous dresses he always made me wear. It perfectly conceals my knife in its thigh holster.

Thoughts of never seeing Dominic again are enough to start the stream of tears. Mascara runs down my cheeks, the perfect addition to the look.

I take a deep breath, then knock on the door.

It swings open, and I'm standing face to face with Yelena. For a second, a look of concern crosses her features then she's ushering me inside.

"Katya, get off the streets. Someone could see you in such a state, and then what would they think!" She pulls me through the threshold then slams the door behind me.

"I... I..." A sob bursts from me, followed by multiple hiccups. "Is... Отец... here? I... need... him!"

Doubt crosses Yelena's features, so I ramp up my performance. I try to fall into her arms, and she pushes me away.

"Come, girl. Your father is in his office." She steers me down the hallway as though I don't know my way around the house I grew up in.

Instead of waiting for her to knock, I throw open the door and stumble inside.

"Yelena, you–" he pauses at the sight of me. "Katerina, what is wrong with you?" There's no concern in his voice, only disgust. His Bratva Princess should never be seen in such a state of distress.

"I... He... Oh, Отец!" I throw myself into one of his chairs.

"Speak up, girl. What happened?" There's a gleam in his eyes that reveals he knows exactly what happened. Of course he does. He orchestrated it.

"He accused me of disloyalty. He kicked me out. Onto the streets. I had nowhere to go." I ramp up my tears, letting them fall freely.

"Katya, my daughter. Of course he threw you out. You were never anything to him. If only you listened to me." He clicks his tongue, scolding me.

"Please, Отец. Please let me come home. I'll do anything." Begging him feels like a betrayal to all the effort I've put into becoming the new, strong me. The words feel like ash on my tongue, but I push them out anyway. I remind myself this is all part of the plan to end him. This is the only way. Playing into his pride. But it kills me that some of my last words to him will be begging.

"Why should we welcome you with open arms? All you've done is betray your family." He sneers at the reminder.

"I'll tell you everything I know about the Syndicate. I'll spill all their secrets." I will do no such thing, but he doesn't need to know that.

"I doubt you know anything important." His words say one thing, but the glint in his eyes say another. This is the best lead he has.

"But I do. He welcomed me into his office, into his Syndicate. I know a lot. And it's all yours." Words of a desperate girl fill the air.

His features are pensive, lost in thought. The wheels turn as he calculates what angle he can exploit this information.

"Very well. Clean yourself up, then come back here. We have work to do."

"Thank you, Отец." There's fire in those words, and I hold my breath. Thankfully, he doesn't catch it, already onto the next thing.

"Remember going forward who your family is." It's a threat wrapped in advice.

"I'm a Sokolov." The words are acid in my throat. I'll never be one of his again.

He hums in agreement, then averts his attention to his desk. He's dismissing me, but I'm not done with this conversation.

"Can I have a hug?" He jerks his head up, a look of bewilderment across his features. We haven't hugged since I was a child. "I could use some comforting." Tears well in my eyes, and I let one slip.

"I suppose so. You've had a rough day." He awkwardly pushes from his desk but remains seated.

Standing on wobbly legs, I make my way to him. Slowly, I wrap my arms around his neck. The smell of smoke wafting off him chokes me, but I hold it in.

He's stiff but tentatively pats my back. After far too long, I pull back and look down at him. This is the moment. Nothing else matters now.

"Tell me something, do you ever think of Мама?" Hardness and hatred spill into my voice. I could never speak of Мама to him with saccharinity. It'd be a betrayal.

"What?" Caught off guard, his gaze jerks up at me.

"Do you ever think of her? After all these years, I've never seen you with another woman. Is it because you miss her?" His answer doesn't matter. But for some reason, I need to know if he still loves her. If he regrets her. It won't change his fate, but maybe it'll answer some of my questions.

"Your mother taught me that all women are a waste. They take and take but never give. If I have needs to be met, I know where to go. You're just a continuation of that useless woman. The one thing you could do for us, you failed at. And here you are, begging for more." His words are vitriol, but little does he know, the poison will be his.

I nod slowly, as if I understand, but inside, I'm screaming. Rage consumes me. This fucker doesn't even care that he drove his wife to her grave.

"I know her ending was brought by her own hand, but it was always you who controlled the knife." I take a step behind his chair. "It was you who pushed her to that point." I run my hands over his scalp. "I always blamed you." I grab his hair and jerk his head back.

"Katerina, what—"

Moving quicker than ever before, I unsheathe my blade and hold it to the base of his neck. I push it in until blood beads for the contact.

"This is for Мама. I could handle all you did to me, but I swore to avenge her. This is me fulfilling that promise." My voice is strong and confident.

"You don't have it in you," he says through a rough chuckle.

"You underestimate my hatred."

"You'll never make it out of here alive."

"That doesn't matter."

"You foolish girl. You really think you can—"

His sentence is cut off by his gurgling. Blood dribbles from his mouth, dancing with the scarlet liquid pooling at the slit in his neck. The shock in his eyes gives way to the void.

The dripping blade falls from my fingers. The *ting* of it hitting the ground falls on deaf ears. All I can make out is the buzzing in my head.

Reaching out with shaky hands, I hesitantly run my fingers through the mess. Once I make contact with the sticky, warm liquid, reality comes crashing down.

I stagger back not stopping until I hit the wall. Slumping against it, I meet the floor. There's only one thing echoing in my mind as I stare at my bloody digits.

It's done. It's over. After nearly two decades of battles, the war is over. We won. I've slain the devil, and now he's home in hell.

Мама, I did it for you. You can rest in peace now.

Chapter 52
Dominic

The drumming of my heart roars in my ears, overpowering my senses. I don't bother with Cecilia's breathing exercises; those damn things don't matter right now. All that matters is finding my wife.

She entered the mansion twenty minutes ago. It's been too long. We should already be in there. But Pyotr's been busy ensuring the team freeing the women at the port are under control. Roman and Bash are with them, so I'm not concerned. The Syndicate men will handle it. All I care about is Katerina.

Bloody images of her being overpowered by Viktor or caught after killing him flash through my mind. Each one darker than the previous.

Despite my confidence in my wife's abilities, so much could go wrong. She's alone in there. I need to be there. I need to be by her side, keeping her safe.

Pyotr gives me a nod then lets himself in. His men follow behind, walking casually as though they aren't staging a coup to overthrow their Pakhan.

After an eternity, the melodic ring of a gunshot carries through the air, and I'm inside instantly. My men trail in. Their duty is to take out any men that fight back.

But not me.

My only goal is finding my wife.

I beeline to Viktor's office. Any man standing between me and my wife goes down. I don't think before pulling the trigger. Headshot after headshot. I couldn't give less of a shit about them.

Finally at the wooden doors, I yank them open. Silence fills the room. The still air sends a shiver down my spine.

Looking around, I meet the blank stare of my sworn enemy. His lifeless eyes stare ahead. The horrific scene before me fills me with pride. My wife was able to complete her mission. She's avenged her mother.

But where is she? If one of these fuckers has her... No mercy will be shown to anyone who touches a hair on her head. Breathing gets difficult as I stress. Where did they take her?

I storm to the door, ready to find my wife, when a soft whimper catches my attention. It comes from behind Viktor's desk.

Gun in hand, I silently investigate. All thoughts leave my head at the heartbreaking sight before me.

My strong, fierce wife sits in a ball hunched against the wall, her knees to her chest. Her stained hands are wrapped around her legs, getting blood all over her hideous dress. But the part that makes my heart stop is the blank look in her eyes.

She's staring into the void, not presently here. She hasn't even registered my presence, and I'm crouched in front of her.

"Tiger, it's me," I try softly, but she doesn't respond. "I'm going to hold you, okay?" Silence meets my words, and I try not to worry.

Wrapping my arms around her, I lift her from her spot and place her in my lap. She struggles against me, but when I whisper in her ear, telling her it's her husband, she collapses into me.

I hold her tightly to my chest, stroking her back while cradling her head in the crook of my shoulder. When she starts shaking, I worry she's gone into hysterics and is laughing. Then I realize she's crying.

My heart cinches. I had my doubts about her killing Viktor. It's been her life's mission, I know this. But patricide, even if you despise him, can be destructive. Killing your abuser has to be distressing.

I whisper encouragements in her ear. I tell her how strong and brave she is. That she's not alone, and I'm right here. That I'll never leave her. I tell her how proud I am of her. And I assure her that the fight is over. She's free.

Eventually, her sobs become less frequent. I don't know if it's acceptance or exhaustion that has her calming. Either way, I'm relieved.

"I'm not crying because I regret killing him," her soft voice whispers. "I'm crying out of relief. It's over. I avenged Мама. He'll never hurt me, or any other woman, ever again."

I rub soothing circles on her back, letting her know I'm here.

"I know, Katerina. I can't imagine what you're feeling right now. Your Мама would be very proud of you. Now she's able to rest in peace." She snuggles deeper into my chest and wraps her arms around my neck, burrowing into me.

Silently, we cling to each other, basking in each other's comforting touches.

Eventually, the office door swings open. Pyotr walks in, looking for us. When his gaze lands on his father's corpse, he staggers backwards. He didn't know Viktor as the monster he was until recently. This has to be hard on him. I avert my gaze, giving him a moment to mourn.

After a few minutes, he catches my stare and rounds the desk.

"It is done. The women have been freed at the docks and will be taken back to Russia. Your brothers and the Syndicate are all to thank. The disloyal men have been rounded up, and Viktor…" He chokes. "I am now Pakhan, thanks to you."

"It had to be done. I'm looking forward to working with you." I don't acknowledge that we're now enemies. It doesn't seem appropriate.

"I want to offer an alliance without any strings. I'd like the Bratva and the Syndicate to be allies instead of enemies. I won't run it how my father did. We will gladly follow the rules." Honesty bleeds into his words, and I realize this is a man I can trust.

"I look forward to peace. We will stick to the previous treaty," I assure him.

"No. I'm absolving that one. We will have a new treaty, one that doesn't require such sacrifice. I'm releasing you two from the arranged marriage. Get a divorce and be free to marry someone you love. We'll have peace without it." His generous smile is a dagger to my heart.

I look down at my wife, but she's too dazed to process his words. There's a pit in my stomach. Divorcing Katerina is the last thing I want. Without her, I am lost. Without her, there's nothing pushing me forward. I can't lose her.

But I can't force her to be mine. So many choices have been taken from her. She's never been truly free. I owe it to her to give her the opportunity.

No matter what she chooses, she'll always be my wife. She'll always claim my heart. Even if I have to watch her settle down with another man, she'll always have my protection.

"I'll talk to her later. She's processing what happened," I tell him.

He nods then leaves the room.

I follow not long after with my wife in my arms. Everything feels so wrong in our world, but everything feels right with her against me.

His offer echoes in my mind as we leave the Bratva house. I can't even take a full breath.

How can I survive when she leaves me?

Chapter 53

Katerina

After sleeping overnight, I feel revived today. A new life has started for me. One where I'm free from the horrors of my past. Unfortunately, Dominic doesn't seem to have the same sentiment.

Dominic's been quiet since the ambush. He's barely looked at me today, and when he does, it's full of anguish.

"What is the matter with you?" I demand at lunch. "Why do you look like someone kicked your puppy?"

"What do you mean?" His head jerks up, and he looks startled, as if my outburst wasn't expected and isn't warranted.

"I mean, why are you acting like this? You should be happy. It's over! The fight is over! And yet, you look tormented. Tell me what's wrong!"

He sighs and runs his fingers through his hair. Dammit, he's nervous about something. It's starting to freak me out.

"Let's go on a walk." He's slow to leave his chair and offers me a hand. I tentatively take it, and he leads me out of the house.

We walk in silence for a few minutes until it overwhelms me.

"Just tell me." It's a plea.

"Yesterday, after everything was over, your brother talked to me. He said he's enforcing peace with the Syndicate no strings attached." He looks crestfallen. "He said he's absolving the peace treaty and that we're free to get a divorce."

"What?" I whisper.

"Divorce. He said we can divorce." He keeps walking, not looking at me. "It's up to you. We'll do whatever you want."

Fuck this.

"Come with me," I order him, grabbing his hand and dragging him.

We enter the gym on the compound, where there are a few Syndicate soldiers working out. That won't do.

"OUT!" I shout, and they all immediately comply. Seems like slashing the enemy's throat gains you some respect around here.

"What's going on, Katerina? Why are we in here?" Dominic looks so lost, and it's pissing me off.

"Do you want to divorce me?" I spit out through gritted teeth.

"It's not about what I want." His shoulders droop.

"Answer the damn question!" I hiss at him.

"I don't want to force you into anything," he confesses. The guilt radiating off him infuriates me further.

"Get in the ring!"

"What?"

"You heard me."

I kick off my shoes and slip between the cords. Silently, he follows behind me. Even if his obedience comes from curiosity, it still makes me victorious that I tamed the great Dominic Montclair.

"What are we doing–"

He's cut off with a round kick to his side.

"Fuck!" he hisses.

"You think you can force me into something I don't want? You really think anyone can force me to do anything?" I circle him, hopping on my toes, ready to fight. My arms are raised in a perfect boxing stance.

"No?"

"That's right!"

"Which is why I'm giving you a choice." His sorrowful eyes earn him another hit. He blocks my jab, so I counter with a cross.

"It's not that simple. You don't get to leave me that easily. You said I'm yours! You promised! So, I'm not going anywhere."

"I don't want you to go anywhere," he sighs heavily. His halfhearted attempt to parry another jab fuels my fire.

"Then fucking fight for me! Be a damn man! Tell me what you what! Make me stay!"

"But–"

I try to kick him again, but he catches my leg and pulls me into him. I swing at him, but he grabs my arms. He quickly rolls us to the floor, trapping me under him.

"You want me to make you stay? Here you go!" He grins sadistically. "You're mine, Katerina Montclair. You're my wife. You have my last name. And you rule over my men. I won't give you up. I won't let you leave. Treaty be damned. It hasn't been about the Syndicate or Bratva in a long time. I'd choose you every time. So, fuck Pyotr and his fucking offer. Divorce isn't an option. You are my wife. Nothing can change that."

"Much better," I purr, pulling him down to me.

He meets me halfway, his lips dancing with mine. The kiss isn't innocent or sweet. It's passion and control. He leads me, cupping my jaw, forcing my mouth where he wants it. His hand moves to cradle the back of my head as he kisses me down into the mat.

"Mine," he growls against my lips.

"Damn straight. You better not forget it," I answer against his.

He pulls back and grins at me. It's a look of utter joy.

"You're everything I never knew I needed."

I moan in agreement. He eyes take on an earnest look as he caresses my cheeks with soft strokes.

"I love you, Katerina. You know that, right?"

"I know." I sigh. His eyes harden as he dares me to reply. "I love you too, husband."

He lets out a guttural groan and attacks my lips. "I fucking love when you call me that." He rips my leggings down my legs, then pauses at my bareness under them.

"Where are your panties?" His accusing tone makes me giggle.

"I don't wear them under my leggings. Panty lines." Smirking, I wiggle my bare pussy catching his heated gaze.

"Don't walk around my men bare," he demands.

"As if I'm taking orders from you, *Dom*." I scoff at him.

"What did you just say?"

"You heard me."

"Naughty wife. Maybe you need a reminder of who your husband, *Dominic*, is." He playfully slaps my thigh. I open them wider and shimmy his pants down his legs. Gripping his member, I guide him to my entrance.

"Someone's impatient," he teases.

"I need my *husband*," I goad him. "Right now."

He pushes inside me in one thrust then keeps rutting into me. I meet his hips just as aggressively. He may be owning my body, but I own his just as much.

The mat crinkles against my back, but it only adds to the sensation. The sound of our bodies meeting echoes through the gym. He wiggles a hand under my bra and tweaks my nipples. I reach up, demanding a kiss.

There's no teasing, no playfulness. We're staking our claims on each other. Burning ourselves into one another.

When we come, we come together. Our sweaty bodies glide against each other in a reverent way. Our moans combine into a melody of pleasure.

And as we come down, we hold each other. With one arm propping himself up, he stares at me adoringly.

"I love you, Katerina. No one compares to you, my fiery, brave, beautiful wife." He gently moves a piece of my hair off of my face.

"Even if I stab you sometimes?" I smirk.

"Even then, because I probably deserve it," he chuckles.

We laugh, and the movement causes me to clench around him. He hardens, still sheathed inside of me, and then we're fucking.

My future looks bright in the arms of Dominic Montclair. My husband saved me from my cage and gave me a life I never could have imagined.

Epilogue I
Katerina

"Mile twelve, eight thirty-seven," I holler to the sweaty man next to me.

"If we do this last mile sub eight, I'll give you a *treat*." My husband's voice is full of promise. I look over, and he arches a brow. I instantly pick up my pace. I'll be damned if I don't get that treat.

We've gotten to a point where Dominic can run with me most days. It's a cathartic way to start our morning. He's even started to look at it as quality time as opposed to 'masochistic torture.'

"Pick up your feet. Come on! You won't want to miss this treat." I glare at him. He's using my own words against me.

"I bet I can beat you to the finish line," I goad.

"You're on–"

Before he can finish, I shove him to the ground, then sprint as fast as I can. I hear his gasp followed by a deep chuckle. He's back on his feet and gaining on me. The slaps of his shoes against the trail echo around us.

"You play dirty, tiger," he whispers from over my shoulder.

We've run this route enough times to know that the tree with the Y-shaped branch marks thirteen miles. I'm only a few steps away. I can taste my victory.

Until I'm hauled in the air and spun around. My husband drops me on the ground and whooshes past me with a laugh.

I turn around with a scowl and cross the last two steps. Glaring at him the entire time, I pause my watch, then stretch my arms.

"Well, did we make sub eight?" he asks.

I glance down, and grin. "Seven fifty-five."

"Great. You've earned your prize, even if you did lose the race," he says casually.

"I didn't lose! You cheated!" I scoff at his indignation.

"You cheated first, tiger. It's only fair." I glare at him, unable to dispute his claim.

"Well, what's my prize?" I demand stubbornly.

Expecting him to seduce me, I take a step forward. To my surprise, he digs into his pocket.

"I know we've done everything backwards. We married before we even met, which isn't conventional. But I wouldn't change anything about our story. Except, maybe this. I should've given it to you a while back, but the timing never felt right. But now, after so many people have questioned us, this is needed on your finger. You deserve to be adorned."

He pulls out a black velvet box and opens it. Sitting inside is a beautiful square-cut, ruby ring adorned with diamonds on the side. My heart stutters a beat as it glints in the sun, a warm blood-red color. It perfectly matches the apology necklace and jewelry from all those months ago. My finger twitches to try it on, but I refrain.

"What are you apologizing for this time?" I tease.

"That's not what this one is. Although for the next set, I'm thinking sapphire." His grin turns serious. "This is to show my love for you."

"Мама told me to never say yes to a man who isn't down on his knee." I fake being appalled.

"I'm not asking you any questions." He scowls.

"Aren't you proposing to me?"

He scoffs. "No, don't be ridiculous. You're already married to me, and that's not going to change." He glares at me, then straightens his features. "I'm giving you a ring to wear with your wedding band every day. Something just as beautiful as you. And so that every man can see from far, far away that you're taken." With the size of the stone and the deep color, no one will miss it.

"So, an engagement ring." I confirm.

"No. We're not getting engaged. We're already married." He huffs. "If you don't like it, just tell me. I'll get you another one."

"Oh, stop being a baby. It's beautiful. Just put it on me already!" I thrust my hand towards him in a not-so-subtle hint. He pulls the ring from the box and slides it onto my finger. It's a perfect fit, which isn't a surprise considering the numerous apology rings he's bought me already.

"So, you like it?" His voice is almost nervous, as though every piece of jewelry he's already bought me hasn't been stunning.

"Of course I do. It's better than the treat I thought I was getting," I tell him in awe, unable to take my gaze off him.

"What treat were you expecting?" His hungry gaze tells me he already knows.

"I was hoping for a man on his knees between my thighs." I sigh wistfully. "But a ring is good too."

"Why not both?" His husky voice sends shivers down my spine.

I part my legs slightly, playing with the hem of my shorts. He's between my thighs, lapping at my slit in the blink of an eye. I have to lean against a tree for support. His tongue sends me over the edge in record time. When he continues after my release, I have to pry him away to catch my breath.

"Come on," I tell him as I pull him to his feet. "We have a meeting with Stefan, Roman, and Pyotr about the new use of the ports."

He sighs as though running his criminal operation is an inconvenience.

"I thought you were a work-oriented man. I didn't marry some lazy guy!" I frown at him.

"I used to be. Now anything that isn't my wife is a chore," he whines.

And despite the absurdity of the sentence, it makes my heart burst. Because I finally have a man who loves me.

Epilogue II
Dominic

The house before me is normal in every single way. It's unassuming and boring. The colors are dull, the lawn maintained, and the paint chipped. It's similar to every house surrounding it.

It evades me why my brother chooses to live here.

Bash moved out of his penthouse abruptly six years ago into this downgrade. The middle-class suburb is well beneath him. But he's never seemed happier.

Katerina knocks on the door while Nik and I stand awkwardly behind her. This visit is an unusual one, but my wife insisted on making my youngest brother feel accepted.

Bash opens the door with a look of confusion.

"What are you guys doing here?" His voice is cautious but happy. My little brother loves his family and enjoys being around us.

Out of the four of us, he's the most reasonable. The most morally sound, besides the hacking he does. For that reason, he doesn't look out of place in this neighborhood, unlike the three of us.

"We wanted to stop by and discuss some things," my wife says lightly. She has a sweet smile on her face, perfectly masking her ambush.

"About the Syndicate?" His confusion is clear. We've never been here before. He's always come to us for Syndicate matters.

"Mmmm," my wife noises uncommittedly.

"Well, come on up to my office." We follow him up two flights of stairs to an open third floor. There are multiple desks with monitors on them. Bookshelves full of books and Legos. TV screens mounted on walls, with framed puzzles under them. All of them with pictures of animals on them. But the oddest thing of all are the telescopes lined against the wall of windows facing his neighbor's house.

"What can I help you with?" He asks cheerfully, and I internally wince. Poor guy has no clue.

"Bash, we wanted to introduce you to my guard and best friend, Nikolai." My wife steps aside to reveal Nik.

I eye him, trying to see what Bash does. He's tall and strong. His hair is thick and light, and his eyes blue. They're not as beautiful and icy as Katerina's though.

"Hi, Nikolai," Bash says with a smile. He reaches forward and offers his hand. They shake.

I can't tell whether Bash is happy because that's his usual demeanor, or if it's because he likes how Nik looks.

Katerina stands next to them smiling wide. I know she feels protective of Nik and wants to include Bash in that.

"I'm sorry to be rude, but what can I do for you?" Bash asks awkwardly.

"Nik is gay," my wife boasts. Her best friend reddens at the announcement, but he agreed to her plan.

"That's... nice?" Bash looks utterly baffled.

"And he's single. We love and accept him just as he is." Katerina looks at Bash expectantly, but the poor man still doesn't understand.

"Bash, we wanted to tell you it's okay to be who you are. The Syndicate doesn't care about sexuality. They thought introducing you to me would help you realize this. Even if it's not with me, you should go out and meet someone." Nik looks so uncomfortable, but he's doing a good job helping Bash feel included.

I honestly never realized Bash was gay, which made me feel like a horrible brother. About seven years ago, he used to be quite the player, but it stopped abruptly. Since then, we haven't seen him with a woman. I never thought about it, but when Katerina pitched it to me, it all made sense.

Bash's eyes widen and he lets out a choked sound.

"You guys think I'm gay?" he squeaks out.

"We love you just how you are. We accept you no matter what," my wife comforts him.

"But I'm not gay," Bash reiterates.

"Sebastian, it's okay." Katerina's using a sweet voice, but it's not calming my brother.

"No, seriously, I'm not–"

"The lizard is in her nest," a robotic voice booms through the room.

It happens in slow motion. The lights in the room dim as the curtains draw almost all the way down. The telescopes adjust to angle towards the house his backs up to, over the short fence. The TV screens turn on and security cameras show a woman walking into her house.

I can't comprehend what I'm seeing. I turn to my brother for clarity, but he's avoiding our gazes.

Bash visibly pales. Guilt contorts his features, and his forehead shines with sweat. He takes his glasses off and rubs the bridge of his nose.

The unsuspecting woman unloads groceries from her car and brings them into her kitchen. I study her, trying to remember a Syndicate order to investigate this woman, but I don't recognize her.

"Bash, who is that?" I ask in a low voice, as if this woman could hear us.

He gulps, eyes wide and lost. "Umm, that's my neighbor."

"Okay. Why are you watching her?" I try to keep the accusation out of my voice. Maybe he's doing extra Syndicate work. But this dorky looking woman doesn't appear to be a threat of any sort. But my equally nerdy brother doesn't look like a threat, and he's one of the Syndicate's best assets, so I don't make assumptions based on appearances.

"Because..." His eyes dart around the room as if it'll give him an answer.

"Bash, why are you watching your neighbor?" I press.

"Because I love her!" His confession is full of anguish. His face is full of longing. His eyes land on one of the screens showing her putting milk in her fridge, and he sighs. "She's my life."

"Oh Bash, that's amazing! Why haven't we met her?" My wife claps her hands in excitement and jumps up. She's glad he has someone, even if it's not Nik.

But Bash winces.

"I... I haven't met her," he confesses.

"What?" Katerina voices my confusion.

"I've never met her... at least not as Bash. She doesn't know I exist." His puppy eyes sadden as he watches the girl.

"What do you mean she doesn't know you exist?" My wife presses, horror dawning on her.

"I keep her safe from afar. I look out for her and protect her. She just... doesn't know about it." His tormented expression tempts my sympathy, but he's done this to himself.

"Bash, that's insane. How long has this been going on?" My wife demands answers.

"Six years."

Dear Reader

Thank you for reading *Vengeful Vows*.

This is my third novel and the third in The Syndicate Series. I'm honored that you've stuck by me and continued reading my works. I know I can't take all the credit; those Montclair brothers have no trouble getting women. My author journey has been incredible, and it wouldn't be possible without readers like you. I'm grateful to each and every one of you.

If you enjoyed this story, I'd be truly grateful if you left a review on your favorite platform(s). Reviews are one of the best ways to support an author. Each one makes a difference.

Want to know what's going on with Bash and his neighbor? Stick around for their story: *Angelic Acts*

Much love,
Ellie

Acknowledgements

There are many people I want to thank in having this book become a reality. Without you, Dominic and Katerina would still be sitting in my laptop, longing for the light of day.

First, Katelyn, thank you for being my vision board and helping me figure everything out. Reading the book back to you as I was writing helped me hear it in a new way. And using doorframes, pillows, and other inanimate objects to figure out *scenes* added so much fun and ridiculousness to the writing process. There isn't anyone I'd rather have by my side during this journey.

Ashley, you mean the world to me. If I didn't have you proofreading my book, 'demeanor' would've been misspelt dozens of times. Maybe one of these days, I'll learn. I'm honored that between med school prep and work, you made time to fit me and my book into your schedule. I'm eternally grateful for our friendship.

Maggie, my big sister. You've always supported me and my dreams. Hearing your positive feedback means the world to me. I need you in this process because I know you'll always keep me grounded and call out anything you find 'absolutely horrible.' I appreciate the time you've spent on my books and all the support you've given along the way.

Parker Drue, you give me what any author wishes for: the reactions of a reader who loves the book. Your notes while beta reading fill me with such joy and hope. If even one reader is as excited as you are to read me books, then I know I've made it as an author. You encourage me to keep going and to chase my dreams. I'll continue to write even if only you read them, because the enjoyment you get from my books fuels me.

Mom, thank you for everything you've done. Not just with my books, but with the outside support. I know author is a long stretch from engineer, but it brings me such fulfillment. Thank you for encouraging me. Your confidence in my writing gives me hope that this is right for me. The way you tell everyone about my writing has brought me more confidence in telling others about my books. Thank you.

Dad, you're still not allowed to read these books, but I wanted to thank you for encouraging me to follow my dreams. Your constant support of me means the world. The way you boast to all your friends about my writing is incredible, despite the raunchiness of these books. Maybe don't recommend them to business associates. I love you.

Mrs. Amy, thank you so much. You've been such an integral part of my life. Having you to talk to and get advice from has helped me in many situations. Thank you for encouraging my writing and supporting me. I'm eager to hear your thoughts on this one. I took your comments into consideration while writing it.

To my ARC team, thank you to the moon and back. The difference even one ARC reader can make is unimaginable. Each and every one of you helps my dreams of a career as an author become a reality. Thank you for spending your time and energy on my books.

To my reader, my lovely readers, this couldn't be done without you. Your comments on my posts and reviews of my books spur me on. You guys are the fuel to my writing fire. Your love for my books keeps me motivated. Thank you.

About the Author

Ellie Hallaron is an author and lifetime storyteller, always turning ordinary moments into something worth retelling.

She fell in love with books early on, and growing up, the only punishment that ever stuck was having them taken away. Novels have always felt like home to her, first as a reader, and now as a writer.

Ellie writes emotionally charged romances with depth, intensity, and heroes you probably shouldn't fall for... but absolutely will.

When she's not writing, she's usually with friends and family who patiently endure her spirals over fictional characters, or she's dreaming up the next story.

She's thrilled to be sharing her words with readers, and there's so much more to come.

Stay in Touch

If you fell in love with *Vengeful Vows* and want more of the Montclair Brothers, come hang out with me online.

I share exclusive updates, upcoming releases, spicy teasers, unreleased scenes, and more!

You can find me here:

Tiktok: @Ellie Hallaron.Author

Instagram: @EllieHallaron.Author

Goodreads: Goodreads.com/EllieHallaron